Claire's Cheeks Felt Hot.

She wasn't sure if she was being teased or insulted, but she'd had about enough. "Listen, my husband is—"

"Oh yes, I know. Your husband is Director of Operations. He could have me diced into little pieces. All you have to do is say the word." He leaned closer again, his voice low and seductive. "But you're not going to do that, are you?"

She could hardly breathe. She knew what she should do. And yet. . . . She wasn't going to tell Howard anything. "You're taking a big chance," she whispered, her eyes very wide as they stared into his.

"Chances are what make life interesting. The question is . . ." He reached for her again, just a finger to her chin, but she felt herself shiver with guilty delight at his touch. "The question is, what kind of chance are you willing to take?"

SILVER LININGS

Helen Conrad

Harper Paperbacks

Harper & Row, Publishers, New York
Grand Rapids, Philadelphia, St. Louis, San Francisco
London, Singapore, Sydney, Tokyo, Toronto

This is a work of fiction. The characters, incidents, and
dialogues are products of the author's imagination and are
not to be construed as real. Any resemblance to actual events
or persons, living or dead, is entirely coincidental.

Harper Paperbacks a division of Harper & Row, Publishers, Inc.
        10 East 53rd Street, New York, N.Y. 10022

This book is published by arrangement with Palace Books, Inc.

Cover art by Jim Griffin

First printing: July, 1990

Printed in the United States of America

HARPER PAPERBACKS and colophon are trademarks of
Harper & Row, Publishers, Inc.

10 9 8 7 6 5 4 3 2 1

CHAPTER

The long, low recreation room was stifling despite the hardworking air conditioner, which was struggling so hard its noise almost drowned out the performance on the stage. Claire Duvall Montgomery shifted uncomfortably in the metal folding chair and pressed out the creases in her skirt with the crimson-tipped fingers of her long, slender hands. She neatly crossed her ankles, only to wince at the scraping sound her soft ivory-leather shoes made against the cement floor.

Sand. It was everywhere, in everything. Sometimes she thought it would drive her mad.

The five little girls on the stage were singing "Every Little Frog Knows" and making froglike leaps back and forth. Her own ten-year-old Katy, frog suit and all, paused long enough to look out at her mother, and Claire waved surreptitiously. Katy's pretty smile was luminous, until her gaze

1

shifted and she saw the empty chair beside her mother. Immediately her smile disappeared and a stricken look took its place. For just a moment, her lower lip trembled. But then it was time for another leap and she dropped to the ground. Claire could breathe again.

Damn Howard, anyway! Why wasn't he here? He had promised he would make it. Even worse, he had sworn up and down to Katy that he wouldn't miss her frog impersonation.

"I won't show it to you now," she'd said the night before, her brown eyes brimming with the joy of anticipation. "I want you to see it right, Daddy. When I have on my green suit with the yellow spots. Please come. Please promise you'll come."

"I wouldn't miss it for the world," he'd said absently, fingering the newspaper he would rather be reading and frowning slightly, hiding his impatience from his daughter, but not from his wife. She'd known how annoying he found these interruptions to his free time. But she'd counted on his love for his daughter coming through. She'd really thought he would find a way to attend the talent show. What was this obstinate place in her heart that kept believing?

The frogs left the stage to thunderous applause and calls of "Ribet!" from the audience of parents. For just a moment Claire, laughing along with the others, felt like part of them. Then reality filtered back, and she remembered where she was— and more importantly, who she was, so she sat a little straighter, knowing she was being watched and commented upon by every other person in the room.

Her thick, coffee-dark hair was tightly coiled, not a wisp out of place. Her soft brown eyes were lightly made up, her pale skin barely covered with powder. The linen suit she wore was tailor-made and looked it, but it hung a bit on her slender shoulders, and bagged where she'd recently lost even more weight. The exquisite gold watch circled a wrist that was too thin, though graceful in form and movement. Except for being so darn bony, she knew she was presentable. There wasn't much to criticize. She was careful about that. But still, she knew they talked about her.

The next act took the stage, three older girls in pink poodle skirts and ponytails, harmonizing fifties-style to "He's a Rebel." Claire's daughter Samantha was the lead singer, her silver-blond hair a streak of light down her back, her pretty face an ice-sculpture version of her mother's. She glanced out at the audience as Katy had done—Claire knew better than to wave at her—and took in the empty chair. But she displayed none of Katy's disappointment. Sam was three years older and subject to a cynicism that should have been way beyond her years. She had already learned not to hope.

Sam's lack of response broke Claire's heart even more than Katy's reaction had. This was not the way it should be. Her children shouldn't have to go through this.

Maybe it was all her own fault. She should have done something. She should have called Howard at noon to remind him. She should have sent along a note in his briefcase. She should have—

No. She took a deep, shuddering breath and began to applaud as the girls made their bows. No, she wasn't going to take on the guilt for this. She'd done that too often in the past. This time, Howard would have to accept responsibility.

Glancing across the room, she caught at least three pairs of eyes on her, the curiosity obvious. Omigod, was her first panicked thought. Did it show? Could they tell how upset she was? She felt cornered, and very alone.

Seven months in this Saudi Arabian outpost, and though she was acquainted with just about everybody, she had not made a single real friend. Howard was Director of Operations for Draxon Oil, and she was the director's wife. Everyone wanted to speak to her. No one wanted to get too close. Except those with ulterior motives.

She'd never been in this uncomfortable situation before. Howard had worked for Draxon for years, but in the States, he had been a hardworking, ambitious employee, first a topnotch petroleum engineer, then a manager, and there had always been others in the same position. Here in Saudi, Howard was the boss. That meant everyone talked about him and his family, envied them, criticized them, and very few had any sympathy with them at all. To make matters almost insufferable, everyone who worked for Draxon lived out here on this same company compound, miles away from the city, miles away from everything. It was like living in a small town, only worse. There was no history to bind them together, no shared experience. It was every man for himself, and no one trusted anyone else.

Claire sat very still, wondering if the sick feeling seeping through her could be attributed to the smell of the room, the slightly sticky blend of cookies, gym socks and spoiled milk—or to the feel of the gazes burning into her? They all knew Howard should be here. Were they pitying her? Probably. Instinctively her Duvall chin rose and her slender shoulders straightened. Pity she could do without.

"Claire."

Startled by the soft voice and the hand on her arm, she jumped and turned to look at the woman seated to her right. Shareen Hunter was married to the Draxon attorney assigned to the Saudi operation. Though she'd been raised in the States and had attended Columbia University, her dark, handsome Arab features gave mute testimony to her heritage. Claire had noticed before that, of all those she came into contact with here in this strange land, Shareen seemed to have the most genuine smile.

"I just wanted to say your daughters are a delight. Katy radiates such a contagious joy. And Samantha—her voice is lovely."

Who could resist hearing her children complimented? Claire smiled happily, her sick feeling evaporating. "Your son's piece on the guitar was wonderful, too. Has he been taking lessons long?"

Shareen's laugh was open and candid. "Not long. Actually that's the only piece Kevin knows. He practiced day and night for this show." She grinned. "We ought to have these things more often. If he had to perform again, he might even learn another piece."

Claire laughed and Shareen leaned closer as the curtain went up on the next act. "We've never really had a chance to talk," she whispered. "Would you like to come over for coffee some morning?"

Claire felt a wave of happiness she hadn't experienced in a long time. "I'd love to," she said honestly. "Let's do it soon."

It was strange how one simple act of kindness could warm her so. She hadn't realized how truly lonely she'd been. The prospect of having a friend, someone she could actually talk to, was exciting, and it filled her mind for a few moments as she sat listening to a small girl at the piano wrestle with Chopin.

There was a sound from the entrance at the back and she turned to look, still hoping to see her husband arrive. She regretted the gesture immediately. Everyone had seen; everyone knew why she was looking. She knew exactly what they said about her.

"Poor Mrs. Montgomery. She was so embarrassed when her husband didn't show up for the talent show. I mean, every other father was there. You would think he could at least put in an appearance. Those poor little girls."

Claire hated being the subject of that sort of talk. It offended her quiet sense of reserve and definitely wounded her dignity. But even worse she hated what it did to Katy and Sam.

She knew Howard wasn't a popular boss. No one had ever told her in so many words, but she could tell. That would be hard for the girls, as well, for surely they heard things at the small school all the children of Draxon employees attended. Every problem that life had only hinted at before seemed to have come to a head here in Saudi Arabia. Sometimes she hated this place, hated having come here.

"It will be a great opportunity," Howard had said all those months ago when she'd first heard they were going. "I'll be in charge of the entire operation and I'll be able to prove my worth to those bastards at the San Francisco home office. One year in the desert, Claire, and we'll be heading for Nob Hill. Trust me."

More than half that year had passed and she still hadn't heard of any plans to transfer them to San Francisco. She was fairly sure Howard had been exaggerating their chances.

The talent show was over. All the children came back on the stage for a curtain call. And then they broke ranks and began to flow down into the audience, finding their parents. Claire rose, smiled goodbye to Shareen, and made her way to the front of the room to speak to Mrs. Farnsworth, the social director who had put the show together.

"You did a wonderful job, Mrs. Farnsworth," she said, as someone handed her some chocolate-chip cookies wrapped in a paper napkin. "I don't know what the children would have done for the last month if they hadn't had this to fill up their summer."

Mrs. Farnsworth beamed, taking the praise from the boss's wife for what it was worth, which was plenty. Claire shrank a bit from the ambiguity of her position. No one liked her very much, but everyone cared what she said. That was inside out from the way she was used to living her life, and she didn't like it.

"Claire, darling, your girls were marvelous."

She turned to meet the tall, strained-looking woman who had approached. "Hello, Frances. How are you?" She didn't ask the obvious question, which was, "What are you doing here?"—Frances Barberry had no children to watch and cheer for— because she knew the woman would have a ready-made answer for that, and for a lot of other questions Claire might throw at her. She knew very well why Frances had come. She'd come to watch the woman whose husband had taken the job she thought her own husband, Gregory, should have had.

In her more paranoid moments, Claire was sure Frances had a little book in which she documented every move Claire made, trying to build a case against her to present to the head office in San Francisco. Frances was a fearless campaigner, and Gregory was her crusade.

They pretended to exchange kisses, each holding herself rigid, and then stood back to eye each other warily. Frances might have been a pretty woman if she had trained herself to get rid of the sneer she employed in place of a smile. Claire didn't like her and might have actually been afraid of her if she'd cared enough.

Perhaps she should care more, she mused now, looking into the watery, spiteful eyes. Perhaps she should be out fighting for her husband and his place in the scheme of things the way Frances did. She had a feeling there were times Howard thought so.

"So Howard couldn't make it?" Frances asked with an edge of malice in her voice. She made a show of brushing away cookie crumbs Claire assumed she thought had fallen on her during their pantomime hug. "Why, all the other fathers are here. Even Gregory managed to take the time off, and he doesn't have any children in the show."

Gregory was the production manager and Howard's main assistant. Although he would know more about Howard's reasons and whereabouts than Claire, she answered gamely, "Howard is so busy right now. You know, Robert Camden is here from the home office, and Howard is tied up with him."

Frances's smirk said, "If you believe that load of bull, there's a bridge I'd like to show you," but her lips said, "Yes, I know all about Robert Camden. He and Gregory were at Stanford together. Howard really should have brought Robert on over to see this. Robert just loves to see the employees having a good time. He would have enjoyed it. I really thought Howard would be smart enough to think of that."

And that explained what Frances and Gregory

were doing here, Claire thought with a sigh of resignation. The cookies were a mess now, crumbled inside the napkin and dropping crumbs everywhere. Using them as an excuse, she took her leave of Frances rather more curtly than was politic, but her head was beginning to throb and she needed fresh air badly.

Finding the trash, she got rid of the cookies, then turned to gather up her girls. She hurried them out the door, wincing at the hot blast of wind that met them, and began the long, silent walk from the recreation center to her car, past the basketball and tennis courts, past the volleyball net, and finally, to her parking place. The girls got in and Claire sat behind the steering wheel, tethering her emotions, trying to think of something to say that would take away the sting of their father's absence.

"Katy, you were the greatest little frog." She turned and smiled at her youngest, who was sitting huddled in the corner of the back seat, her eyes red, her face puffy. "You jumped the highest of anyone. And Sam—" she turned to her older daughter and met the icy blue eyes that challenged her to find plausible excuses "—Sam, your voice was wonderful. Everyone said so."

Sam shrugged, her mouth a straight, tight line in her pretty face. "Who cares? It was dumb. I want to go home."

"It wasn't dumb. It was terrific. And I know your father would have been here if he could have gotten away."

"He promised," Katy said, her voice quavering. "I made him promise and he said he would."

Sam glanced back in disgust. "Grow up, Katy. It was just a kids' show. He forgot. That's all."

"He was busy," Claire said, growing desperate. How many times had she said that before? The excuses were sounding hollow in her ears, too, and she didn't have the heart to make them all again. "He was tied up," she said lamely, then turned the key in the engine and started the car.

She couldn't pinpoint when things had begun to fall apart. She only knew this wasn't what she had planned. She had two daughters who were beautiful and bright and talented. Was it asking too much that they have a happy home life?

She'd been so determined her children would have the warm, loving, caring, supportive family unit she herself had missed growing up. But perhaps that was the problem right there. She'd never had it, so maybe she didn't know how to make it happen, didn't have the knack. She spent most of her time blaming the tensions on Howard. Could it be it was really her own fault?

No, damn it. Howard was going to have to try harder. She would have it out with him tonight.

Their house was the nicest one in the compound. A two-story ranch-style with a three-car garage, it looked very much like any of the better tract homes built in the States. But to Claire, the walls seemed like cardboard, the rooms had the feel of a movie set. Somehow, it just didn't ring true.

It wasn't her and it wasn't hers. She missed her Ethan Allen furniture, her canopy bed, her rose garden. And she felt guilty for missing them.

Things. Superficial, material things. Lately the lack of them had loomed large in her consciousness and she wasn't proud of the fact. She'd never been one to place a lot of importance on possessions before. Years ago, in college, she'd claimed to need nothing but a pallet to sleep on, as long as she had her music.

And now here she was, missing her baby-grand piano, missing her rosewood writing desk, missing them all with an aching longing that clawed at her insides.

She walked quickly to the stainless-steel compact disk player and selected a bright, shiny disk. Beethoven's *Eroica*. At least she could still have music.

The first magic chords that swept through her were pure physical pleasure. She closed her eyes and swayed, letting the music possess her. Yes, without this, she would probably have shriveled up and died in this hot, dry land.

Samantha came into the room, Walkman earphones already attached to her ears, gave her mother a look of disgust, and promptly turned up the volume on whatever variety of sonic-boom noise she was currently destroying her hearing with, then left the room. Katy came running through in play clothes, mouthing something that Claire knew was a request for permission to play with the little boy next door. She nodded and watched Katy run out, her face already glowing with pleasure, her disappointment in her father forgotten.

But not really forgotten, Claire reminded herself. No, just pushed to the back of her young mind. She sighed and turned down her own music, then picked up the telephone and dialed.

She'd been trying to get through to Atlanta for the past two days, and now the numbers clicked in and she heard the familiar ring of her parents' home phone. Her heart beat a bit faster as she waited for someone to answer. Calling home was her one vice, her one luxury.

She needed to talk to her father. In a strange way, they'd become closer now that she was out of reach.

For most of her life, Richard Duvall had been a shadowy figure, rather unapproachable, completely reserved. Her mother had been her contact, her touchstone. Bright and lively, she'd shielded Richard from the parts of family life he didn't have the patience to handle. And Claire, the oldest of three, had never felt she'd really known her father.

For most of her life, she'd been sure he hated her. Her sister Laura had been plump and blond and pretty. Everyone loved Laura. But Claire had been a dark, scrawny, skinny little thing, with big feet and a large nose, always knocking things down, always stepping on someone's toes. Whenever her father saw her, a deep contemplative line would appear between his brows. She was sure he was thinking how much better things would be without her, and she tried to oblige by keeping out of his way.

She'd never dared tell anyone what she thought. She'd gone on for years, holding the knowledge tight inside, not letting anyone in on the secret. Her father hated her. Who would want to tell that to anyone?

Every now and then he would do something that made her wonder if she'd read him wrong, if maybe there wasn't still hope that they could have a father-daughter relationship. And then he would frown at her and growl out some caustic comment that reinforced her belief. Her father hated her. She could never be good enough for him.

Strangely, after thirty years of being sure her fears were based on fact, everything had suddenly turned around. A whole new relationship had sprung up between them across the thousands of miles of satellite feed and telephone wire. He was retired now, and often when she called, he was the only one home. Their conversations had started out tentatively. But they'd both been lonely, and little by little, the topics had grown. Now they had reached a point where they could talk for hours about life and beauty—and music. She realized with a new sense of joy that he was the one she took after. He was the one who could see into her soul. She was looking forward to how it would be when she returned to Atlanta, how close they would become, how much they would have to share. Meanwhile, she lived for their telephone conversations.

But this time there was no answer to her call. She sighed with exasperation and dialed her sister's number, only to get the same result. Where were they? She glanced at her watch. It was just a little past eight in the morning at home. They should be there.

The worry that trickled through her was forgotten when she heard the sliding-glass door open in the family room and a familiar voice ring out.

"Hi there! Hey, where is everybody?"

Claire sighed, half with annoyance, half with amused resignation. It was Margo Kincaid, her neighbor and constant visitor. Joe Kincaid was a mechanic and head of the Draxon motor pool, a busy man who looked as though he carried the weight of the entire Saudi operation on his square shoulders. And Margo was bored. At home she'd run her own restaurant and been darn good at it. But here there was nothing much for her to do.

Claire appreciated her to a certain extent, because she was the only person who had tried to help the Montgomery family settle in. Relentlessly friendly, she had a raucous sense of humor that was often grating, and Claire always felt just a little uncomfortable around her. She talked about everybody in and out of sight, and Claire was pretty sure she talked about Claire and her family when Claire was out of earshot. Besides, she wasn't crazy about the way the woman came in without waiting to be greeted at the door.

But she managed a welcoming smile as Margo came into the living room. "Hello, Margo. What's new?"

As if she needed to ask. Margo didn't require an opening to get her started. "Did you hear about Suzanne?" she cried, dropping onto the overstuffed couch and propping her feet up on the coffee table. "She's gone, honey. She's no longer among us. She's outa here. Vamoose." Margo grinned happily, her head of platinum-blond curls bouncing with her enthusiasm. About ten years older than Claire, she always dressed in pantsuits that snugly fit her trim but well-rounded figure. "She told old Bob she wasn't going to spend one more day in this Godforsaken country, and he could come along or not as he pleased."

Claire sank reluctantly into the chair across from the couch. Suzanne's husband was the chief petroleum engineer on the surveying team. News of a wife deserting her husband and heading for home was not unusual at any foreign outpost. Some women hated life away from home so much they were willing to risk their marriages to escape. Claire had some sympathy with the desire, but a certain horror for the deed. Family was everything. One had to make sacrifices to keep it together.

"What about her kids?" she asked.

Margo shook her head. "She took them with her."

Claire felt a heavy sadness seeping in. "So Bob's all alone?"

Margo grinned lasciviously. "Yeah. Dreamy hunk, isn't he? I wonder if he needs some company."

Claire looked up, startled, then decided she was joking. "Margo, cut that out. Sometimes I almost think you're serious."

"I am, honey. If I could find myself some cute little guy who wasn't scared to death of my husband, I'd be on him like a bluejay on a June bug." She squirmed in her seat and shuddered deliciously. "Ooh, it makes me feel good just to think about it."

Claire hid her smile. She was pretty sure Margo was all talk.

"Have you seen that bunch of roughnecks they

just brought in from working on rigs in the Gulf?"
Margo threw her head back and whistled. "I drove
by them today on my way to the market. They were
walking around in little bitty shorts, no shirts. I'm
telling you, honey, any one of those beauties could
jumpstart my daydreams." She threw her arms
open wide and cried, "I'm easy. Come and get me!"

Claire laughed. It was hard to take Margo seriously. "Margo, sometimes I think you're fixated on
sex."

"What else is there to be fixated on, honey? I
mean, my husband no longer comes home. My kids
have hit the teenage years, which means they no
longer recognize me. I feel like some cleaning
woman they've hired just to set food on the table."

"It can't be that bad."

"Are you kidding? My kids come into the house
and nudge each other and say, 'Who is that crazy
lady over in the corner? Think she'll be staying
long? Hope she doesn't drink all the Cokes.' "

Claire laughed again, but with some sympathy.
She'd seen Margo's two teenage boys, David and
Jesse, and she knew they were considered wild by
the others in the compound. How did you deal with
that in Saudi Arabia? She was having a hard-enough
time trying to deal with prepubescent girls.

She'd found Samantha talking to Jesse once,
alongside the garage after dark, and it had given her
a moment of unease. The boy looked like he belonged on a motorcycle. And Samantha's eyes had
been so bright, so full of wonder. She'd wanted to
take her little girl in her arms and whisper, "No,

please, no. There will be plenty of time for boys later. Don't grow up too soon."

But Sam had turned into someone who did not allow hugging. Or whispered confidences, for that matter. And so Claire had said nothing, other than telling her to come into the house.

"How about you?" Margo was asking, her gaze suddenly intense and curious. "You ever think about getting a little on the side?"

It took Claire a moment to understand the "little" Margo was alluding to, and when she did, she reacted automatically. "Oh, no! Of course not. I'm a happily married woman."

Margo made a face and intoned mockingly, "And it would be wrong."

Claire straightened in her chair, her fingers curling around the curved arms, her bright red nails almost cutting into the fabric of the upholstery. "Of course it would."

Margo's laughter filled the room. "Are you trying to tell me you've never even been tempted?" she asked scornfully.

Determined that she was not going to let the woman get to her, Claire made a solemn show of sighing and shaking her head. "Margo, my dear," she said, getting up and pouring her neighbor a glass of iced tea. "The secret is not to let yourself be tempted. The possibility doesn't even enter my mind."

"Because you're locking it out. Wow." Margo shook her head in derision and mocked Claire's words and tone when she answered, "Claire my dear, the secret is to use it before you lose it. You can't tell me that blustery, angry man you're married to is keeping you satisfied."

Claire felt a flush creep up her cheeks and she cursed herself for showing how offensive she found Margo's words. Sitting down again, she held on to her own glass of iced tea, wishing she could put it to her throbbing temple. "I'm perfectly happy . . ." she began, but Margo was hooting.

"Perfectly bored, you mean. Come on. Get real. Or better yet, get yourself a lover. That would fix you up in no time. Something short and sweet, with no entanglements. Someone along the lines, say, of those roughnecks I saw today."

"Roughnecks." Claire's tone was noncommittal, but Margo bristled, taking it as disapproval.

"Oh, I see. They're not good enough for you, is that it? Well, let me tell you, honey, every man looks the same in bed. What he does for a living doesn't matter when it comes to how much he knows about pleasing a woman. Believe me, at the moment of truth, that's all that counts. Join the real world, sweetie."

Claire sat back, her arms folded against her chest, repelled by the things this woman was saying. It all sounded so cut and dried, so animalistic, so selfish, as if all that mattered was the physical pleasure, as if relationships and caring had no place in lovemaking. If that was what the real world was all about, she didn't want to join it.

She was ready for Margo to go, and she was about to tell her so, but before she could say anything, the sound of a car coming up the drive filled the room.

"Oops, here's your lord and master." Margo jumped up and started for the sliding glass door, going out the way she came in. "At least yours comes home, honey. Consider yourself lucky." She grinned and disappeared around the corner, leaving Claire to stare after her, mulling over her last remark.

Lucky? Was that what she was? She didn't feel very lucky. Howard came home all right, but his arrival was seldom cause for rejoicing these days. Tonight was going to be even worse than usual, because she was going to have it out with him about missing the talent show. She was tired of letting him get away with these lapses. It was time he took responsibility for what he was doing to his family.

She sat very still, her hands folded in her lap, her face composed and calm, and waited, listening to Beethoven and waiting for the storm.

❧

Howard turned off the engine of his luxury car and sat staring straight ahead, his arms leaning on the steering wheel. He had to get control of this rage boiling inside him before he went into the house. He had to get a handle on it. Sitting very still, he concentrated all his mental strength on the problem, the cords in his neck standing out with the effort, forcing it down. Control. That was the secret. Control.

It had been a hellish day. Robert Camden had gone over the books like a polite but canny Mr.

Scrooge, jotting down notes and frowning. Then he had called a meeting of the department heads and proceeded to call into question every decision Howard had made since he'd arrived in Saudi. Every last one. Howard's hands began to tremble as he went back over the things Camden had said: ". . . perhaps Howard didn't fully understand the implications . . . it has never been Draxon company policy to . . . fifty years of carefully cultivated relations might be wiped out by one thoughtless gesture. . . ."

His hands tightened on the steering wheel, the knuckles white, as the rage surged up again. Damn Camden! He had always hated him. Camden and all the other blue bloods who ran Draxon Oil formed an impenetrable golden core, a private club that required certain background qualifications, such as being born into the best San Francisco families, such as a childhood spent in Bensonhurst, transcripts from only the best schools, and of course, a degree from Stanford University.

Howard didn't have any of those things. What he did have were brains and moxy and a love for the business. That was supposed to be enough. He'd thought he could make it on ability and ambition. Just to be safe, he'd added marriage to Claire. She wasn't from a San Francisco family, but her Atlanta roots were as blue as any others, and her quiet elegance had seemed to strike just the right note.

He'd done everything he could. Why hadn't it been enough? Why did they still want something he could never provide? The harder he worked, the nastier the sneers became. He'd invested his life in this company and, he was beginning to realize, he'd probably backed the wrong horse.

"Goddamn bastards," he muttered, his hands threatening to rip the steering wheel from its moorings. Every one of them was against him. He could see them all standing over him, their patrician noses in the air. And for some reason, Claire was with them, her pale smile as mocking as the rest. "Goddamn bastards!" he snarled, staring straight ahead as though his gaze could burn through wood. "I hate every one of you."

As she watched her husband come into the room, Claire studied him in a way she hadn't for a long, long time. His dark hair was steel gray at the temples now, cut a bit too short for her taste, and his shoulders seemed to hunch in a defeated way. She was struck by how much he'd aged, how careworn he looked. Was this really the same person as the young, bright-eyed idealist she'd married thirteen years before? His gun-metal blue eyes were flat now, cold, staring at her as though he wasn't quite sure who she was, either.

No, she realized with a start, nothing that benign. He was staring at her as though she was the enemy.

His gaze drew away from her, and without a word he turned toward the cabinet where he kept the liquor they had so carefully smuggled into this dry country. "Turn off that damn music," he muttered as he poured himself a drink.

It was a familiar greeting. She ignored it. "We missed you this afternoon," she said quietly.

He turned back, frowning. "This afternoon?" he repeated.

"The talent show," she reminded him, accusation in her tone and in her eyes.

"Oh, my God." For just a moment, pure distress washed across his face. Obviously he had totally forgotten.

Claire immediately felt a pang of remorse. She should have called him. After all, he had so much to do, so much to think about, maybe it wasn't fair to expect him to . . .

Then something inside her hardened. Yes, it *was* fair to expect him to remember something that important to his child. Katy had told him again and again how much his going meant to her. It was as though he hadn't listened to a word she'd said. Hadn't listened, or hadn't cared.

Howard became defensive. "Claire, you know Robert Camden is here from San Francisco. You know I have to devote every minute to him. I don't have time for children's shows in the afternoon."

Claire didn't often argue with Howard. There was no percentage in it. But this time she felt she had to make him understand, and she twisted her fingers together tightly as she forced herself to speak out. "If you knew you would have no time, why didn't you tell the girls that last night? Why did you let them build up their hopes?"

He looked at her as though he couldn't believe she might question his motives. "I thought I could get away myself. But it didn't happen." He tossed back his drink and reached again for the bottle of scotch. "Damn it, Claire, I've got more important things to do than sit and watch a bunch of stupid kids prance around on a stage."

They both realized at the same time that Katy was in the room, and they swung their gazes toward her. Katy was looking from one to the other of them, her eyes wide with hurt and distress.

Claire rose and said quickly, "Hello, darling. Daddy's home."

"Hi, Daddy," she said, her voice quavering slightly.

"Hi, Kitten." His voice was a little too loud, a little too jovial. "Listen, I'm sorry I missed your talent show today. I . . . I couldn't get away from the office in time."

"Oh, it's okay." She shrugged her little shoulders and began to walk across the room to the stairway.

Claire stared at Howard and he looked back resentfully, grimaced, then turned with a false smile to stop Katy before she left the room.

"Hey, I've got a great idea," he told her. "Why don't you and your sister get into your costumes and give me a talent show of my very own? Huh? What do you say?"

"Oh." Katy hesitated, then shook her head. "No, it's really not worth it, Daddy," she said. "It was just a dumb show. Never mind." She gave her father a quick hug and ran up the stairs.

Howard turned to Claire, triumph in his eyes.

"You see? They don't really care. You're the only one who cares."

Claire held her tongue. Was he really so blind, or did he just not want to see the truth? There was no use in trying to tell him what he wouldn't even try to understand. She turned away, no longer intent on getting him to face up to his responsibilities. What was the use?

But Howard wasn't ready to let the subject go. He was drinking now, throwing back one shot of liquor, then another. "You're always trying to sabotage me," he was saying bitterly. "God knows I've provided a good living for you. But that's not enough, is it? You've got to tear me down . . ."

Claire rose and started for the stairs. There was no point staying when he took this turn. He could go on for hours about what a lousy wife she'd been to him, how unsupportive she was. She didn't need to hear it again.

"That's right, run away like you always do. The truth hurts, doesn't it?" He snorted. "I hope you're going up to get ready for the party," he said. She stopped, hand on the bannister.

She turned. "Party?" Then she remembered the reception for Robert Camden and her heart sank. She was going to have to go out again tonight and see all those people who despised her. Squaring her shoulders, she smiled at her husband. "Of course," she said evenly. "That's exactly what I'm going to do."

Hurrying upstairs, she slipped out of her clothes and into the shower, letting the warm water wash her anger away. Anger wouldn't help. Anger only developed new problems. The trouble was, she had no idea what would help. And help was what they needed.

The incident with the talent show was not an isolated event. Life here in Saudi Arabia, without her family to dilute the mix, without her job to take up much of her time, without the usual diversions she had at home, had brought her face-to-face with facts from which she'd been trying to hide for years. She no longer loved Howard. Sometimes she wondered if she ever really had.

But that didn't matter. It was too late to go looking for love. She had a family, and her commitment was to the girls and their father. It was her job to keep them together. If only she knew how.

She thought again about the phone call she'd been trying to put through to her father. She missed him. She needed to talk to him. They'd become so close lately, she'd been thinking of telling him how things were with Howard, of asking his advice. Right now that looked like just about her last chance to find a way to make things right. She only hoped it wasn't too late.

CHAPTER

3

Claire eased her car into a parking place and turned off the engine, then looked out at the long expanse of walkway to the recreation center. The same building that had housed the talent show this afternoon was now going to accommodate the cocktail party reception for Robert Camden. She was sure it had been nicely decorated in the past few hours; still, there was something inherently depressing about the fact that there was only this one building that had to make do for just about every social function in the community and in her life.

She was alone. Howard had sent her on ahead while he went back to the office to pick up some papers he wanted to work on. He would be along shortly, but for now, she was going to have to face the crowd alone.

Alone. It seemed she was always alone lately.

Her hands were shaking. Was it nerves? Shyness? Anger at Howard? She wasn't sure.

She'd dressed very carefully, choosing a light silk chemise that flattered her too-thin body. She'd spent half an hour on her makeup, carefully outlining her eyes, then her lips. She always tried for a perfection she never reached. But she kept on trying.

Gathering together her small black purse and the light, filmy wrap she'd brought to wear about her shoulders, she stepped out of the air-conditioned car and into a blast of desert wind so dry and hot, it seemed to peel away her skin.

Lord, didn't it ever rain here? She longed for a huge summer thunderstorm to come charging through the way it did at home, an act of nature to clear the air and clean the landscape. Nothing ever seemed to change here. Every day was hot and dry and miserable, with the sun beating down and the wind sweeping in menacingly.

She closed the car door and stepped carefully and precisely onto the walkway, and that was when she noticed that the volleyball court she would have to pass was occupied by more than the usual children. There were six or seven men playing about the net—large, tanned, muscular men without shirts.

These must be the roughnecks Margo had seen earlier. Claire realized she was going to have to walk past this group. She felt like a teenager again, embarrassed to be noticed by the boys.

Don't be ridiculous, she told herself firmly.

You're a mature, married woman. These young men will have absolutely no interest in you. You can walk by and they'll never notice.

Still, she felt awkward, and she pulled the shawl tightly about her shoulders for protection. But it was all right. As she drew nearer to where the men were shouting good-naturedly at one another, her eyes began to glaze over and her patrician chin rose. It was either that or let herself blush, and so telegraph right away how much those sweaty, muscular bodies affected her. The classic, elegant approach had always been her forte, and she fell back on it now, walking by carefully, focusing her eyes on the sky. Just a few more steps, and she would be past them. Just a few . . .

She'd almost carried it off when the volleyball sailed out of the court, landing right in front of her. It would have hit her in the face if she hadn't caught it.

As though a switch had been thrown, suddenly everything changed. The volleyball felt light and lovely in her hands, and she flashed back to high school when she'd been on the team that had gone to state finals in the game. Some of the happiest days of her life had been spent on the court. She tested the ball experimentally, tossing it from one hand to the other, her purse pushed up under her arm.

One of the men had detached himself from the group and was coming her way, his blue eyes smiling, his hand held out for the ball.

"Thanks," he said.

She smiled and tossed it to him, letting it fly lightly from her fingertips.

"Nice pass," he said, catching it. His eyes traveled appreciatively over the picture she made in her clinging silk. "Want to play?"

She didn't really see him. Her mind was back sixteen years. The crowd was roaring in the stands. She and her teammates, full of hope, were caught up in the excitement of the game.

"Could I . . . would you mind if I tried one serve?"

They made way for her, murmuring. She dropped her purse and shawl to the ground and was glad she'd worn low-heeled shoes. The young man tossed the ball to her and she went to the baseline, testing it, then sending it up and giving it a stinging slap that sent it hard across the net, rebounding off the defender's hands. Delight shivered through her. She still had the touch.

The young man with the blue eyes grinned. "Hey, we get her for our team. First pick." He moved closer. "You want to try another one?"

She nodded, laughing. This was wonderful. She had forgotten how clean and pure sports were. You either came through or you didn't. You could feel when you were on, and it was a feeling like no other. "One more time," she said, taking the ball and repeating the expert serve, scoring another point for her side.

The men around her cheered, but the cheers and laughter were quickly stilled by a new voice.

"Claire, what the hell do you think you're doing?"

She whirled to face her husband. Palpably angry, Howard was striding toward her, his hands clenched into fists, his face contorted darkly. Panic flashed through her. In an instant, she could see this scene as he saw it and she knew she'd been a fool to let down her guard this way.

Turning to the blue-eyed man, she threw him a brief smile. "Thank you," she said formally. "It was kind of you to let me have a turn." Picking up her purse and shawl, she stepped quickly to Howard's side.

He put a possessive arm around her shoulders and led her away from the court toward the building. "Goddamn it, Claire, you look like some cheap tart cavorting with those bums. You're making a spectacle of yourself right in front of Robert Camden." His fingers dug painfully into her shoulder and his furious gaze burned into her. "You really are trying to sabotage me, aren't you?"

His words stung. She wanted to cry out a denial, make him see how harmless her actions had been. But she bit her lip and held her tongue. Howard was possessed by a demon right now. He couldn't hear logic, couldn't think rationally. Maybe when Robert Camden left, things would get better. Maybe.

Peter Arnold stood balancing the volleyball in one hand and watched Claire leave with the man who was obviously her husband. He'd been fascinated watching her cool exterior melt as she played ball. And then reappear the moment she heard her husband's voice.

Interesting. Very interesting. He wasn't sure what it was that appealed to him, but he enjoyed watching the way her skirt slapped against her trim legs, the way her chin was still high and proud, even though her husband seemed to be spewing an earful of recriminations at her. She looked good in a way that reminded him of something. How long had it been since he'd been with a woman like that?

Long months spent on oil rigs in the Gulf had left him tough, tanned, and hungering for a change. He'd been living a rock-and-roll life for years, and this woman reminded him of a Chopin nocturne.

How long had it been since he'd been with a woman who smelled clean and sweet and approached lovemaking with a hesitance, as though it were a mysterious undertaking that deserved a bit of reverence? He knew this woman would be like that. It was written in her dark eyes.

"Hey, Arnold, get your head out of your . . ."

"Cough up the ball, sucker, or we'll use your . . ."

Hardly hearing the casual insults, he tossed the ball back into the game, but he turned away himself, still watching as the woman disappeared into the recreation center. He believed in dreams, and he could have sworn he'd dreamed about her, somewhere, sometime.

"That's just a sample of what's waiting for us around here, boy."

He turned, startled, to find that Malcolm Edwards had come up beside him and was watching, as well. At forty, Malcolm was considered the old man of the crew. He'd been working Gulf rigs for twenty years. He'd been everywhere, seen everything. At least, that was what he would like the others to believe.

"That place over there—" he pointed a bony finger at the rec center "—that room is full of hungry women."

Peter laughed aloud, shoving his hands into the pockets of his shorts. "What?" He looked toward the building and sobered as he noticed that there was a row of female faces at each window, staring out at the volleyball game still in progress. "What are you talking about?" he asked doubtfully.

Malcolm shrugged as though it were all the same to him whether or not Peter believed him. "Think about it. All those wives. Here they are in this little closed society. They aren't allowed to have jobs in town. They aren't even allowed to go into town unless some husband drives them. They see the same faces every day. They don't dare mess around with each other's husbands, because everyone would know about it in two seconds. So it's not like it is at home, where you can always go to the other side of town where nobody knows you to shack up, or meet at some motel out on the highway. There's nowhere to go here. Every damn one of them is stuck with nothing but her own husband. They're sick of each other by now. Just look at the way those women are eyeing us, boy. We're fresh meat. We got it made if we work it right."

Peter grinned. "I take it you speak from experience."

"You'd better believe it. Listen, the fact is, to them, we're safe. We'll only be here for a few days, then we're gone. You find yourself a nice little hiding place, you can count on it. You've got a gold mine."

Peter shook his head. "Thanks for the advice, Malc. But my days of chasing quantity are in the past. I think I'll hold out for quality next time."

His gaze returned to the double doors Claire had disappeared through. Maybe it was just his imagination, but there seemed to be a new, softer feeling to the air. Yes, he was sure he'd dreamed about her. Someone that classy would be hard to forget.

She was a married woman, but that didn't bother him. Her marriage was far from happy, he could see that at a glance. Besides, he wasn't looking for anything long-term, and he would never pretend otherwise. Her life was her business. It was better that way.

❧

Claire had herself under control by the time they entered the room. She let Howard introduce her to Robert Camden and chatted with him quite pleasantly, then invited him to dinner for the following night, an invitation he seemed pleased to accept. Duty done, she turned away, slipping out of Howard's line of vision, and sighed with relief.

But that was short-lived. Ralph Quartern, Arab Relations and Liaison for Draxon, cornered her for one of his usual lectures. It was his job to smooth relations between the visitors and the host country, but he seemed to have made it a crusade. The man was obsessed with getting the oil people to understand the Arab point of view.

"This country is the birthplace of Muhammad and the Islamic religion," he informed her, as though there was no way she could have known this before he announced it. "This country has a past as grand as any in the world, a past filled with struggles and victories, domination by the Turks, and wars of liberation. They conquered Spain, these people. They rode across the vast deserts in huge camel caravans during the days of the frankincense trade. Just a few years ago, they were a nation of tribesmen roaming the sandy dunes, and now, look at the beautiful modern nation they're carving out of the desert."

"All thanks," Claire broke in wisely, "to the great god oil."

"Oil, yes, of course, oil." He shook his shaggy head of white hair as though it were indeed a mixed blessing. "They are letting us in now, you know, because they still need us. But the day will come when they don't need us at all, and then we'll be gone, like the Turks, like the winds that sweep across the sand, like the—"

"Uh, excuse me. I see someone I must talk to." Claire spotted Shareen Hunter and made good her escape. It wasn't that she didn't agree with the man.

But she knew these things already, and he always acted as though he were preaching to the heathens.

Shareen saw her, too, and came close with a secret smile to whisper, "Dragon alert, dragon alert. Beware. Dragon at one o'clock."

Claire turned to see Frances coming at her from the opposite side of the room. Reaching out, she grabbed Shareen by the wrist so she couldn't escape.

"You're a super sentry," she whispered back, half laughing, and very happy to have what was starting to look like the beginnings of a real friendship. "How are you at playing bodyguard?"

Shareen grinned. "Not bad. I can kidney punch along with the best of them. Want to see a sample on the dragon lady?"

"Only if she hits below the belt."

Frances arrived and Claire turned to give a pretend welcome with a forced smile. They made small talk for only a few moments before Frances got to the meat of the matter.

"Claire, dear, I did want to talk to you about something." She threw a baleful glance Shareen's way, but when Claire shook her head slightly, letting Shareen know she didn't want her to go, Frances went on anyway. "You're new here, and of course there are things you can't be expected to know about. I try to help you out when I can. You know I've done it in the past."

"Oh, yes." Claire smiled bleekly. "You were most helpful before I even arrived, when you had them send back the new furniture that was supposed to go in my house and put back in the old stuff that had been in the house for years."

"Oh. Well, you know, that new furniture was completely unsuited to the climate here. I knew it would make you miserable, so I had them return it. . . ."

"And when you hired that houseboy for me, the one who had lice. And sticky fingers."

Frances shook her head, undaunted. "That's the chance we all take, my dear."

Claire's eyes flashed. She didn't usually let herself catalogue her grievances this way, but now that she'd opened the floodgates, she didn't want to close them. "And when you advised Howard to send my girls away to boarding school in England, and even went so far as to submit applications."

Frances looked pained, as though she thought it quite bad form of Claire to bring up these past instances of her intrusiveness.

"Let's forget all that, Claire. I'm quite serious. This is something you obviously don't know, and should. For your own good."

Claire sighed. She'd said her piece. Frances had the hide of an elephant. "All right. What is it?"

Frances leaned closer and spoke conspiratorially. "The fact is, my dear, wives of Draxon executives are not supposed to fraternize with roughnecks."

Claire blinked and thought, My God, I'm never going to live this down, am I? A few glorious moments playing a sport I once loved, and the rest of the world is going to hold it over my head forever. "Fraternize?" she echoed aloud.

Frances nodded, her eyes glittering maliciously. It was obvious she smelled blood and was ready to go for the kill.

"Everyone saw you out there. Can you imagine what Robert Camden must think? And then, to find out you're the wife of the Director of Operations . . ."

Claire started to shake her head, but there really wasn't much she could say. Frances was probably only articulating what all the others were thinking. She only wished she didn't have to care. But Robert Camden was important. So she had to.

"So unsuitable, so gauche. Really, darling, you should show more judgment. You know this reflects on Howard. Why, he might lose a promotion because of this. Can you imagine what Robert Camden is going to tell them back at the home office?"

"Yes," Shareen broke in suddenly, surprising them both. Claire had forgotten she was there. "As a matter of fact, I know exactly what Robert Camden is going to tell them back at the home office. Because—" Shareen smiled pleasantly. "—you see, I was standing right beside him when he looked out the window and saw Claire." She paused dramatically, then grinned. "He said, 'What a lovely woman. And athletic, too. I like the way she keeps herself busy. I'm sure she's an example to all the wives here in the compound.' "

Claire and Frances both stared at her, then looked at each other. Laughter bubbled up in

Claire's throat and she could hardly contain it. "Gee, thanks, Frances, for your concern," she said, eyes sparkling. "But I guess once again, I don't really need you."

Frances looked as though she wanted to say more, but Shareen's words had robbed her of her moment. Finally, she gave up. "Hmph," she sniffed, and moved on to torture someone else.

"He didn't really say that, did he?" Claire asked when she was out of earshot.

"How should I know?" Shareen admitted, laughing. "I was on the other side of the room at the time."

Claire gasped. "Say, you are a good bodyguard. I ought to put you on a payroll."

Laughing, they walked together toward the table where appetizers had been set out on crystal plates. "Why is it that we haven't become better friends before this?" Claire asked, genuinely curious. They seemed to get along so well on such a short acquaintance.

Shareen picked out a stuffed mushroom and popped it into her mouth. "I haven't been here much since you arrived," she told Claire. "Now that we're living in this part of the world, I take every chance I get to zip up to Beirut and visit my family."

"You have family there?"

"I'm Lebanese. My parents took me to the States when I was young, but I still have aunts and uncles . . . and my grandmother."

They both began to fill plates with tiny delicacies.

"Isn't it awfully dangerous there these days?" Claire asked.

"Oh, yes. That's one reason I go."

Claire shook her head. "I don't get it."

They found a place to sit outside beneath the canopy. Everyone else was still inside in the air-conditioning, so they had privacy.

"It's like this," Shareen told her quietly, sitting with her beautiful embroidered skirt spread out around her. "My grandmother has a huge villa on the hill overlooking the ocean. It was once full of paintings and sculpture and tapestries, and there were fountains in the courtyard. A fleet of servants polished everything every day. My grandmother reigned over them, and over the rest of her family, like the queen of a small country. Then, almost twenty years ago, the war came. Little by little, she lost almost everything. The servants were the first to go. Then the artwork. By now, most of the members of her family have vanished, either killed in the fighting, or emigrated to some safer land. She's alone in her big old empty house, and she sits in the hallway that faces the front door. She holds a rifle on her lap. And she waits for intruders."

Claire was intrigued by her story, horrified by what it implied. She thought of her own grandmother sitting in her black crepe and eating strawberries in her sunny living room. "But that's terrible. Can't you get her out of there?"

Shareen shrugged. "She won't leave. Her whole life is in that house. She hasn't left it in years. She just sits, waiting to fight off the vandals."

"Vandals! Are there . . . ?"

"Oh, yes. And squatters. That's why she hasn't left the house. It's happened to friends of hers. They left for only hours, and when they returned, they found their homes full of squatters. Once they get inside, it's almost impossible to get rid of them." She smiled, though her eyes held an eternal sadness. "Like human cockroaches."

Claire had read about the situation in parts of Lebanon, but Shareen's tale brought it home to her in a way it had never done before. "Why do they keep fighting?"

"They've been at it so long now, I don't think they know how to live any other way. Beirut was once called the Paris of the Middle East." She sighed. "Now it's more like Hiroshima after the bomb."

Silently, they mulled that over. Claire thought of the old woman fighting to maintain the family home she'd cared for over the years, holding on to the core as it all unraveled around her, and she felt infinitely sad. The people the old woman had loved were gone. What was she holding on to? The memories? The ghosts?

Suddenly the quiet was shattered by shouting, and they rose and went back inside to see what was going on.

The shouts were coming from Bob Sanders, whose wife, Suzanne, had just left him. He appeared to be calling out through the double front doors to the roughnecks, still playing volleyball.

Frances was wandering through the room, a

drink wobbling in her hand. She turned toward Claire in horror. "He's inviting them to join the party," she cried. "Can you believe it? The man is drunk as a skunk. The Director of Operations surely should do something about him."

Claire ignored her words, watching Bob's frenzied antics instead. Actually, the whole situation was pretty comical, with Bob jumping up and down and the other men trying to restrain him. The roughnecks were pulling on shirts and walking toward the building. They were coming in.

A ripple of excitement ran through the assembled crowd. It wasn't often that they mixed with the blue-collar workers. This would be something new, something to add a little spice to the same old party round they were so used to.

Bob greeted the men at the door, draping an arm around one neck, then another, giving maudlin speeches about how he was one of them now. Claire couldn't help but laugh. Poor Bob. He was taking his wife's desertion hard.

As she turned away, her gaze met that of one of the roughnecks who had just come in. It was the blue-eyed young man who had allowed her to play with the group for a few moments. He'd put a khaki shirt on over his denim shorts, but it was open halfway down his chest, revealing plenty of smooth tanned skin. She stared at him a bit too long, and he stared back. Turning, she made her way quickly to another part of the room. But from then on, whenever she saw him, he was looking at her with a particularly intent gaze that made her feel strange for a reason she couldn't pin down.

Finally, she realized what it was. There was a man other than her husband who was very much aware of her.

At first she thought she must be mistaken. She'd had men call her beautiful in her younger days, but she'd never felt beautiful. And now that she'd become so skinny, she often felt awkward rather than attractive. Women were supposed to grow more womanly with age, rounder, softer, comfortable. And she only seemed to get more angular, flatter, bonier. Men weren't supposed to be attracted to her.

But this man was looking in a way she hadn't had a man look at her in years. She had to admit it was a bit exciting—even if, she told herself quickly, it didn't mean a thing. But every time she caught his eye, his glances spoke of hot steamy nights with saxophones wailing in the background—things she'd never experienced but was curious about. She laughed at herself for getting caught up in the fantasy. A roughneck! Really!

Finally, she was ready to go home. She'd made all the small talk she was capable of for one evening. The room's atmosphere was getting heavier and heavier as the mingled scents of perfume and cigarettes began to thicken into a palpable cloud.

Approaching Howard, she tried to signal to him, but he was looking singularly harried. He was talking to Robert Camden and Gregory and gesturing wildly with his hands, which made her wonder if he'd had a little too much to drink. She gave up trying to catch his eye and slipped outside instead, hoping for some fresh air, going under the canopy where she and Shareen had sat before. It was dark outside now, and it was a moment before she realized the blue-eyed man from the volleyball court was sitting on the bench as though he'd been waiting for her.

He rose and stepped toward her, just inches away, before she'd had a chance to register his presence and beat a hasty retreat.

"Ah," he said, and even in the gloom she could see the amusement sparkling in his eyes. "The lovely lady with the killer serve—and the tyrannical husband."

She smiled nervously and looked behind her, wondering if it would look odd if she dashed back inside right now. Yes, she decided. Good grief, she was the director's wife. She should be able to converse calmly with one of her husband's employees.

Drawing upon her reservoir of Duvall dignity, she calmed herself and said, "Thank you so much for letting me have a chance out there. It's been years, but I used to love volleyball."

"I can tell. You play very well."

"We had a pretty good team in high school."

His large strong hand was coming toward her and she stared at it for a long moment, admiring his long, beautifully tapered fingers, before she realized he wanted to shake hands.

"I'm Peter Arnold," he told her as she hastily met his hand with her own slender one.

"Claire Montgomery," she replied, then wondered if she ought to have given her first name. But that thought was lost as she realized he wasn't letting go of her hand.

She stared up at him, puzzled. He was awfully good-looking, with a straight nose, wide full lips, eyes that sparkled with humor and intelligence, blond hair left a bit shaggy, skin bronzed by the sun. He wasn't much taller than she was, but his shoulders seemed to stretch a mile wide. And surely he couldn't have been more than twenty-six or -seven.

"I . . . uh . . . it's very nice to meet you," she managed, glancing down at how his hand held hers, then looking back into his eyes. "Have you been in Saudi Arabia long?"

"Off and on for the last three years. I just got in from six months on a rig in the Gulf."

"Six months."

Why wouldn't the man let go of her hand? He was standing there, so close, so solidly male, and holding on to her hand as though it was the most natural thing in the world to do. She tugged slightly, but he showed no intention of releasing her, and she felt like laughing. It was absurd.

"Six months," she repeated. "My, that is a long time to be without—" She stopped. Without what? She had no idea what life was like on an oil rig.

But he seemed to have read more into her aborted statement than she'd intended, and his smile was knowing in a way that might have disturbed her if she'd been able to think clearly. "You're damn right it's a long time," he said softly, his voice husky in a way that made her dress feel too tight. "Six months without a real bath, without being able to really let loose—and worst of all, without a woman."

Oh, so that was it. She tried to laugh, but her voice sounded strange to her ears. When was he going to release her hand? This was utterly ridiculous. What if someone came out and saw them like this? "Well, I'm sure there must be plenty of girls in town who . . ."

He grinned and somehow managed to pull her even closer. "You haven't been in the Middle East very long, have you, Claire?"

She felt a small shock at his use of her first name, but it was certainly consistent. He was acting much too familiar. Funny, though, instead of putting her off, it was turning her on. She was really going to have to get control of herself. Just a moment or two more to enjoy this, well, thrill, she supposed it was. He was so handsome and it had been so long since a man had seemed at all attracted to her. Just a moment more, and then it would be back to normal. She would tell Shareen about this, and they would laugh together.

"I, uh, well . . . no, I've only been here for a few months."

"Then maybe you aren't aware of how protective Arab men are of their women. If I so much as looked at an Arab girl sideways, I'd probably wake up with a knife in my chest."

She knew that, of course. She'd been told. But she hadn't thought of the ramifications for men like these roughnecks. What did they do, anyway? Surely they didn't just . . . abstain?

"The Middle East is a dangerous place. That's what makes it so exciting to live here."

"Exciting?" Claire's smile came and went nervously. "I don't find it very exciting. In fact, I think it's fairly boring."

"That's because you hide yourself away in this compound, a little piece of the States set down in the middle of the desert. If you went out into the country and mixed with the people, you'd see what I mean." He cocked his head to the side, his eyes probing hers. "I could take you out. I could show you what I mean."

His face was in shadows, but she could feel the intensity of his gaze, and her heart began to beat quickly. A gust of wind ripped at her hair, and he curled his hand more tightly around hers, bringing it to his chest, resting it against his heart.

"Listen," he said huskily, turning his head as though he heard a distant sound, though all she could hear was the lonesome whistling of the wind. "The song of the desert. It reminds me of Rimsky-Korsakov's *Scheherazade*. Do you know the piece?"

Her eyes widened in surprise. "Of course. But how do you . . . ? I mean, that's a classical piece, a symphonic suite. Where did you hear it?"

He was laughing at her. "Mysterious, isn't it? What with me being a roughneck and all. And God knows, we roughnecks ain't got no culture nohow. That's a rule."

She flushed with embarrassment. "I didn't say that."

"But you meant it." He shrugged, then forced her hand to flatten over his heart. "So I break the rules. I love classical music. Especially opera. When that tenor starts in on 'La donna e mobile,' it never fails to raise the hair on my neck."

She stared at him, not quite daring to be delighted to find a kindred spirit in such an unlikely form, waiting to hear the catch.

"Shocking, isn't it?" he teased, his face getting closer to hers, so close she felt his breath when he spoke.

She shook her head, dazed. "No. Not really. But it is . . . surprising."

"I'm a surprising kind of guy. You'll find that out as you get to know me better."

His free hand was suddenly at her neck, his fingers playing with the wisps of hair that had pulled away from the knot, and she seemed paralyzed, powerless to remind him that he had no right to touch her this way. The insanity of it all was overwhelming, yet she couldn't pull away. Her breath was coming in small, awkward gasps, and her heart was beating fast. And at the same time, she felt alive in a way she never had before, tingling and aware. It was deliciously intoxicating.

He was going to kiss her. He couldn't do that. It wasn't right. But his face was coming closer and her eyes were beginning to close as she melted toward him.

And then she realized what was really going on

here. Of course. How could she have been so blind, so gullible? These men didn't dare approach Arab girls. So what was there left but company wives? The man was hoping to seduce her!

She was horrified, flattered, repulsed and insulted all at once, and that revelation gave her the strength, at last, to do something other than sink into his spell.

"Oh," she said, stopping cold, her eyes open wide. "Uh . . . wait a minute." She pulled back, adjusting her composure. "Excuse me," she managed to say coolly, twisting from his grasp, regaining possession of her own hand and stepping back. "But I think you ought to know, my husband isn't much more accommodating than Arab men are. At least not where his wife and family are concerned."

She looked at him quickly, her heart still pounding, and there he was, laughing, not at all chagrined. His smile was lopsided, assured, infuriatingly arrogant. "Don't get the idea I'm begging, lovely lady," he said softly. "I do have my resources. We're only here for a stopover. We're on our way to Athens for some R and R. There will be plenty of volunteers there."

Was he talking about what she thought he was talking about? It took her breath away that he could be so frank about it, and she didn't know what to say.

His smile faded and something that looked like sincerity grew in his eyes. "I'm sorry if I come on a little strong," he said softly. "I think you're the most beautiful thing I've seen in a long, long time.

I just had to touch you—the way you want to run your hand over an exquisite piece of sculpture, or dig your fingers into thick, lustrous fur." His gaze explored her face. "I didn't mean to scare you."

She wanted to touch him, too, but she would never have managed the honesty he brought to the gesture, so she stood stiffly and clenched her hands into fists at her sides. "You didn't scare me," she lied, looking around, trying not to show how her heart was beating. "But my husband will be looking for me."

"Ah, yes, your husband." He positioned himself so that she would have to push him out of the way in order to leave the area. The light in his eyes had gone from amusement to cynicism. "Do you always do everything he says? Do you always jump just as high as he tells you to?"

Her Duvall blood rose as her eyes narrowed. Who did this impertinent young man think he was? It was true he was fatally attractive, but that didn't give him the right to goad her this way. "That is none of your business," she snapped.

"Probably not. But I can't help being curious. You see, I've been conducting a survey of sorts. We Westerners are so sure that Arab women are totally dominated by men and that our women are completely free. I've been looking into the situation and I've been sort of formulating a different theory. When I see husbands order their wives around like your husband did you, I think of a sheik with his harem. You know what I mean? And I begin to wonder just how much freer you really are."

Claire's cheeks felt hot. She wasn't sure if she was being teased or insulted, but she'd had about enough of this irreverent chit-chat. "Listen, you, my husband is—"

"Oh, yes, I know. Your husband is Director of Operations. He could make or break me. He could have me fired. He could have me diced into little pieces. All you have to do is say the word." He leaned closer again, his voice low and seductive. "But you're not going to do that, are you? You wouldn't want to ruin my survey."

She could hardly breathe. She knew what she should do. Howard would be only too glad to use Peter Arnold as a whipping boy. And yet, the roughneck was right. She wasn't going to tell Howard anything. "You're taking a big chance," she whispered, her eyes very wide as they stared into his.

"Chances are what make life interesting. The question is . . ." He reached for her again, just a finger to her chin, but she felt herself shiver with guilty delight at his touch. "The question is, what kind of chance are you willing to take?"

He smiled, and then he turned and left her standing there, still shivering with the sense of him.

CHAPTER

Claire sat before her mirror, a brush in her hand. She stared at the woman in the reflection, hardly recognizing her. She had the horrible, sinking feeling that perhaps she had changed as much as Howard had. Was it merely the passage of time that had cut those hard little lines along the sides of her mouth? Or was it unhappiness?

Unhappiness. She shivered, hardly daring to articulate the emotion. Unhappiness. What right did she have to be unhappy? She was married to, well, in many ways, a wonderful man, who provided a very good living and had given her two wonderful children. Wonderful, wonderful. Life should be like that, too. Why wasn't it?

Maybe she was asking too much. After all, who said you had to be happy all the time? Being a good person and doing what was right and making other people happy—wasn't that what it was all about?

But she felt cold as she thought of Katy and Sam and even Howard, and she realized she was failing even there. They weren't any happier than she was. What was she doing wrong?

She looked back into the mirror and wondered if Peter Arnold had seen the unhappiness. Perhaps that was what had keyed him in, made him think he could approach her with his provocative suggestions. He'd sensed she was missing something—that she would be easy prey.

Shaking her head, she almost laughed aloud at the worried-looking woman in the mirror. She was certainly getting fanciful. Peter Arnold was just a young man looking around for a woman, and she happened to get in the line of fire. That was all there was to it. She would probably never see him again.

"Let's get to bed," Howard said gruffly from the bathroom.

Claire stiffened. She recognized the tone. He wanted to make love. Everything in her rose in protest. The last thing she wanted right now was his touch. Feelings of resentment and confusion were churning in her, and it was going to be very difficult to hold them back and pretend desire.

She tried to think of a way out. But there was none. It was her duty to hold this family together, and that meant sleeping with Howard. As her mother used to say, she'd made her bed—so what if she couldn't manage to sleep in it?

Howard came out of the bathroom and

brushed by her. "Come on," he muttered. "Let's go."

Claire had a sudden picture of an Arab wife, veiled and subservient, being ordered into the bedroom by her husband. Was Peter Arnold right? Was this any better?

She had the urge to stand up and refuse, to tell Howard he could sleep in the den, that she couldn't stand the thought of his hands on her body right now. But she knew before the thought was fully formed that she wouldn't do it. Experience had taught her that Howard did not like to be rejected. He didn't handle it well at all, no matter how tactfully it was done. Headaches didn't cut any ice with him. "Don't worry. You've got a headache because you're tense. A good dose of sex will fix it right up." How often had she heard that one?

No, he was walking around like a bomb about to go off as it was. She couldn't risk antagonizing him further. Besides, she was desperately trying to think of ways to draw this family back together. Refusing sex would only pull them further apart.

She rose reluctantly and followed her husband to the large double bed. He lay back, completely naked, his eyes cold but greedy as they examined her. She lay beside him in her cotton nightgown and began to do the things he liked her to do, despite the protest that rose in her throat. After all, she thought with a touch of humor—which was her saving grace in these situations—she was a *woman*, and therefore used to holding back disgust as she changed diapers, picked up after the dog, cleaned

up the sick room when small children had the flu.
She could do this, too.

"Take off your nightgown."

Her hand went to the cloth at her throat. She
hated to reveal her thin body. "Can we turn off the
light?" she countered.

"No." He moved impatiently. "Come on. Take
it off. You shouldn't be ashamed of your body. It's
not that bad."

Thank you, dear Howard, she thought wearily.
But what did she care really? He'd seen her a thousand times. Steeling herself, she slipped out of the
garment and returned to her duty, trying to block
out her discomfort.

Peter Arnold's face swam into her mind again.
He was laughing mockingly at what she was doing.
"Free as a bird, aren't you?" she could imagine him
taunting. "Free to do any little thing your hubby
wants you to do."

The thought of the handsome blond hanging
over the bedpost giving her advice at this point
made her smile. Unfortunately, Howard caught
sight of her face. His hand reached out roughly to
stop what she was doing.

"What the hell's so funny?" he demanded.

"N-nothing. Howard, I wasn't laughing at
you."

"The hell you weren't." Rage contorted his
features. "Damn you! You're just like all the rest
of them." He pulled away from her, his eyes aflame
with irrational anger and the need to get revenge
for the pain he obviously felt himself. "Stay away

from me, you bitch. Who would want you anyway? You're flat as a board. Making love to you is like screwing Peter Pan."

He rolled off the bed and onto his feet, grabbing his robe as he flung himself out of the room. Claire pulled the sheet up over her chest. Her eyes stung with tears. Inside, she cringed from the injuries his words had inflicted. He'd sliced her to ribbons before, but somehow this time was worse. This time, something deep inside her was cut to the quick by his venom, and she lay back aching, wounded and losing hope. Was there any way to rebuild something that had been splintered so badly?

❧

The sound of the telephone split the silence of the predawn. Claire sat up in bed, not sure for a moment what it was. Then she ran and grabbed the receiver. "Hello?"

"Claire?" It was Laura, her sister in Georgia. Claire's blood froze.

"What is it?" she demanded without preamble. "What's happened?"

Laura's voice was strained. "It's Daddy, Claire. He's . . . he's had a heart attack and they don't think he's going to last much longer."

Her world rocked against its moorings.

"When did it happen? Is he conscious? Where is he?"

"Just come home, Claire. Make it fast."

She was pulling a suitcase out of the closet before Howard was fully awake.

"What's going on?"

"My father's had a heart attack. I'm going home."

"Home? You mean back to Atlanta? You can't do that."

She whirled and stared at him, still lying in bed, up on his elbow, his hair mussed and sticking out at odd angles. He looked confused and defenseless. Had she ever really loved this man? If so, she couldn't remember how or why.

"I'm going, Howard. Can you call the airport for me? I'm leaving on the first flight to anywhere with connections."

He made no effort to move. "You can't go," he said flatly. "You invited Robert Camden for dinner."

If she didn't handle this very carefully, she would start to cry, and once she started to cry, she wasn't sure if she could go on. Steeling herself, she said very evenly, "To hell with Robert Camden. My father's had a heart attack. They say . . . they say it's real bad. He may die. I'm going, Howard. I have to."

"But what about me? Your first responsibility is to me, after all. What am I going to do with you gone?"

She wasn't sure if he was just being annoying or if he really meant it, so she ignored his question and went on pulling clothes out of drawers and stuffing them into the case.

"You can't go without my permission, you know."

She stopped and turned slowly to look at him. "What did you say?"

His smile was oddly malicious. "The Saudi Arabian government won't let you leave without my permission. You know that. A woman in this country needs her husband's permission to get on an airplane."

She sank slowly into a chair, desperation beginning to build. "Howard, please . . ."

"Why should I let you go? If your father's dying, your being there isn't going to stop it. All that way, all that money just to say goodbye to an old man you never exactly doted on in the first place? It doesn't make any sense. You'd better stay here."

For the first time, she felt actual hatred for this man. "Howard . . ." Her voice was strangled. She'd been married to him for thirteen years. How well did she know him? What would work best? Crying? Pleading? Demanding? Maybe she could threaten to call the home office in San Francisco. Or run out into the night and knock on Robert Camden's door. She had to go. She forced herself to be calm and then said as slowly and quietly as she could, "Howard, I must go. Surely you can see that. Please don't be difficult. Please."

He stared at her for a long moment, then shrugged. "Okay, what the hell. Go, if you have to. But I can't take care of the girls," he went on. "Who's going to take care of them?"

She rose, relief flooding her. "They're going with me. He's their grandfather, remember?"

Howard was quiet for a moment as she worked, sorting through items, finding shoes, searching for earrings. "Good idea," he said at last. "Listen, why don't you find a way to leave them with your mother when you come back? They just get in the way here, anyway. Maybe if the kids weren't underfoot all the time, we could get along better."

His words cut little notches of hopelessness in her soul, but she didn't have time to deal with that now. "I can't believe you're saying this," she said tonelessly as she worked. "You would dump the girls on my mother at a time like this?"

"She's always liked having them around."

Claire turned on him, her face blank, and spoke to him as she never had before. "My father may be dying. I don't have time for this. Make our reservations and get out of my way."

The Atlanta airport was the gateway to home. When Claire emerged from the debarking runway, flanked by Katy and Sam, Laura let out a screech and ran to take them all into her arms at once.

"How is he?" Claire asked anxiously.

Laura pulled back. "Bad. Very bad. We'd better hurry."

Laura chattered on the long drive to the hospital, more nervous than anything else, and the girls answered and asked questions, catching up on things they'd missed being half a world away. But Claire didn't hear a word of it. She couldn't enjoy the Atlanta skyline, nor the beautiful Smoky Mountains. It was all a black mist to her. She was racing to the side of the most important man in her life, and he was dying.

They rushed across town on the freeways, rushed from the parking lot, rushed down the long, sterile hallways. And suddenly, when Claire was just outside his room, the rushing came to a stop. For a moment she thought it would be impossible to take that last step.

Finally she forced herself through the doorway. The room was dimly lit. Her mother sat beside the bed, her eyes red and swollen. Her brother, Gary, stood at the window, looking out. And there on the bed was her father—not the strong vital man she remembered, but a gray sagging shell of the man he had been, a shadow of a life stuck with tubes and monitored by wires.

Claire froze, denial running through her. This couldn't be her father. It didn't even look like him. There had to have been some mistake. . . .

"Claire." Her mother was up and moving toward her with a watery smile. "I'm so glad you made it."

Her arms went around her mother's shoulders. When had they become so frail? Guilt assailed her, guilt for having been gone for the past few months while her family had been going through these changes.

"Mama . . ." Her voice was choked with tears.

"Come say something to your father."

Her mother led her to the bedside. Claire went reluctantly, still not convinced this man was really her father. Sitting down on the edge of the bed, she tried to think of something to say, something to do. And then his eyes opened, and in their glimmer she saw the man she loved so very much.

"Daddy," she whispered, leaning close. "Oh, Daddy . . ."

"Claire." His hand moved and she grasped it. "You got here. Thank God."

"Daddy." She was smiling through her tears. "I love you. We have so much to talk about. I have so much to ask you."

His fingers curled weakly around hers. "You'll do it, baby," he whispered, his voice barely audible. "You'll find a way."

She had no idea what he was talking about, but there was no time to ask him. His eyes closed and his hand went limp in hers. The doctor stepped forward and asked them all to clear the room. He didn't expect her father to be able to talk any more that evening.

They went home for a sad dinner, then came back and took turns sitting by him through the night. When it was her turn, Claire took his hand in hers and whispered to him, though she knew he couldn't hear her. She looked at the waxy skin of his face and anger filled her. It was too soon for him to go. She wasn't finished with him yet.

A memory slid into her consciousness. She'd been little, six or seven years old, and she could remember running through the house, looking for a place to hide. She'd just dropped a glass of milk on her mother's brand-new, egg-shell blue carpeting in the family room, and instead of sticking around to take her lumps, she'd run, full of panic and remorse. Dashing in through an open door, she'd found herself in her father's den, and she'd rushed to hide in the leg space of his desk.

She heard him come into the room and shut the door, and her heart thumped so loudly she was sure he could hear her. She couldn't have picked a worse place to hide than the private place of the man she feared so. At that time he had been so distant, so removed from their daily lives, that even on good days he terrified her. Shivering, she waited for the worst to happen, her face pressed against the wood, her eyes closed, her heart in her throat.

And suddenly, music filled the room. He had turned on the stereo. The sweet, high sound of violins curled through the air, and Claire opened her eyes and listened, enthralled. The music was beautiful, so different from the light pop tunes her mother listened to. It seemed to speak directly to her heart in a way she'd never experienced before. She sat huddled very still, listening, and she had no idea how much time passed. She was transported.

And then he found her, his large hand reaching under the desk to pull her out, and she was terrified again, tears running down her cheeks. She stared up into his fierce eyes and was sure this must be what God looked like.

"What the hell are you doing here? Spying on me?" he'd demanded.

She'd begun to cry. He'd been exasperated, but she realized now, not cruel. He'd put her in his big easy chair and handed her a handkerchief.

"Stop your blubbering," he'd growled at her. "Here, dry up before I send you back to your mother."

Slowly, the sobs had subsided. She kept the cloth to her face so she wouldn't have to look at him again. But the music—that was what she remembered most vividly from that scene. The soaring violins, the crashing chords as the piano joined in. And when she finally dared to look up into his eyes again, it was as though some message flashed between them.

He stared at her, then gestured toward the record player. "You like that?" he asked gruffly.

She stared back, aware of how small and skinny she was, still sure he disliked her because of it. But she nodded.

"What do you know," he'd muttered. "I may have got one of you, after all."

She hadn't understood what he meant then, and he hadn't explained. He'd sent her out of his private domain, back to the rest of the house where her mother held sway, and she hadn't dared to go back into his den again for years. But then one day she was told she was to begin piano lessons. The lessons changed her life.

All those years when he had been gruff and aloof and locked himself away from the rest of the family, she'd known what he was doing in there— listening to his music. And even though no one ever heard it, for he never turned it up very loud, it was there in his head, where he lived, where he wanted to live. And she had been the only one who had understood that.

"Oh, Daddy," she whispered now, leaning over his still form. "Why didn't you tell me then? Why didn't you invite me into your den to listen with you?" There was still so much to know. He couldn't leave her now.

But he never regained consciousness. In the early morning, his heart stopped beating and he slipped away.

Claire was in a state of shock. How could it have happened so fast? She had the irrational feeling that she could have prevented it somehow, if only she had been here. Again and again she asked Laura for details, trying to puzzle out how this could have happened, how it could have been stopped in its tracks if only someone had seen it coming.

"There is absolutely nothing you could have done," Laura insisted. "Don't be silly, Claire. You have your own family to take care of. You couldn't be expected to take care of this one, too."

But it wasn't what people expected of her; it was what she expected of herself. She had hero-worshipped her father from afar and finally had been within reach of really knowing the man—and then he had left her. Now the relationship she had so looked forward to would never be. She was finding it very difficult to let go of the anguish of that reality.

Laura had very little patience with this line of thought. Two years older than Claire, she had always had a very matter-of-fact relationship with her father, and in her view it was one that had never needed deepening and strengthening.

Married to Jim Craymore, an ambitious industrialist who still had time to coach their two boys in Little League baseball and bring his wife flowers for no reason at all, she handled the family investments, sat on a few boards, managed a small interior-decorating business, and generally had a wonderful life. It was something she wanted her sister to have, as well, and it annoyed her that Claire didn't strive for such perfection.

Laura had been prone to asides and sarcastic comments on the state of Claire's marriage almost from the beginning. A one-week visit to the Montgomery family in Saudi Arabia a few months before had crystalized her attitude and she was now very open about her hostility toward the state of affairs in Claire's life.

"Claire, you are really taking this too hard. Daddy was not a young man. His dying was a pretty natural occurrence, all things considered."

They'd gone to the Peachtree Center, shopping for something for Claire to wear to the funeral, and had stopped for a cup of tea before heading back to their mother's house. From the window of the tea room, they could see the traffic swirling by. A siren wailed. The modern world was moving at a frantic pace. Claire couldn't help but think of the ancient land where she had been living for the past few months. The contrast was appalling, and she wasn't sure which place she liked least.

"I'll tell you what I think," Laura went on.

"Don't you always?" Claire murmured, rolling her eyes.

Her sister ignored her thrust. "I think you would be able to let Daddy go more easily if you had a decent relationship with a man."

Claire stared at her. "What are you talking about?"

"You're just the type of woman who needs a good strong man in her life. Howard isn't there for you anymore. You're not the sort to go out and find someone on the side, so you turned back to Daddy." Laura's green eyes sparkled with appreciation for her own theory. "Now Daddy's gone and you're feeling deserted."

"Thank you, Dr. Craymore. Bill me, won't you? It's so good to know why I'm neurotic."

It struck Claire that Laura just might have something there, but she wasn't about to give her the satisfaction of hearing that. She smiled enigmatically and stirred sugar into her tea.

Laura wasn't ready to let the subject rest. "I'll tell you what you need, Claire, and I know you're not going to want to hear this, but here goes." She took a deep breath. "Dump Howard and get yourself a new husband."

Claire's dark eyes rose in shock. "What are you saying?" The hand that held the teaspoon began to shake slightly, knocking the spoon against the china cup, making a light ringing sound, like tiny chimes. Claire put down the spoon and flattened her hand on the table, willing herself to stop shaking.

Laura was leaning toward her earnestly and didn't seem to notice. "Only the truth. Darling, you know I love you and that's the only reason I'm saying this. I know it upsets you. But it upsets me to see you with that man. You deserve so much better. When I think of how different it is for me than it is for you . . ." She reached across the table and took her sister's hand in hers. "It's not fair. You . . . you're better than I am in so many ways. You always have been. And you deserve a better life than the one you have with Howard."

Half-angry, half-despairing, Claire stared at Laura. What good did it do to talk this way? Nothing was going to change. She was married to Howard. That was a fact, a condition she'd set in her life, and there wasn't anything she could do about it now.

"Let's go," she said crisply, gathering her packages. "Mother will be starting to fix dinner, and I promised to help."

Laura read Claire's reaction accurately, and she sighed, but she didn't give up. For the next few days, she got in a comment whenever she had a chance.

"It's not true that I've always hated Howard," Laura claimed at one point, as they worked on dinner together, Claire peeling potatoes, Laura sprinkling tenderizer on lean steaks. "It is true that I've never really liked the man. But I only started hating him when I spent that week in Saudi Arabia and saw what he was doing to you and the girls."

"Drop it, Laura."

"If you would just let me do one little thing, I swear I'll quit bugging you. Just let me introduce you to some men. . . ."

Claire glared at her sister and waved the peeler at her. "Drop it, Laura, or I will walk away right here and now and never speak to you again."

Laura gave her an impish grin. "You can't do that. You haven't finished peeling the potatoes."

"Hasn't anyone ever told you? The skin is the most nutritious part." Claire reached for the sash on her apron, while Laura squealed out an apology. The only thing she hated worse than her sister's marriage was fixing dinner by herself. "I'll be good, I promise. At least for tonight."

And she was. At least for the night.

But Laura's determination had stirred up another memory. Claire had been a college girl and sure she had outgrown her fear of her father. And so, when she and Howard had begun to talk about getting married, she'd gone to her father to tell him. For some reason she had thought her news would impress him, make him see her as, well, not just a scrawny girl, but a woman worthy of a man's attention. His reaction had squelched that dream.

"Marry Howard?" he'd sneered, barely sparing her a glance. "Go ahead, if that's the best you think you can do. But don't expect to be happy."

At the time she'd cried all night and cursed him for an unfeeling bastard. But now, looking back, she realized he had been right all along. How had he known? Where had those perceptions come

from? It was only later, when she knew him better,
that she understood how he knew the things he did.

But Howard—who could understand Howard?
And he wasn't in the past. He was here and now.

CHAPTER

5

The funeral was beautiful and very sad, but Claire wasn't crying any longer. She'd cried for hours the day her father had died, but now the tears seemed to have come together to form a huge lump in the middle of her chest and she couldn't get rid of them. The minister gave a warm, loving eulogy and others stood to describe things about her father she'd never known—his charity work, his quiet sense of humor, his exploits as a young man, when he had played hobo and ridden the rails all over the country. Deep inside, she mourned for this man, as much for what she'd never known as for the part of him she loved.

After the funeral came the ordeal of the buffet at the house, and then finally only the family members remained. Claire's brother, Gary, and Laura's husband, Jim, spoke in hushed tones about the reading of the will and stock options and transfers of ownership, while Claire and her sister took a walk in the yard, arm in arm, and whispered about what their mother would do now.

"She should travel, don't you think? Get some friends together and take off for Europe or Australia or Japan."

"And have the house renovated while she's gone, done over in the bright colors she loves."

"The colors Daddy couldn't stand."

They rounded the corner of the house, and the evening gloom made it possible to see right into the library where their mother was sitting all alone on a leather couch, staring at her husband's eclectic collection of books that lined the walls. Her face was etched with agony, and Claire and Laura caught hold of one another and backed away.

"I wouldn't have thought she would take it this hard," Laura said. "Surely on some level she must feel as though she's been released from prison. After the way he was always holding her back. . . ."

"She cared about him, just as she cares about all of us."

"I suppose so," Laura answered doubtfully. "But we all knew she should never have married him. She's probably just as sad about all those wasted years as anything else." Laura shook her head and looked at her sister. "Did you see her sitting there?" Suddenly she seized Claire's upper arms in her hands, almost shaking her. "I will not allow you to follow in her footsteps and waste your life married to a man who makes you miserable!"

"Laura—"

"I won't let you, Claire. It's not right. You should have learned from her example."

Claire turned on her sister, her defensive side coming through. She was tired of Laura's nagging. But more than that, she was tired of Laura's seeing everyone else's relationship through the prism of her own experience. Different people needed different things. It was time her sister learned that.

"But I did learn, Laura," she told her firmly. "You don't get it, do you?"

It was Claire's turn to grab Laura, and she forced her back to the corner of the house where they could just see their mother in the library. "Look at her. Don't you see the beauty there? She did it for us—and for him. She dedicated her life to making others happy. She's a heroine, Laura. She's almost holy. She's so far above the rest of us with our petty greed and demands for instant gratification—"

"So you want to be just like her?" Laura cried.

Claire nodded, releasing her sister and turning away. "I only wish I were half as good a person."

That worked to silence Laura only for that evening. By the next day, she was back in gear, itemizing the men Claire might have married instead of Howard and urging her to give one or another of them a call. "Just to say hello."

Claire ignored her. It was time to go back to Saudi Arabia, but she couldn't force herself to make the reservations. Howard was all alone there. If she were going to be more like her mother, more giving, more supportive, dedicated to holding the family together and strengthening it, she should have been winging her way back to him as fast as she could. But the days began to drift by and she couldn't seem to make that one little telephone call to the airline.

"You don't have to go back." Laura was so helpful, she thought dryly, during times of moral dilemma. "You and the girls can stay with me. We'll get you your old job back at the music department at the university and you can take the time to think things through."

"I would be deserting my husband."

"So what? He deserves a little desertion."

"I can't do that."

Laura gestured pathetically. "Don't you think it would be a good thing if you made contact with other men? You would see you still have a lot to offer. Out on the singles scene, I mean."

"That's very kind of you, Laura." Claire's voice was icily polite. "But, you see, it hardly matters about my value on the singles scene. Because it just so happens I'm not single. Or did you forget that little fact?"

Laura may not have forgotten, but she managed quite handily to ignore it, inviting Claire to dinner and just coincidentally also including three recently divorced and very eligible men. Claire went home early and refused all Laura's subsequent ideas for social evenings.

It was almost funny, really, this attempt of Laura's to get her to take a look at other men. She didn't seem to understand that other men were not the issue at all. If she were susceptible to them, she would have fallen head over heels for that roughneck—what was his name?—Peter Arnold. She had to admit, whenever she thought of him, something inside began to tingle. But so what? That only meant she was human. He was an attractive man, and she was a normal woman. Even if she was madly in love with Howard, Peter Arnold would have still conjured up some sort of reaction in her. And she would have laughed and ignored it and gone on with her life. That was the sane thing to do.

The only flaw that ruined that tidy theory was the fact that she dreamed about Peter Arnold that night, a dream as hot and sexy as any she'd ever had, a dream that left her a little shaken. But it didn't change her mind, or her goals. Men like Peter Arnold were fun to think about, but deadly to play with. She would stick to her guns and rebuild her marriage.

In the meantime, she had thought of something she wanted to do, a project that would hold the need to return to Howard at bay for another few days. Samantha and Katy were saddened by their grandfather's death, but as they had never got to know him well, their sorrow was basically superficial. That bothered Claire. She wanted them to know the man she had been beginning to know.

With her mother's permission, she began sifting through his papers, old pictures, old documents, until she had compiled a fairly comprehensive overview of his life. Feeding quarters into the copy machine at the library, she managed to put together five copies of the work, and then found a place where she was able to have them bound on short notice. She gave a copy each to her sister, her brother and her mother. Then she gave the last two copies to her daughters.

Katy was delighted. "Is this really Grandfather?" She asked questions about every picture, wanted to know more about every account of travel or career advancement or special social gathering she found. Sam sat very quietly through it all, the unopened book in her lap. When she finally got up and left the room, Claire followed her to her bedroom, where she found her packing the volume away in the bottom of her suitcase.

Claire didn't say anything to her about it. Sam had been growing more and more remote. Something was wrong, and it occurred to Claire that perhaps her older daughter was confused about her family and her place in it. She couldn't think of anything she might say that would do anything but push her daughter further away, so all she did was put her arms around her little girl, rock her gently and whisper, "I love you," into her silver-blond hair.

Sam allowed the affectionate gesture, but did nothing in response, and Claire drew back, the lump of despair in her chest throbbing painfully.

That night Katy came to her bed in the middle of the night, and Claire drew her daughter close. They whispered for a while about her grandfather and about life and death and how fragile things were. And then Katy went to sleep in her arms, and

Claire lay very still, watching the moonlight travel across Katy's precious face and worrying about Samantha.

But all that was forgotten the next day. She took the girls to the ballet in the afternoon, and then out to eat, just the three of them, and for a while, Samantha was the little girl she'd known for twelve years, and not the withdrawn adolescent she'd become. Claire wished she could take them to the ballet every day. Anything to have her girl back.

Laura made a few more inventive attempts to get her to think about other men, attempts she deftly parried. But her patience was just about worn to a frazzle.

"She means well," her mother said soothingly a bit later when she'd taken her anger back to her mother's house and poured it out to the woman who had listened to her confidences for so many years. They sat at the kitchen table with steaming cups of decaffeinated coffee before them. "She loves you so much. She would do just about anything for you."

"And all I want her to do is leave me alone." Claire pushed back her hair with a weary hand. "I have to deal with my marriage in my own way. And dates on the side aren't it."

"Claire." Her mother looked at her with her probing dark eyes. "Is there really a problem with you and Howard?"

Claire hesitated only a split second before smiling and saying, "Of course not, Mother." This was no time to lay another burden on her mother's shoulders. "Howard is just working very hard and the country is so strange. It's taking some time to adjust, that's all. We're fine."

Her smile felt plastered on and she wasn't sure if her mother was buying her words. Marla's shrewd eyes studied her daughter's for a long moment, and then she shook her head. "That's all very well, Claire. And perhaps Howard needs to be there in that strange country. But you and the girls don't need to go back. Why don't you stay here?"

Shock clouded Claire's eyes. Of all the people to say such a thing! "But, Mother, I can't leave Howard alone. I'm his wife. It's my duty to stay with him."

Her mother stared at her again, then sighed. "It's just so dangerous in that part of the world," she said vaguely. "Bad things always seem to be happening to people. I'd feel safer with you and the girls here." She shook her head. "And you're getting so thin."

They went on to other topics, but Claire's thoughts kept returning again and again to her mother's words. Was it just that in losing her husband so suddenly, she'd become fearful of losing others in her family? Or was it more than that? Maybe she was trying to give Claire a signal of sorts. Did she regret her own marriage? Was she proud of the sacrifices she'd made? Or did she feel that she'd been cheated?

Claire desperately wanted answers to those questions. But she couldn't bring herself to ask them. Not yet. Her mother was too emotional right now.

And weren't they all? The tears Claire couldn't shed were still lodged in her chest like a heavy, aching lump. Sometimes it struck her as almost obscene the way everyone could go on with life as though nothing had happened. And yet, her grief was always with her. If only she could cry again!

Another thing she couldn't bring herself to do was play the piano. She wandered into the music room again and again and sat at the piano where she'd spent long hours practicing as a little girl. The music was still there. But she couldn't touch the keys. The music had always been her one connection to her father. Something was blocking her, something she couldn't name, couldn't identify.

But no matter what, she was going home to Howard. There was no doubt in her mind. She was a wife. She was a mother. It was her job to hold things together. He was her husband, the father of her children. She would work hard, and things would be better.

The airline reservations for the flight back to Saudi were finally made, and Claire began to prepare for the trip. Katy and Samantha would be staying at Laura's for two weeks after Claire's departure, and then would follow. She called Howard to tell him of the plans. He was polite, but distant. It was like talking to a stranger.

She had one final social obligation left to perform. Laura had tickets to a concert by the Emerson Chamber Orchestra at the university. Though she loved the music, she went reluctantly, not sure what her sister might have up her sleeve. The music was exquisite—Mozart's *Overture to the Magic Flute,* Beethoven's *Sixth Symphony*—and it swept her onto the euphoric plane of existence that said all was right with the world because music reigned.

As a result, her defenses were down when Laura convinced her to come to an after-concert reception in Beeker Hall. The room was lovely and the refreshments included champagne and caviar. It was fun to see old friends and acquaintances, to catch up on their lives.

Dressed in ivory lace and dark green velvet, a black velvet ribbon tying back her hair, and she felt rather classical herself tonight. The music had put her in a dreamy mood. For the first time in days, her smiles were genuine.

The only fly in the ointment was Gustav Menninger, the conductor. He seemed overly attentive, even going so far as to give her a sly wink now and then when he was pulled away by others and had to leave her side. She found his behavior merely puzzling—until he caught her alone at the table, putting a cracker with caviar into her mouth.

Leaning close, he whispered, "I'm trying to get rid of these people, but if need be, we can escape together. My room is very close. The bed is very large."

The shock of his words didn't fully sink in, even when she felt his hand slip into the folds of the back of her velvet skirt. She stood very still as his fingers found her bottom and moved, giving her a sharp pinch. And then he turned away to speak to someone else.

Claire stood where she was, the caviar still on her tongue, stunned. Frank Norman, an old friend of hers from the music department, had witnessed the entire scene. He grinned at her and said, "He's just been divorced, you know. And I overheard Laura talking about how much you two would have in common."

Fury surged through Claire. That did it. She'd had enough. Not bothering to speak to anyone at all, she grabbed her wrap and stormed out of the hall, walking briskly toward home, even though she knew it would take hours on foot.

But she'd probably need those hours just to cool down. Damn Laura, anyway! She didn't know how to take no for an answer, and she was too pushy, too nosy, too arrogant. This setting Claire up with every available male was completely unacceptable. She was glad she was leaving for Saudi Arabia in the morning!

Claire was off the campus now and walking through a quiet neighborhood. Trees lined the street and houses sat cozily behind picket fences, while old-fashioned streetlights held the darkness at bay. But she knew that only a few blocks away was an area where she was going to look more than a little out of place. The prospect was chilling, but nothing would make her go back and beg a ride home from Laura. Nothing in the world.

She heard a car approach and slow, but she kept her eyes straight ahead.

"Hello."

It was a male voice. She refused to look around. He would get bored keeping pace with her and drive on.

"Hello. Aren't you one of the Duvalls? You're Laura's sister. Claire Montgomery, isn't it?"

Not another one! Laura had probably sent him. Claire whirled and glared at the man. He was good-looking, a few years older than she was, with prematurely gray hair that looked silver in the moonlight. His car was a convertible and the top was down. And he had a nice smile. Didn't all of Laura's candidates?

Men—who needed them, anyway? Hands on her hips, she gave him a piece of her mind. "I've had enough of this. I'm fed up. I don't need another man in my life. Don't you understand? I am not in the market for romance. Please leave me alone."

He looked a bit startled. "Uh . . . okay."

Satisfied, she turned and continued her march. But the car was still following her, and he spoke again.

"I'm really not trying to pester you. You're not in the market for romance, I know. But I thought you might be in the market for a ride home."

A persistent one. She whirled again. "Do I really look like a brainless bimbo to you? I can walk, thank you."

"Brainless bimbo or not," he drawled, a trace of humor in his tone, "that's a pretty long walk back to your section of town."

"I can make it," she threw back over her shoulder, striding along energetically. "I need the exercise." She could still see the nose of the car from the corner of her eye.

"Come on. Take the ride. It's not like we're complete strangers. I saw you at the concert, and at the reception afterward. And I know your sister. We're good friends."

And he thought that would convince her? Hah!

"Get lost," she demanded, walking faster. Was there a male under seventy-five in Atlanta Laura had not solicited for her?

He pulled the car a little ahead and looked back.

"Listen, I swear to God, I'm not an ax murderer. I'm not a rapist, either. I don't even have much of a reputation as a seducer, to my shame. I'm harmless. Take a chance."

The area ahead was looming dark and shadowy. The buildings were no longer neat little houses, but rundown storehouses and industrial structures with broken windows and sagging iron gates.

"Listen," the man was going on, "I've got references. Credit cards. See?"

She could see that he'd thrown out a string of them in his plastic holder. She looked ahead. The way definitely appeared threatening.

"Here's my driver's license."

Her steps slowed and she glanced at the card he was holding up for her to see. Matt Stevens, she noted.

"I've got a library card. No outstanding fines, honest."

She let herself veer slightly toward the car. He did seem nice.

"And this. Look! Would a rapist have a Red Cross donor card? I gave blood just last week."

She took the card from him and peered at it suspiciously, then looked him full in the face. There was no doubt about it. This was a good guy. The fact that he was also a friend of Laura's should not be held against him.

"All right," she said grudgingly. "I'll let you drive me home."

"Thank you."

She knew he was laughing at her, but was too angry with Laura to care. Getting into the car, she flounced into the seat, spreading her wide skirt around her.

"Let's get one thing clear from the start," she stated firmly. "I am a happily married woman."

"Congratulations," he responded softly. "You're one of the lucky ones."

"I really mean it. And I don't need comforting. And I don't need to catch up on all the fun I missed while I was away. And I have no tension that needs relieving."

"You sound like a healthy specimen to me."

She gave him a piercing gaze. "You're really not trying to pick me up, are you?" she said at last.

His grin was very attractive. "Only literally. Not in any broader sense."

She sighed with relief and relaxed against the

soft leather of the seat. "Great. You don't know how sick I am of fighting off Laura's 'friends'—guys she's trying to set me up with. I'm surprised she's left you out of it. You look like a prime target."

"Oh, she approached me about taking you out." He started the car toward the freeway on ramp.

"Not surprising. She's approached most of the men in Georgia by now. Next week she's starting on the neighboring states."

He laughed and she threw him an appreciative look. "I suppose you're recently divorced."

"Actually, my wife died a few years ago."

Claire wished she'd kept quiet. "Oh, my God. I'm sorry."

His blue eyes met her brown ones and his smile warmed her. "Don't be. We had a great life together while it lasted. Most people don't get as much as we had."

This was a man who looked on the bright side instead of seeing all the monsters in the shadows. Why hadn't she married a man like this? Claire shook her head, smiling to herself, then said, to fill the silence, "Here's what I can't figure out. What exactly does Laura say to people to interest them in me?"

His grin should have been a warning. "In Laura's eyes, you're a beautiful but unloved woman who just needs the right man in her life to get her going again." He shook his head as Claire let out an exasperated sigh. "She must really have it in for your husband. At the time, I told her I didn't like blind dates." He glanced over at her, then back to his driving. "And now that I find out you're a happily married woman, I'm glad I turned her down."

Claire sighed again. She was liking this one better than the others. There was something accepting about him. She felt as though she could talk to him.

"What is wrong with people nowadays?" she fretted. "Here I've got my neighbor in Saudi trying to talk me into having an affair with a roughneck, and I've got my sister trying to get me remarried before I've even divorced my husband."

"Are you planning to divorce your husband?"

"No. No! Of course not. You see, that's the point. That's where it all breaks down. I'm not free."

"I know, I know. You're a happily married woman."

"Right."

Their gazes met and suddenly they were laughing together, though Claire wasn't sure why. She directed him to her mother's house, and when they stopped in front of it, she was almost reluctant to leave him.

He seemed to feel the same way. "Listen, maybe we can get together again. Not for a date," he added hastily. "I mean, just a friendly visit, another concert or dinner, maybe with Laura and her husband."

Genuine regret filled Claire. "I'm sorry. I'm leaving for Saudi Arabia tomorrow."

"Oh. Well, let me take you to the airport."

She was tempted, but knew her family was

coming to see her off. "Thanks, but I've already got a ride."

He smiled, took her hand and leaned over it, brushing her fingers lightly with his lips. "It's been a pleasure meeting you, Claire," he said softly. "I wouldn't have missed it."

His smile stayed with her for a long time after she went into the house. And at the same time, she couldn't remember what Howard's smile looked like at all.

CHAPTER

6

It was not until she was over the middle of the Atlantic that the full desolation at the loss of her father hit her.

She was alone. The girls wouldn't be with her for another two weeks. Until she found herself sitting in the pressurized cabin without them, she hadn't realized how much support they had been on the flight to Atlanta.

She looked out the window, and the tranquil blue sky, the churning gray sea, seemed to go on forever. From one horizon to another, there was no land in sight. That was exactly the way she felt, adrift with nothing and no one to hold on to. When she got back to Saudi Arabia, things would be so different. Where once she had counted on comforting telephone calls from her father to shore up her days, there would be nothing. She had grown used to collecting all the little amusing incidents of the days to share with him, and now there would be no point. Howard didn't want to hear them. There was no one left who did. And who was she going to talk to about her music?

She knew plenty of people who liked music, but no one who spoke about music the way her father had with her. The depth of her sadness was overwhelming, and the lump of grief in her chest felt as hard as stone.

Her flight landed in Frankfurt and she changed planes, flying on to Athens, where she would connect to Riyadh. She wasn't looking forward to seeing Howard again. Despite all her intentions, she knew it wasn't going to be easy to try to rebuild their marriage. She was coming back, carrying a heavy load of sadness, and wondering how she was going to deal with Howard's anger when she hadn't yet recuperated from the loss of her father. As she got nearer to the reunion, she became more and more uneasy about it.

The Athens airport was crowded with tourists and business travelers. When she was informed that her layover had been extended from the two hours she was expecting, to four hours, she sagged with disappointment. What was she going to do for such a long time? Sit in a hard metal chair and work up even more dread at the coming confrontation with Howard?

She wasn't sure why she was so certain their reunion was going to be closer to a fight than a reconciliation, but she was. It was so important that they get off on the right foot right away, but how could that happen? She wasn't strong, she wasn't ready. She needed nurturing to help heal her, and it had been so long since Howard had given her that.

Her carry-on bag got heavier and heavier as she wandered through the airport, looking for a good place to make a temporary nest. Sound seemed to echo around her. Faces were cold and unfeeling. A beautiful woman in a designer dress rushed by, followed by shouting paparazzi. An international film star? Claire wondered, then collided with a woman carrying an old suitcase, which bumped hard against Claire's leg. The woman went on without a glance, much less an apology. Claire winced at the pain and watched her go, feeling very much alone and abandoned. Pulling herself together, she passed a knot of men gesticulating wildly and shouting at each other in what she assumed must be Greek, and she turned away to find a quieter spot. There, on a row of benches, sat a group of men who looked instantly familiar.

It was five of the roughnecks who had been playing volleyball in the court outside the recreation center that night, which seemed so long ago now. They hadn't seen her and she stared, torn between the need to find someone she knew in this strange place, and the realization that these men were not really appropriate friends.

They had young women with them—pouty, pretty women, dressed to cheaply provocative perfection—apparently there to see the roughnecks off. They were hanging all over the men, who generally seemed pleased to have them along. All except for one, who was turned a bit away. Claire saw a curvaceous redhead reach out and touch his cheek. He turned, pushing her hand away with a look of annoyance on his face, and as he did so, she realized it was Peter Arnold, the one who had disturbed her so at the party.

He raised his eyes at the same moment, and their gazes met. Claire stood frozen, a flicker of panic in her breast. She was alone in an unfamiliar airport, in a strange country where she knew no one, and she felt vulnerable. She was still shaky from her ordeal in Atlanta, and she was dreading the coming meeting with Howard. Her strength was low.

These were not the circumstances under which she could face meeting this man again. His impudent sensuality had threatened her. Ordinarily, she might have dealt with it easily. But not now. They stared at one another for several seconds, and then she turned and hurried through the crowd, hoping he would let her go.

The ticket booths were on the opposite side of the airport, and she headed that way, searching for a restroom, the only place she might be able to hide. When she felt a hand on her arm, stopping her and pulling her around, she knew she wasn't going to succeed.

"You can't do that."

She looked up, blinking into his laughing blue eyes. "What?" she asked.

"Escape. You can run, but you can't hide."

She felt trapped. He was just as overwhelm-

ingly attractive as he had been the last time she'd
seen him. She had to get rid of him, but how? "I
don't know what you're talking about," she murmured vaguely, looking around for a way out.

"Don't you?" His hand was still on her arm and
the fingers moved seductively. "Then what was this
mad dash away from me all about?"

A wave of resentment swept over her. She'd
been through enough; she didn't need to justify her
actions to this near stranger.

"Listen," she said icily, pulling away from his
grip. "I don't have the stamina to play games with
you. I just want to be left alone."

His head drew back and he grabbed her arm
again. Sure he was angry, she looked up quickly,
ready to say something even stronger if she had to.
But instead of the anger she expected to see in his
eyes, she saw sudden concern and sympathy, and
the hand on her arm was gentle.

"What is it, Claire?" he said softly, frowning,
his blue eyes searching hers. "What's happened?"

Despite herself, she was touched by his reaction. How long had it been since Howard had actually noticed something was troubling her? Or had
he ever? But this man whom she barely knew had
the perception to see right to the heart of things.
He knew there was something wrong.

She found herself weakening. "I . . . I've just
come back from Atlanta. I went home because . . .
because my father was dying. . . ."

Her voice choked and, suddenly the tears she'd
been holding back since that awful day welled up.

"Not now," she wanted to cry out. "Not here. This isn't the right place." But it seemed she wasn't being given a choice.

Her control had melted away and all she felt at the moment was grief. Overwhelming grief. Peter's arms came around her smoothly and naturally, as though they were old friends. The strap of her bag slipped from her hands, and before she knew what was happening, her face was pressed to his chest and she was sobbing like a child.

He held her, right there in the middle of the airport, rocking her slightly, whispering comfort as he stroked her hair, and she let her sadness and despair gush out. She wept on and on in the shelter of his arms, and she'd never felt so safe before. The words he murmured meant nothing to her, but the sound of his voice was so soothing she felt herself relax against him, needing his comfort. His hand stroked her cheek, her neck, and she melted against him as though she were letting a gentle current carry her down a river.

Eventually her crying ceased. Her pent-up grief was released. She caught her breath, and then tried to pull away from him. But he wasn't ready to let her go.

"Come over here." He led her to a row of attached chairs and settled her in one of them. "You're on your way back to Saudi?"

She nodded, wiping her eyes with the handkerchief he'd offered her, thinking she should feel foolish for the way she'd acted, but feeling relieved instead. She hadn't felt so protected by someone who seemed to care since she'd been a little girl. It was tempting to cling to it, though she knew it was time to tear herself away. "I've got a four-hour layover."

His face darkened and he swore softly. "Wait here. I have something I've got to do."

In a daze, she watched as he went to the ticket counter, spoke rapidly to the clerk, counted out some bills and was back again. "It's going to be okay," he told her, stroking her cheek with his long fingers. She looked up at him, not sure what he was talking about, but infinitely comforted by his presence.

A flight to Abu Dhabi was called on the public-address system. Peter looked up. "Just one more thing," he told Claire. Striding quickly away, he went to where his friends were still sitting, though they were beginning to gather their bags, for the recent announcement had been of their flight. He spoke a few words to them, and picked up his own bag before turning back to her.

"What are you doing?" she asked as he re-joined her. "Didn't they just call your flight?"

"They called my *old* flight." He smiled as he sat down beside her. "The boys and I were on our way back to the oil rigs in the Gulf, to Abu Dhabi, for our next assignment. We've just had a couple of weeks' vacation here in Athens and it's time to get back to work."

"Then you're leaving?" She couldn't stem her rush of disappointment.

"No." He rose and picked up her bag. "I'm not

leaving. I'm taking you to lunch." He pulled her up with his free hand. "Let's take a cab into town. I know a place where they make the most fabulous moussaka you've ever tasted."

"But your flight—"

"All taken care of. I canceled it. I'm going with you."

This was wrong. This was crazy. But it was also irresistible. She stood very still, staring at him. It was her choice, she realized. She could go with him or not, as she chose.

"All right," she said at last, knowing she was stepping into uncharted territory, yet at that moment, not caring. "Let's go."

A warm feeling seeped into Claire as she hurried along beside Peter, something she hadn't known for a very long time. This man hardly knew her, and yet he cared enough to go to these lengths to make her feel better. How could she help but be moved?

❧

He watched her as she reacted to the scenery of Athens. The rickety cab went up and down streets that were often so clogged with pedestrians. The driver had to weave in and out, leaning often on his horn. Claire rested against the door to look out the open window, delighted with the people, the row upon row of whitewashed buildings, the pastel colors here and there. She was coming alive again, softening, warming, opening up.

"Is that . . . ?"

"The Acropolis. See the Parthenon there in the sunlight?"

"Unbelievable."

He smiled at her awe. When he'd looked into her eyes back at the airport, he'd been struck by her vulnerability. From the first time he'd seen her, he'd known she possessed a deep vein of emotion she kept hidden from the world. His instincts told him her passion would be just as strong. He intended to find out if he was right.

"Oh, look!" she cried, pointing out a lovely fountain as the cab bounced past. "There's a little boy in the water. Look at that smile!"

Peter looked at Claire instead. He liked her laugh and the way her soft brown eyes lit up when she saw something she appreciated. He liked the small gold cross that dangled in the hollow at her throat, and the way her hands moved like graceful birds, and the light, downy hair on her slender forearms. He'd been thinking about her ever since that night at the reception for Camden, thinking of her in a strange, wistful way that he didn't remember ever experiencing before.

He wasn't supposed to think about women that way. He'd decided a long time ago that no woman was worth losing sleep over. There were just too darn many of them to worry about any one unduly.

The women in his life lately had been available, lusty—and interchangeable, with no strings attached. That was the way he'd thought he wanted it. And then he'd seen Claire with her quiet beauty, her classic features, and he'd . . . what? Fallen for her?

No, not that. But he'd been intrigued by her and the challenge she represented. For the past two weeks he'd been bored stiff with the women he and his buddies had found for themselves. Claire's face had haunted him. He wanted her.

"Here we are."

They got out of the taxi and made their way through an alley lined with vendors and musicians and dogs. The sounds and smells were exotic, exciting. Vendors cried out at them as they passed, brought out cloth and jewelry and copper goods to dangle before them, pulled at Claire's jacket. Laughing, she avoided them and tried to take in everything at once—the colors, the people, the music.

"This way."

Peter's arm slipped around her shoulders and gently directed her toward a small café with a large sign that said Taverna. She looked up at him and smiled, wondering if he could feel how thin she was, then suppressing that thought. It didn't matter how thin she was. It didn't matter what he thought about it. This wasn't a date. . . .

He led her into the restaurant. The tables were empty. A young woman came out from behind a counter, speaking rapidly in Greek to Peter. He spoke back in the same language and the woman looked at Claire, rolled her eyes and shouted something to someone unseen. A gruff male voice called back, and everyone laughed. Everyone except

Claire, who was beginning to feel slightly embarrassed.

"What is it?" she asked Peter. "What are they saying?"

"Nothing." He grinned at her. "Don't worry about it. They like to joke. Come on through here."

He led her into a back room and she stood hesitantly, looking around. The walls were hung with faded tapestries. Three large couches were grouped around a low round table in the corner. Strange spicy scents filled the air, and the light filtered in through high barred windows. Claire had visions of old movies with Peter Lorre skulking in the shadows.

"Can't we sit at one of those tables out in the restaurant?" she asked the Peter she was with, beginning to distrust the setup.

"No," he told her, shaking his head. "The whole neighborhood would come in to take a look at us. It'll be better here. We'll have privacy."

"Better" was a relative term and Claire wasn't sure she agreed with his assessment, but she let him show her to one of the low couches. The young woman said something to Peter that sounded impudently challenging, even though Claire couldn't understand the words. Peter laughed and pinched her cheek, and she flounced out, petticoats swinging. He turned and sank onto the couch beside Claire.

"She'll bring us something to drink. And fix us something to eat. You won't believe the food here. It's out of this world."

Claire smiled back tentatively, tugging the skirt

of her light wool suit down over her knees. She was beginning to wonder if she'd been crazy to come along with this man. She was supposed to be sitting in the airport, waiting for her flight to Riyadh. Instead, she'd let a virtual stranger take over and whisk her away to God-knows-where, with no guarantees that she would be taken back in time—no guarantees of anything, in fact.

She'd been acting as though he were a friend, and he was actually nothing of the sort. Suddenly she remembered how he'd held her hand that night, how provocative he'd been. He'd been well behaved so far today, but when she thought back to the sensual threat he'd posed that night not so very long ago, she felt shaken. She shouldn't have come here.

She looked at Peter. He was sitting only inches away. Was he too close? She tried to analyze his smile, looking for hints of danger, wondering just what he expected to get out of all this. But all she saw was friendly concern.

"Now, tell me all about your father," he said, leaning back comfortably against the huge cushions, his arms spread wide, his face open and not at all threatening.

Tell him, this perfect stranger, all about her father? Was he joking? Why on earth would she do a thing like that? It wasn't her style to open up to people she didn't know well.

But before she knew what was happening, she was doing exactly that. There was something about this man that released her usual inhibitions. Her tears started again, though this time they were a gentle stream rather than a raging torrent, and she released all her regrets and resentments for his inspection. He didn't comment, other than to murmur sympathy, and when she was done, he put an arm around her shoulders and stroked her hair.

The young woman came with the drinks and went again, and Claire didn't even notice. But by the time the food began to arrive, one plate after another, she'd dried her eyes and found her smile. And she was ravenous.

"This is all so good. How did you find this place?"

She noticed he wasn't eating much, but he seemed to enjoy watching her. But once she started asking questions about him, a wariness crept into his blue-eyed gaze, and his smile became noncommittal. "I've been coming here for years," he offered casually, instead of answering.

She waited a moment, but he didn't amplify his offhand statement, so she tried again. "You speak Greek, I see."

He shrugged. "A little. Languages are pretty easy for me. I pick up a smattering in every country I work in."

She sighed and pushed away her plate, still piled high with food. If she didn't stop soon, she would explode. "How many countries have you worked in?"

"Quite a few." He wasn't giving anything away.

She stared at him, remembering how he'd compared the night air to Scheherazade. A roughneck who was into classical music. That was a puzzle just waiting to be solved. But something told her he wasn't going to give away the solution easily.

"Do you play the piano?" she asked abruptly.

His eyes widened slightly. "Why? Do you need a piano player?"

"Ah-ah." She waggled a finger at him. "No fair. You can't answer a question with a question."

He grinned. "Okay, you win. I once played the piano. How's that?"

She glanced at his hands, appreciating the long, tapered fingers. "I guess you don't get much chance to play when you're out on oil rigs."

"Not much." Amusement flickered in his blue eyes, but there was something else in there, too. Something Claire couldn't quite identify.

She was going to find out more about him if she had to drag it out with tongs. "Do you ever play anymore?"

"Not really."

She looked at him searchingly. "Did your mother make you practice when the other kids were out playing baseball?" she asked.

He threw back his head and laughed. "You're not going to give up, are you?" Not waiting for an answer, he went on, "Okay, here goes. I grew up in a small town outside of Portland, Oregon. My father was the town doctor. My grandmother taught piano when she wasn't filling in for the nurse in my father's office. I practiced long and hard, because that was what you did in my family. But I don't really play any longer. Although I did put my fingers to the ivories a few days ago when I found a piano in a cantina and had some fun messing around with it. Okay? Did I leave anything out?"

She watched him with a smile while he recited his piano-playing background, and when he finished, she shook her head regretfully. "I'll bet you were good once, weren't you?"

His blue eyes deepened and he said with seeming reluctance, "I was all right. I could hold my own."

"Talent shows and recitals?" she guessed.

He nodded. "And then the district symphony and the high-school jazz band."

"Really?" She was impressed, and a tiny bit excited. Here was someone who might speak her language. "And what did you specialize in? What's your favorite?"

He stared back at her for a moment, then a strange spasm quirked the corners of his mouth. "The Rolling Stones and Charley Pride," he said shortly. "That was then and this is now."

Disappointment clouded her dark eyes. He was closing himself off from her again. The fact that he seemed to feel the need to do that was puzzling; it didn't fit with his general openness. "I guess I still live in the 'then,'" she said quietly. "My family loved music, too. My father was an amateur conductor. His family established the philharmonic orchestra at Clayton University in Atlanta, and when I was a little girl, I used to go to see my father conduct in the summer for outdoor concerts on the green, when the real conductor was on vacation. I sat in the grass and ate fried chicken and let the music sweep me into the clouds. That was when I began to realize what all that hard work at the piano was all about." She smiled. "Now I turn on my compact disk player and try to recapture that feeling."

A smoky look had come into his eyes, and though she couldn't quite read it, the feelings it engendered made her uneasy. "So tell me," she said brightly, "what made you leave Oregon and head out into the big wide world?"

"Jobs," he said shortly.

"But there are jobs in Oregon. You must have been infected with wanderlust as a child."

"Not really."

"No? When did it hit you, then?"

He shrugged. "About my second year of college, I'd say."

"What college?" she shot back at him.

He groaned and leaned back. "Enough," he said. "What does all that ancient history matter?" He turned to look at her, his eyes deepening. "I live in the present tense. How about you?"

She felt as though he had reached out and touched her. A prickle of anticipation shivered through her. She looked at him, at the casual way the sleeves of his light jacket were turned back, the casual way his blond hair fell, the sensuality in his face as he looked at her. Her pulse began to quicken. There was no way to avoid the thought— what would it be like to make love with this man?

Something twisted inside her and she turned

away quickly, searching for a neutral topic of conversation.

"So," she said breathlessly, "I guess you've been soaking up Athens and getting your fill of wine, women and song."

He waited a beat too long before answering, but she steeled herself not to look back into his eyes.

"Not exactly," he drawled at last. "It was a somewhat disappointing R and R, to tell you the truth."

She smiled nervously and began playing with the napkin in her lap. "Why was that?" she asked, since that seemed the obvious question.

He moved closer to her on the couch and suddenly his hand was flattened between her shoulder blades. Her light wool suit coat provided only a little insulation. It seemed to her that she could feel the heat of his palm from the first, like a brand against her skin.

"I'll tell you why," he was saying, his voice low and husky. "Every time I would start to get . . . friendly with a woman, something would go wrong."

"Oh." She wasn't sure she wanted to hear this. She glanced sideways at him, then away again, desperately trying to think of a graceful way to announce she wanted to leave.

He moved still closer and at the same time, his hand slid down and came back up under her jacket, with only the thin silk of her blouse between his flesh and hers. She arched a bit, wishing he couldn't feel her spine, but she forgot that quickly when he said, "The same thing would happen every time. Your face would get in the way."

Her head swung back and she met his gaze. "What do you mean, my face?" she asked, bewildered.

"I would think about you. I wouldn't be able to get you out of my mind."

She gazed at him incredulously, then a smile began to sneak into her expression. "Oh, come on." She knew he had to be joking. Or else this was a central part of his seductive technique. "You expect me to believe that?"

He was smiling, too, but his look had a smoldering quality that made her breath come quickly. "I could prove it to you."

Keep things light, she told herself, trying to control her breathing. "How are you going to do that?" she asked, demolishing her own defenses.

"Like this."

He used the hand on her back to propel her to him so quickly she didn't have time to set up opposition. His mouth took hers as though he had a right to it, taking advantage of her surprise. His need, his desire, his vitality and male strength all poured into her in that moment, stunning her, arousing her. A trembling excitement swept through her. Had she ever been kissed like this before?

And then his free hand cupped her breast and she jerked away. The response was automatic. She didn't want him to discover how thin she was. And at the same time, she knew that defied logic, for he surely knew. He'd held her and comforted her, and her clothes couldn't hide the way her bones stuck out. Still, she cringed from direct contact, and suddenly, crazily, she cared very much what he thought of her.

She was breathing heavily and his eyes were stormy. The total insanity of the situation overwhelmed her. This wasn't where she belonged. How could she have let things go this far?

"Peter—" she looked toward the doorway, still holding him off with her arm "—please don't."

He touched her cheek with his index finger. "Don't worry," he said in his low, husky voice. "No one will come in now."

She stiffened and turned to look into his face. "Why not? How do you know?"

"I told them we wanted to be alone. They understand things like that here."

She pulled away as far as she could go on the couch, looking back at him doubtfully, forcing her breathing to even out. "They may understand. I'm not sure I do."

He could still reach her, and his hand caressed the back of her neck. "Claire, please understand this. I just want to make you happy."

"Peter." She wrenched herself away from his touch, twisting on the couch. "I don't want this. I'm a married woman. You know that."

He leaned back against the cushions and groaned. "You're not in love with him. If you were, you wouldn't be here with me now."

She opened her mouth to protest. She'd only come with him because of the layover, because he'd offered her lunch, because it was so reassuring to see a familiar face in a foreign country.

But before she had said a word, she knew that was all beside the point. He was right. If she had thought she would receive the comfort she needed from Howard, if she'd known he would be loving and understanding, she would have saved her grief to spill on his shoulders. She would have waited to do her mourning at home. Her marriage had deteriorated to the point that she couldn't count on anything from Howard any longer. And most of all, she wasn't in love with him.

"Howard and I have had our problems," she admitted, her voice shaking slightly. "But I have to tell you, I am determined to patch things up when I get home. I am committed to saving my marriage."

His handsome face twisted. "What makes you think it's worth saving?" he asked softly.

A flash of physical pain wrenched her chest. Her marriage had to be worth saving. "We have children. Two daughters. And I firmly believe that children are always the big losers when there's a divorce. I won't do that to my girls." She made herself smile. "Things are going to be different when I get back. I'm going to make them better. I'm starting over. Like New Year's Day."

His lids were heavy on his gorgeous eyes as he watched her, a smile just barely curling his lips.

"Claire Montgomery is going to emerge from her cocoon like a butterfly."

"You've got it. That's me. A whole new person."

He raised his hand and suddenly the backs of his fingers were smoothing the wisps of hair that had escaped her knot and now sprang wildly along her neckline.

"I'll be looking forward to that," he said softly. He stared at her for a long moment, then began to move closer to her again. She sat very still, paralyzed. His lips brushed hers softly, his hand skimming across her cheek, and his clean, male scent filled her head as the touch of his lips filled her senses.

"Okay, lovely lady," he said softly, his face still close to hers. "We'll play it your way. But if it's all the same to you, I think I'll hang around for a while. Just to make sure you're all right."

It wasn't until much later that she realized how seriously he'd meant his promise. For the time being, she only knew that he was treating her with incredible tenderness, and that once they were back in another cab and on the way to the airport, he announced he was flying to Riyadh with her.

"In the same airplane?" she asked, stricken.

"Yes. I reserved myself the seat next to yours at the airport before we left."

The cab was careening down the streets. This driver seemed to be in a bigger hurry than the last. The ruts in the road sent the two of them bouncing inches into the air at almost every turn.

"You can't do that," Claire gasped, her hands clutching the edge of the ratty seat.

"Why not?" He'd braced himself with his legs against the seat in front of him.

"Someone might see you. Someone who knows Howard."

He looked at her blankly. "So what?"

They went around a particularly sharp corner and Claire slid across the seat until she landed hard against Peter, pinning him against the side of the car.

"Claire, Claire," he whispered, holding her to him, his face pressed against her hair. "Don't you know how much I want you?"

She moved back quickly, feeling trapped, as much by her own response as to his words. What could she do to convince him not to take the flight with her? How could she sit down on the plane next to this handsome roughneck when there might very well be people on board who knew her, or at least, knew Howard?

"Don't worry," he said, reaching out to squeeze her hand. "I'll talk to your husband when we arrive. I'll tell him you were emotional at the airport and I didn't want to leave you alone."

Talking to Howard was the last thing she wanted from him. But she stayed quiet. She would think of something to say to dissuade him. Maybe.

CHAPTER

She passed health control, and then passport control, without incident, but the customs officials managed to make her feel as guilty as a smuggler, even though she had nothing illegal in her bags. Every harsh sound, every suspicious look, made her more jumpy. As she walked out into the terminal, the metal detectors looked more menacing here than any others. Was it her mood? Men in white robes, women in black, hurried past her. As she stepped out onto the curb, a hot dry wind tore at her hair and she knew she was back.

Howard was late, and she'd so needed him to be early. She'd hoped he would be waiting for her so that she could hop in the car and be whisked away before Peter got through customs. Beyond all else, she wanted to avoid having Howard see Peter.

She tapped her foot impatiently, ignoring the taxi drivers vying for her attention, looking up and down the road in front of the terminal. If Howard didn't hurry, Peter would come out of the building and try to talk her into riding in from the airport with him—and that would never do.

"Hurry, Howard, hurry, Howard," she chanted softly.

Too late. She heard Peter calling her name. Turning, she saw him coming toward her.

"No husband, huh?" he said with a grin. "Great. I'll rent a car and take you in. . . ."

His sentence hung in the air as a long, black Lincoln Continental came to a skidding stop beside Claire. Gregory Barberry emerged from behind the wheel, his patrician profile exaggerated by the way he held his head, his thin mustache quivering as he disdainfully examined Peter, his voice high and thin as he addressed Claire.

"Claire, my dear. Howard is involved in telephone negotiations with three heads of state at the moment, and couldn't tear himself away. So I've been delegated to meet and greet, as it were."

He came around the car to get her bag, still casting curious glances at Peter. "Beauty before business, I always say. And so you see, I do have the better end of the deal."

He pulled open the door for her to get in and stepped back, turning to Peter. "Is there something I can do for you, young man?" he asked icily. "You do look a bit lost."

For one brief moment, the temptation to climb into the car and never look back flashed through Claire. She didn't want anyone to see her with

Peter. She didn't want anyone to talk about her, speculate about him. And more than anyone, other than Howard himself, she didn't want Frances's husband to get a hint of there being anything between them. How easy it would be to pretend she'd never seen Peter before, that he'd merely come up to her just then.

One look at his face told her she couldn't do that. Instead, she smiled at her husband's assistant. "Oh, I'm sorry. Gregory Barberry, let me introduce you to Peter Arnold. He's been very helpful to me, in the Athens airport and on the flight home. Peter, this is Gregory Barberry, Draxon's Production Manager, and my husband's righthand man."

The two men shook hands warily and Claire slipped into the car. Gregory came around and got behind the wheel. Peter stood where he was, and as they drove away from the curb, his intense blue eyes met Claire's and his lips moved. She couldn't hear what he was saying, but she was sure it was a promise of some sort.

Stay away from me, Peter, she cried silently. Please stay away.

Gregory drove her back to the compound, talking all the while. She barely heard a word he said. Her mind was on only one thing.

"What time will Howard be coming home?" she asked as he helped her out of the car in front of her own house.

"Not until evening, I would think," Gregory responded cheerfully. "Would you like me to help you in with your things?"

She stood with her bags and shook her head, desperate for Gregory to leave before her carefully cultivated mask of normalcy slipped and left her naked to his scrutiny. "I can manage. Thanks."

"I'll be off, then," he responded. "Onward and upward. Cheerio."

She watched him drive away, then turned and went into the house. She was met by an almost eerie silence. No Howard. No girls. No music.

She left the bags in the living room and went into the family room to put something on the compact disk player—anything to drown out this awful silence. She'd reached for a disk before she realized the player looked strange. It looked as if it had been smashed with something heavy. Someone had deliberately destroyed it.

Her first thought was burglary, but who had ever heard of a burglar in this small compound? Besides, why would a burglar destroy the player instead of taking it? Fast upon the heels of that doubt came the growing realization of what must have happened.

She hurried into the kitchen, but everything looked perfectly normal there. Her heart beat wildly as she raced up the stairs. Sam's room was untouched, and so was Katy's. She opened the door to the bedroom she shared with Howard with shaking hands.

The room was a mess. The mirror had been smashed and pieces lay all over the floor. Some of her dresses had been pulled off hangers and ripped to shreds. Her pillow had been gutted, and down feathers covered the room like a blanket of peaceful snow, a bizarre coverup to the violence they represented.

She left the room quickly and closed the door behind her, then doubled up as though her stomach hurt, gasping for breath.

Howard. It had to be Howard. The first emotion beyond pure shock was fear. If he had done this to her things, what might he do to her?

A hundred thoughts flashed through her head. She had to get out of here. She had to go back to Atlanta. No, she had to go stay with Shareen until this was all explained. No, she should stay and face Howard with what he had done. No . . .

Little by little, she regained control, and with it came a cold, methodical calm. She went back into the bedroom and began to clean it, stuffing the shredded dresses into the trash, picking up the jagged pieces of glass one by one, and finally, vacuuming up the feathers.

She was functioning perfectly normally, but she couldn't think. She couldn't sort out what had happened and put it into a context to be dealt with. She would have to wait for Howard to come home and make some sense of it all.

It was dusk before he arrived. She'd been sitting very still, but rose to her feet as he came into the room. He looked haggard and she felt immediate compassion. But she didn't say a word. She stood and waited, watching every nuance of expression that passed over his face, trying to analyze him. If he would take a step toward her, if he would hold out his arms—if he would explain, offer comfort, anything—she was ready to wipe the slate clean and start over.

One gesture.

Anything.

He stood and stared at her and his eyes seemed full of nothing but resentment. "So, you finally managed to come back," he said coldly. "I was beginning to think I was going to have to forgo the pleasure of your company for the rest of this tour."

"Of course I came back. I belong with you."

His short laugh was remarkably free of any trace of humor. Turning, he glanced at the compact disk player. "Oh, sorry about the player. It fell."

It was on the tip of her tongue to ask if the bedroom had fallen as well, but she managed to hold it back. "Have you eaten?" she asked instead.

"I had something brought in at the office." He turned back to look at her. "I suppose you've seen the bedroom."

"Yes."

"It happened the night Bob Camden left. I got drunk and got a little carried away. I left it for you to clean up, because—" he shrugged "—that's what wives are for, aren't they?" He glared at her. "Am I right?"

Was there anything left of this marriage to salvage? She had to believe there was, and she pushed the question back into the recesses of her mind.

Ignoring what he'd asked, she countered with, "Where have you been sleeping all this time?"

"In the den. It's quite cozy in there." Something she recognized flickered in his eyes. "In fact," he said, moving closer, "why don't we go on in there right now? The foldout bed has room for two." His hand brushed her cheek roughly, and then his fingers closed down on her shoulder. "It's been a long time, Claire. Let's go see if we still know how to do it."

Dread poured through Claire, along with bittersweet memories of other reunions, other times. She could remember running into his arms when he returned from a long trip, of holding him and laughing and falling on the floor of their little apartment to make love right then and there, because they had missed each other so much, because they needed to show each other how much they cared. What had happened to those emotions? What had happened to those people?

This was not the man she'd once loved, the man she'd promised to cherish. But she was still his wife. Didn't she owe him this?

He pulled her toward the den, and she went, reluctant but unable to think of a way out of this duty. He pulled out the bed and turned to her, his eyes burning.

"Come on, Claire," he said, his voice stinging with sarcasm. "Show me just how much you missed me."

She wanted the light off but she knew better than to ask for that. His hands were rough, pulling at her clothes, and a hard knot rose in her throat.

"Wait. Let me do it," she pleaded, trying to unbutton her blouse before he ripped it.

He paid no attention and she heard the fabric tear. "Come on, come on," he urged. "You owe me this." The blouse fell to the floor, ruined.

But she wouldn't think about that. She would set her mind on making her husband happy. Her hands went to the closure on her skirt, but he was quicker than she was, yanking at the zipper and swearing.

"Howard!" She tried to push his hands away, but that only made him more determined to do it himself. He grabbed at the skirt, his fingers hard and hurtful, and something snapped inside Claire.

Fury surged in her. She used both hands to push him away. "Leave me alone," she told him evenly, her eyes flashing dark fire, her voice rough as sandpaper. "Don't touch me."

She wasn't at all sure what he would do. After what he had done to her things, a little voice inside her head was crying out a warning. The violence he harbored inside was evident in those actions. She stood her ground and held her breath, waiting for the worst.

He stood very still, but his anger was unmistakable, his eyes cold as steel, his hands clenched in white-knuckled rage.

"What's the matter with you?" he demanded.

"You," she said, her voice quavering but firm. There was no denying she was afraid of him. He was larger and stronger than she was. If he decided to force her, there wasn't much she could do about it, except to make it as unpleasant an experience as possible for him. She took a deep breath and said something she had never said to him before. "I . . . I'm not going to make love with you, Howard."

"What?" His shock at her words was clear to see. His face was contorted. "What are you talking about?" he cried harshly.

She forced herself to hold his glare with her own gaze. If she couldn't face him down, how could she ever hope to make him understand? "I can't make love with you," she repeated. "Not now, not this way."

A sound came out of him, something low and ugly, almost an animal snarl. "The hell you can't," he spat. "You're my wife. You do what I say."

She was shaking so badly, she thought her knees would give way. He was going to hit her. She could sense it coming.

"No," she said anyway, loud and clear. "No." And her Duvall chin rose.

He stared at her, and then, to her surprise, the fury seemed to die in his eyes, and a puzzled helplessness took its place.

"Why?" he asked, his voice rough but low. "What's the matter?"

She didn't dare feel relief yet, but her shoulders sagged. Leaning down, she took the strips of fabric that had once been her blouse and she held them to her chest before she looked at him again.

She was still shaking, but the strong calm was back, holding her up.

"You've become a stranger to me, Howard," she said. "You're a hard, cold man who doesn't love me. Bring the old Howard back if you want me. I'll make love to him. But not to this stranger."

"Don't be ridiculous," he growled, but he made no move to touch her again.

"You don't care about me," she went on. "You haven't asked one question about the funeral, about Daddy. You haven't told me you were sorry I lost him. You haven't even asked how my trip was. Nor did you care enough to show up at the airport when I arrived."

He looked almost happy to grasp at her last statement as the real reason. "Oh, is that all this is? You're miffed because I sent Gregory?"

"No." She pushed back her hair, which had torn free in the struggle. "No, Howard. It's much more than that. We're aliens living together and pretending to belong."

She felt tired suddenly, bone-weary, and it was only with supreme effort that she managed to keep from swaying and reaching for something to hold herself up.

"The pretense has fallen through, Howard. Something has to change to save us."

"You're talking garbage as usual." But his eyes were hurt, almost vulnerable. And his body language told her he wouldn't come after her again right now.

"We need time to think, Howard. To think, and to regroup and decide what we want from each other. Until we come to some kind of understanding, I . . . I think I'll sleep in the bedroom. And maybe you should sleep down here. All right?"

She didn't wait to hear his answer. Holding the remnants of her blouse firmly to her, she turned and left him, taking the stairs quickly, closing the door to her room, and then waiting, heart pounding, to see if he would follow.

The minutes inched by. Suddenly there came the sound of glass shattering, and she held her breath. But everything was quiet again. Minute by minute she waited, and there wasn't another sound.

Finally she got up from the bed. Moving as quietly as she was able, she locked the bedroom door and went to the bathroom, drawing water and sinking into the thick, white suds that smelled like spring flowers. She soaked for a long time, trying to think, trying not to think.

Eventually she got out, dried herself with a fluffy towel and listened, hard. There wasn't a sound in the house. Could Howard have left? She tried to see the driveway from the bedroom window, but there was a palm tree in the way. Steeling herself, she unlocked the door and tiptoed down the staircase.

Howard was in the den, sitting at the desk. Splinters from something—probably a glass—thrown against the wall lay glinting on the carpet. A large bottle of scotch sat before him, its contents almost gone.

She went into the room, holding her robe tightly around her. He looked up blearily and saw her there, silhouetted in the doorway.

"Well, hello, Claire," he said loudly, waving a half-empty glass at her. His smile was lopsided and he looked unsteady on the chair. "Welcome to my nightmare, darling. Come right on in and pull up a coffin. We're having a wake."

Claire stood uncertainly. "Howard, don't you think you've had enough?"

"Eh-eh-eh." He waggled a finger at her and then motioned for her to sit down. "None of that. If you won't sleep with me, you can't nag me. The two go hand in hand, you know."

Claire sat on the edge of the chair and wondered how she was going to get him to go to bed.

"Would you like to join me in a toast?" Without waiting for her answer, he poured her a drink and held it out for her. "Here. Take it anyway." He plopped it into her hand. "We're toasting the late, great career of Howard Montgomery."

"Howard—"

"Be quiet, dear. I'm going to tell you a story." He settled back and stared at her, threw back the contents of his glass, winced, and began to talk.

"Once upon a time there was a little boy named Howie. He lived in a two-bedroom cold-water flat above a garage in a very bad section of Newark. His mother was a waitress. And his daddy was an inventor who could never hold down a job and never seemed to get patents on his inventions in time to make any money off them."

Claire had always known Howard came from humble beginnings. He'd always told her his parents were dead and that they had been poor, but she'd never heard this version before.

"Little Howie went to school and he learned

about the American Dream and he decided to make it work for him. You can be anything, he told himself. All you have to do is be smart and work hard, and you can be anything.''

He paused, staring at a place behind Claire's head as though he could see that little boy there. Claire was tempted to turn around and look.

"So he did. He was smart and he worked hard and he left that cold-water flat and went to a big university and studied even harder, and before you know it, he was hired by Draxon Oil and told to expect to make it all the way to the top someday.''

His gaze dropped and he stared into Claire's eyes. "And then he met a beautiful princess who seemed to have all the class and background he lacked, and he married her. Now everything would be perfect, he thought. And he worked and he worked and he waited to make it all the way to the top.''

"But a funny thing happened on the way. They didn't come right out and tell him at first. But finally, he began to realize the truth. They lied when they said he could get to the top. You see, the top was reserved for a certain class of people. And since he'd been born poor, with nothing to brag about in the way of breeding, that superior stratum would be forever out of his reach. No matter how hard he worked, he was only spinning his wheels.'' Howard sighed and laughed hollowly. "End of story. A real tear-jerker, isn't it?''

"Howard . . .'' She reached out and took his

hand in her own. "Oh, Howard, I didn't realize. . . ."

"No big deal. I'm learning to live with it. I hope you like Saudi Arabia. It looks as though we may be here for a while."

Her heart was filled with pity. Now that he had articulated the facts as he saw them, she realized she had always suspected there was a subtle prejudice against Howard among the upper echelons at Draxon. She'd tried to ignore those feelings all these years. But now little incidents sprang to mind, digs at Howard behind his back, looks from top officials of the company, glances meant to convey to Claire that, though she was one of them, her husband was not. They'd bought him for his talent and proceeded to milk him for all they could get. But they had never intended for him to be one of them. Why hadn't she seen it?

The unfairness of this situation burned like a brand inside her. Her sympathies were all with Howard once again. No wonder he was so hard to live with these days. She would help him. They would fight this thing together, and it would be as it had been in those first years of their marriage—the two of them against the world. Maybe hope wasn't dead, after all.

"If you really believe that this is the way it is at Draxon, why don't you quit?" she urged, starting to feel excited about the idea. "We can start over. We can go back to the States and find another company. . . ."

Howard was shaking his head, his face dark and hopeless. "They're all alike," he muttered.

"No. No, they're not." She had to make him see that. "There are companies where talent and hard work are rewarded."

His head came up and he glared at her, his eyes bleary and full of resentment.

"How would you know what it's like? All your life, you've had it all—money, position, respect of the people around you. I've had to earn it, Claire, to earn every scrap of respect I ever had. I had to be twice as good as the next guy."

"And you *were* twice as good as the next guy. And you could be again, in a new setting. We'll start over. We'll go to California. Anything, Howard. Anything it takes to pull this family back together and make you happy again."

But he couldn't seem to catch hold of the fire of her enthusiasm. He shook his head, making a face of disgust.

"Are you crazy? I can't quit Draxon. This is what I've worked for all my life."

She felt her future slipping away again. "But if it's hopeless . . ."

He shook his head, dismissing her ideas. "It can't be hopeless," he muttered, completely negating his earlier contention. "It just can't be. There's got to be a way."

She sat back and stared at him. She hardly knew this man. Had she ever? Had she been fooling herself all these years, pretending he was something he never was?

"Claire." He was looking at her again, pushing the bottle aside. He reached out his hand, pleading. "Claire, sleep with me."

Her heart lurched in her chest. How could she deny him when he asked like this? He looked pitiful—beaten, hurt, needy, as though he knew he was wounded but couldn't figure out quite how it had happened. She should comfort him. And sleeping with him was one way she could do that. She was his wife. How could she turn him away? She would have to go with him.

She looked up, about to tell him she would do whatever he wanted, but her words stuck in her throat. She couldn't get them out. Suddenly she knew she had to stick to the decision she'd made.

If she gave in now, she would never have a chance to deal on this firm a foundation of resolve again. It was the only right thing to do. There could be no lovemaking between them simply out of pity. There had to be a bond, a real relationship.

Was there any hope such a thing might happen? No. Not really. It was time she faced that truth. This marriage, to all intents and purposes, was over. Only the form remained, the appearance.

She took a deep breath and hardened herself. "No, Howard," she said. "I can't do that."

He stared at her for a long moment, swore with obscene vehemence, then reached for the bottle again. She got up and left the room, heading for the stairway and her bedroom, where she planned to lock the door. The pain of what she was doing twisted inside her, and for a moment she almost hated herself. But she had to make a stand. If she couldn't do it now, she would never be able to gather the strength to do it. She went up the stairs quickly, running from the mess her life had become.

She slept as though she'd been drugged, and when she awoke, the bright sunlight streaming through the window couldn't lighten the leaden atmosphere.

Peter. She'd been dreaming about him. Lying there alone in her bed, she felt herself blushing. Oh, Lord, she had to stop this.

Wiping him out of her mind, she dressed and went downstairs to rouse Howard and get him off to work. They went through the motions, barely speaking, barely connecting at all.

"I'm going to Cairo for a meeting on Friday," he told her gruffly as he left. "Pack me some things. I'll be coming back on Sunday."

He started out the door, then looked back. "I'll get someone over here to hang a new mirror," he said. "Maybe I can find someone handy enough to finally fix all the other things that have gone wrong around here."

"Great," she said, though she wasn't hopeful that there was any such person. "Have a nice day."

He left and she sat down with a cup of coffee to try to make some sense out of her future, to think through the tangled muddle of her present. It was over. What now?

The bleak question of her future was still wavering before her eyes when she heard a knocking on the sliding glass door in the family room. She sighed, knowing who it must be. At least Howard had locked the door, so Margo couldn't barge in. Claire went to let her in and found herself smiling at the perky woman, glad for the company, despite everything.

Margo bounced in and grinned at her. "So you came back after all."

"I came back after all." She began to lead the way to the kitchen. "Where did you think I would go?"

"Who knows? Once you got out of this place, I thought you'd never look back." She flopped onto a kitchen chair with a heartfelt sigh and watched while Claire poured her a cup of coffee.

"But I'm glad you're back. I've been dying for another adult to talk to. I was going crazy at home, so I decided to come over here and hide out for a while."

Claire sat down across from her, glad to immerse herself in someone else's problems. "School will start up again soon," she reminded Margo. "You'll have David and Jesse out of your hair."

Margo shook her head, rolling her eyes. "This isn't just one of those end-of-summer-blues things," she stated emphatically. "It's much worse than that. My kids have taken over my house." She took a sip of coffee and put her chin in her hand, contemplating her misery.

"Jesse ordered one of those infernal drum machines from Japan. It arrived last week, and life has been hell ever since. The two of them fancy themselves rock-and-roll stars of some sort." She threw up her hands in despair.

"I don't know," she went on. "Who am I to say? They sound awful to me, but what do I know? They spend their days shouting obscene lyrics into microphones with the drum machines going hell-for-leather in the background. I can't hear myself think."

Claire laughed at her neighbor's description. "Have they ever had music lessons?"

"Music lessons? What do they need music lessons for? You buy the expertise these days. It comes in a little machine with knobs and levers. You just turn it on and you yell something into a microphone, and that's called music." She shook her blond curls. "I swear, you wouldn't believe the god-awful noise they make."

"I'll bet it's better than you give them credit for."

"No. It is not." She had no doubts on that score. "The funny thing is, they both think they're going to take this act on the road. I don't know. Maybe they know something I don't. But I'll tell you one thing—songs aren't what they used to be. Remember the old days, when almost all the lyrics rhymed with moon and June and spoon?" She shook her head sadly. "Those days are gone, honey. Nowadays, everything has to rhyme with a word I won't repeat, but it ends in *ck.*"

Margo's stories about her hair-raising adventures bringing up two teenage boys made Claire laugh—but they also made her glad her daughters weren't around to get caught in the boys' wake.

Margo stayed all morning, only leaving when Frances came to the door. For Margo knew she was invisible to the woman. Frances didn't mix with anyone but white collar professionals.

Frances refused a cup of coffee and took out a bottle of spring water she carried with her.

"So . . . you decided to come back," she said. Her eyes gleamed with exaggerated sympathy.

Claire was getting a bit tired of this surprise at her return. "Of course. Why wouldn't I come back?"

Frances waved a negligent hand in the air. "I'm sure I don't know. But you know what they say about deserting a sinking ship."

A hard knot suddenly appeared in Claire's stomach. "What sinking ship are you talking about?"

Frances leaned closer to her across the kitchen table. "Let's be honest. You and I both know Howard is having problems."

Claire found herself leaning backward to get as far away from the woman as possible. "I've heard something along those lines." She managed to fake a sweet smile. "But I'm sure Gregory is doing everything he can to help Howard with those problems." She arched a questioning eyebrow. "Isn't he?"

Frances had the grace to look uncomfortable for a split second, but no longer. "Certainly. But the good of the company is always uppermost in Gregory's mind. Surely you know that. Draxon is the most important consideration here."

"Is it?"

"You know it is. Well, let me tell you, Gregory is worried about Howard. He's losing concentration, Claire. His mind isn't on his work. Gregory and I think the best thing he could do would be to take a leave of absence and go back to the States for a while. Believe me, Gregory is willing to step in and take over for him—on a temporary basis, of course. Just until Howard gets himself together again." Her smile reminded Claire of a crocodile opening its jaws. "I want you to think about it. I'm sure you can influence him to do it. And with Gregory so willing to make the sacrifice to help out, it's the perfect solution."

Claire began to laugh. It started out slow, just a slight chuckle. But as Frances wound up her pitch, the chuckle became a hearty laugh, one she couldn't have stopped if she'd wanted to. Frances reddened, cleared her throat and finally got up to leave.

"I was only trying to help," she sputtered as she made her own way to the door.

Claire didn't answer. She was still laughing.

"It was just so funny," she said later that afternoon, trying to explain it to Shareen. "She actually had convinced herself that I would believe she had my best interests at heart."

"You did the perfect thing," Shareen replied sensibly. "If you had argued or shouted, she would have stayed forever. She would have relished a good excuse to do some screaming. Laughter she wouldn't know how to handle. So she got out as fast as she was able."

"Yes, this will definitely come in handy in the future." Claire grinned. "Laughter to Frances is as garlic to a vampire."

"Apt comparison," said Shareen. "Green skin and all."

They were relaxing on the terrace at Shareen's house, a block from Claire's The light slanting across the desert gave the afternoon the color of a golden peach.

"I've been gone, too, you know," Shareen informed her. "I went to see my grandmother last week."

"In Beirut?"

She nodded. "I told her about you. And she wanted me to give you this." She reached into the pocket of her skirt and took out a thin gold chain bearing a small, exquisitely molded gold heart.

Claire took it wonderingly. "It's beautiful."

She threw Shareen a questioning look. "What did you tell her about me?"

"How hard it is for you here. How you have to hold off the gossip-mongers while trying to support your husband."

Claire hadn't known anyone else had noticed. She smiled and looked at the heart. "How nice of her," she said softly.

"I told her about you because I wanted her to see that other women were having a hard time, too. That she wasn't the only one. And she felt very badly for you. She wanted me to tell you—you'll find a way."

Claire's heart skipped a beat. "She said those exact words?" she asked quickly, looking up to search Shareen's dark eyes.

Shareen looked surprised. "Yes, I think so. Why?"

Claire hesitated, then told her. "My father said the same thing to me. Just before he died."

Shareen went very still. "The same words? You're sure?"

Claire shrugged. "Very nearly. Isn't that odd?"

"Yes," Shareen echoed faintly. "It *is* odd."

She considered telling Shareen about Peter, but she hesitated. After all, Peter was forbidden fruit, the sort of temptation good wives avoided like the plague. The fact that she couldn't get him out of her mind, that she was always seeing his blue eyes, his muscular shoulders, the way his pants fit on her rear end, was a trial, not a pleasure. Or so she tried to tell herself.

She had dinner with Shareen and her husband, Larry, one night a week later when Howard worked late. Larry turned out to have a delightful sense of humor, as well as a collection of vintage sheet music, popular tunes from the twenties and thirties, that kept them at the piano, playing and singing, until almost midnight.

Claire wished Howard could have come along and joined in the fun. But she knew there was very little hope of anything like that happening soon, if ever. Was this the pattern for the rest of her life? Would she have to make her own way socially? The prospect chilled her. And yet, she realized, that was exactly what her mother had done all those years.

What was next for Howard and her? She hadn't come, as yet, to any firm conclusion. They passed back and forth like two strangers. He came home late, left early, and barely noticed her.

The girls would be back soon. She could hardly wait. The loneliness she felt without them was beginning to get to her.

But she still hadn't formulated a real plan. Did she really want to live as her mother had, a separate life that revolved around her children and ignored her husband? No. She hated the thought of it. But her only other choice was divorce. And she couldn't quite bring herself to take that step just yet.

❧

The front doorbell rang during breakfast the next morning. Claire looked at Howard in surprise.

"That must be the handyman I hired to come

over and do some work," he said, starting to get up. "I'll get it."

Claire was pleased he had come through on his promise. "I hope you hired someone who knows what he's doing this time," she said, smiling faintly. "That houseboy Frances got for us the first month we were here . . ."

"No, I think this one has a little more on the ball," he replied over his shoulder as he left the room. "He's a roughneck currently between assignments, and I think he's doing this more because he's bored and needs something to do than anything else."

Claire stood very still as she heard him open the front door and talk quietly to their visitor. She had a strange, prickly feeling, an ominous premonition, and by the time the two men returned to the kitchen, her heart was beating rapidly.

"Here he is, Claire. Peter Arnold. He says he can fix everything from mirrors to plumbing. Is that right?"

Peter's blue eyes were sparkling with mischief and his grin was wide and devilish. "I can fix whatever's broken," he said. "Just give me a chance."

Claire looked from one to the other of them, the blood draining from her face. Didn't Howard remember Peter? Obviously not. But then, why should he have? Peter had just been one of the roughnecks playing volleyball, nothing special.

Peter, on the other hand, knew better. She stared into his eyes, her own asking, Am I supposed to pretend we've never met? Why are you here?

"It's nice to meet you, Mrs. Montgomery." His hand was stretched out to her and she took it quickly. "I'll have your house feeling just like it's back in the States in no time."

He was dressed in tight denim jeans and an open shirt, and a tool belt was slung low on his hips. She had never imagined she would ever see him in her house. The room seemed to spin for a moment as she tried to get her bearings.

Her husband seemed oblivious to the emotions being generated all around him.

"Take him up to the bedroom, Claire," Howard was saying as he sat down for his second cup of coffee. "I have a new mirror being delivered. Show him where to install it."

Numbly she led the way to the stairs, holding the rail as she went up, acutely aware of the man behind her. She hesitated at the door to her bedroom. Howard hadn't been in here since she'd come back from Atlanta. And now he was encouraging her to let Peter Arnold in. This was crazy. She turned and looked at Peter.

"You've got to get out of here," she whispered urgently.

He grinned. "Why, ma'am, what are you saying?" he drawled. "I came to work. Your husband hired me." He shrugged. "If you really want me out of here, I think he should be the one to fire me."

She gazed at him in despair. "I thought you'd be in Abu Dhabi by now," she wailed softly.

His gaze caressed her face. "I can't go to Abu Dhabi yet. I haven't got what I came for."

She looked at him warily, not sure she wanted to hear this. "Well," she said impatiently. "What did you come for?"

He moved too close, looking down at her. "You know what I came for, Claire. I came for you."

She backed away quickly, inadvertently pushing open the door to her bedroom as she did so. He went on in and she didn't have any choice but to follow.

"Here's where the mirror was," she said, giving in to the inevitable.

He nodded, but didn't seem much interested. "Is someone staying with you?" He turned to watch her eyes as she answered.

"No. Why?"

He smiled. "As you were taking me through to the stairs, I noticed a foldout bed in the den. A bed that was slept in last night." He looked around the bedroom, taking in the nightgown thrown carelessly on the end of the bed, her shoes kicked off across the floor. "You and Howie aren't sleeping together, are you?"

She drew in a trembling breath and turned away. "That is none of your business."

"Claire . . ." He stopped her, taking her chin in his hand and gazing down into her eyes. "I intend to make it my business."

She was suddenly aware of how dowdy she must look, in her old blue T-shirt and corduroy shorts, with her hair pulled back into a careless braid, hanging down her back, no makeup. She hadn't been expecting to care what the handyman thought of her appearance. Now it seemed critically important.

No, she took that back, pulling away from him and chastizing herself silently. She was attracted to Peter. He made her blood sing like no other man ever had. But that didn't mean she was ready to jeopardize her family's reputation for the thrill of having a man like this pursue her.

"Leave me alone," she said through clenched teeth. "Don't touch me again." Gesturing toward the wall where the mirror had been, she went on, "You're the one who wants to be a handyman. Do your handyman things. I won't get in your way."

She proceeded to dash about the room, picking up clothes and magazines, and when she looked back to see what he was doing, she found him in her open closet, gathering an armful of her dresses, pulling them to him and burying his face in the fabric.

"What are are you doing?" she hissed.

"These smell just like you do," he murmured. "Chanel No. 5 and pearls."

"Pearls don't smell."

"No, but they have a lustre and a richness . . ."

What were they doing here, talking about pearls? Was she crazy? She had to get rid of him.

"Oh, will you get out of that closet?" she pleaded. "Howard might come up and see you."

He looked up from her clothes with a wicked smile. "But Howard doesn't 'live' here anymore," he reminded her.

"That certainly doesn't mean you are moving

in." Resentment rose in her. Men! Mere devices to complicate women's lives. "I'm getting out of here," she said, turning to go. "I'm not going to stay while you're here."

He took her arm as she tried to pass him. "Come on, I only came here for you."

She looked up into his eyes and slowly shook her head. "I can't. It's not right. I can't stay here with you in the house. I'm leaving."

Claire took the stairs at a run and flew into the kitchen. Howard looked up from his paper in surprise. "Going somewhere?"

She stopped, catching her breath and trying not to look as though she were fleeing danger, although she knew that was exactly the case.

"I . . . I thought I'd go over to Shareen's for a while." She tried to smile. "I don't want to hang around here with that man in the house."

Howard folded his paper carefully and looked at her, his eyes cold and forbidding. "That's exactly why you're going to have to stay here," he said evenly, rising and straightening his jacket. "There's a stranger in the house. Doesn't it mean anything to you that he could steal everything we've got?"

No, Howard, she thought, staring back at him. Everything we've got is already gone. There's nothing left for him to steal. But instead of saying that plainly, she turned away and said, "He works for Draxon. He wouldn't steal from you."

"That doesn't matter, Claire. The fact is, if you want a job done right, you have to supervise it. I don't ask a whole lot of you around here these days. At the very least, you could guard our interests."

She watched as Howard left, listened as he started the car and drove away down the driveway. It was almost as though he were giving her permission, wasn't it? Well, that was just too bad. What she would or would not do was her decision.

Still, she stayed in the house. When Peter came down the stairs a few minutes later, she was dusting the bookshelves in the family room.

He looked at her but didn't gloat, for which she was grateful. Then his glance fell on the damaged compact disk player, which she had left right where it had always been in a mute reproach, a petty decision she now fully regretted.

"Uh-oh. Your player has had an accident."

She met Peter's gaze and knew he understood exactly what had happened. His eyes flashed anger for a moment and he took a step toward her, but she retreated behind the couch and began dusting pictures with furious intensity.

He hesitated and turned away, looking at the room again. "Where's your piano?" he asked.

She looked up briefly and went back to her dusting. "I don't have one here."

"I bet you miss playing the piano." He grinned, catching her by the waist as she moved past him. "You want to play around with me instead?"

She pushed his hands aside. "No." She said the word loudly, crisply, so that there could be no misunderstanding.

He shook his head sadly. "All this housework is making you grumpy," he diagnosed. "Let's cut out."

She turned to stare at him. "Peter . . ."

He took her hands in his. "I have an idea. I'm going to take you out into the desert. I want to show you the nomadic tribes, the Bedouins, the camel races, the horses. Will you come with me?"

His eyes were as deep as a crystal sea. She could drown in there if she weren't careful. "I can't go with you."

"Yes, you can. I'll take care of everything."

She shook her head, wanting to laugh. He was so tempting in such a childlike way. The urge to let herself be a child again was intense, and she had to work hard to resist it. "From what I've heard, they don't think much of Western women racing about the desert with handsome young rough-necks," she told him.

He grinned. "Silly of them to be so picky. I suppose if I was ugly it would be okay?"

She couldn't help it. He made her laugh. "You couldn't be ugly if you tried."

His eyes sobered. "I could be anything I have to be, for you."

She was beginning to tremble. She pulled away from him, turning to look out the window at the street. "Oh, Peter," she said softly, anguish in her tone, "why are you here? Why are you doing this?"

He came up behind her and put his hands on her shoulders. "I'll tell you why. You want me to be totally honest?"

She closed her eyes. "Aren't you always?"

"I like you, Claire. I like the way you move. I like the way you look. I want to make love with you."

His words sliced through her, leaving her breathless. "Just like that," she whispered.

"Exactly like that." He leaned down and kissed the back of her neck. "Anytime, anyplace you say."

She turned and looked into his eyes, searching his gaze. "Why? Why me? Why not someone else? One of the other wives, maybe, or one of the older teenaged girls. Or Kim Striper, the new secretary at the office. She's not married, and she's very pretty. Why not her?"

"Because they're not you."

She studied him, hardly able to believe he could be serious. She'd never had a man this persistent before. She couldn't help but imagine certain ulterior motives.

"What am I, some kind of sick challenge to you? The director's wife. Is that it? You want to bed the director's wife in order to prove something to someone."

He stared back, then lowered his head and began to nuzzle her neck. "I don't care about beds, Claire," he whispered against her skin. "I'll do it anywhere you say."

He kissed her earlobe, her cheek, her lips. "Just as long as we touch, and you have me, and I have you, and we share that one moment in time."

She could hardly breathe, and the room was spinning again. Was this real, or some crazy dream?

This wasn't Claire Duvall, it couldn't be. Claire Duvall did not do things like this. Helpless, she clung to her one line of defense. "But you don't deny that you're doing this to prove something."

He looked at her again. "What do I have to prove, Claire?" he said. "All I want is to connect with you." His heavy lids lowered, giving him a dreamy look as his gaze drifted slowly over her. "I want to see your face when it happens," he whispered seductively. "I want to see your eyes cloud, see your hands clench, feel your hips pull me in."

He pressed her tightly against his hard young body and she gasped.

"I want to hear you cry out my name and feel your fingers digging into my back. I want every part of you to scream for me."

She was drowning. No one had ever talked to her this way before. No one had ever made her feel so desirable. She still couldn't quite believe it.

"But why?" she insisted. "Why do you want that?"

He looked straight at her and it was evident to her suddenly that he didn't even know himself.

She pulled away and took a few steps backward. It was too much. She couldn't trust herself. "I've got to get out of here," she said hollowly, turning so that she wouldn't have to look into his eyes again. "I won't come back until you're gone."

She expected him to try to stop her, but he didn't. She walked quickly from the house and headed for Shareen's, praying that she wouldn't run into Frances before she made it to a safe haven. She was shaken to the core, and she needed time to regroup.

CHAPTER

9

Katy and Samantha were back. Howard went with Claire to the airport to meet them only because she insisted. The girls came out looking older in just the two weeks she'd been away from them. Katy turned right back into her little girl in no time, but Samantha held her cool reserve all the way home, her blue eyes glazed over like a pond in winter, not giving anything away. Claire ached to get close to her again. Sam was just thirteen—was there no child left in her? Was she destined to live with a teenage stranger for the next six or seven years?

Sam was turning into a beauty, with her wide-spaced blue eyes and her silvery blond hair almost down to her tailbone. There would be boyfriends soon. Would she sit still for a mother-to-daughter chat about the birds and the bees, and how far to let boys go, and how you know when you're really in love? Claire hardly thought so. She could see

Sam rolling her eyes already and saying, "Mother! I already know all that stuff. Come on."

Maybe she ought to get that little duty done with Katy now, before the teenage curse was cast over her, as well. But looking at her smiling youngest, she couldn't imagine her withdrawing the way Samantha had. Katy would always be a cuddler, her confidante, the one with emotions right near the surface, ready to love, to cry, to cherish.

If only she could get through to Sam that way. Remembering her when she was very young, with curls all over her head and a ready smile, running in the sunshine, screaming with laughter in the sprinklers, throwing herself into her mother's lap when a stranger came near, Claire ached for what she was missing now.

Barely hours into the homecoming, Samantha was already voicing the age-old teenage cry. "It is so boring here. There's nothing to do."

Claire came back with her standard response, even though she knew it was useless. It was automatic. Push her Mother button and out it came.

"If you can't find anything to do, I have plenty of jobs that need doing."

"Mother!"

"Well, school will start again next week. Read a book. Watch a movie. Go visit some of your friends."

Samantha was too old and too proud to pout, but she did a good imitation anyway. "I don't have any friends here. They're all in Atlanta."

"What about those girls you sang with in the talent show?"

"They're nerds. I can't stand them."

Then stay here by yourself and be miserable, Claire thought. After counting silently to ten, she said, "Shareen Hunter has organized a shopping trip into Riyadh tomorrow. A group of women from the compound are going. How would you like to come along?"

Had she actually seen a spark of interest in those eyes? "Maybe," Sam said.

Claire was hopeful. A mother-daughter outing might just do the trick. She rose early the next day, prepared breakfast for Howard and sent him off, then dressed carefully and knocked on Sam's door.

"What is it?" came the sleepy voice.

"Sam? May I come in?"

There was a shuffling noise, as though she were hiding something. Claire bit her lip, reminding herself of when she went through the stage of reading true-confession magazines and hid them under her bed so her mother wouldn't know. Everyone was allowed to have some secrets.

Finally Sam's voice called out, "Okay."

Claire went in. Sam was lying in her bed, the frilly pink covers an odd contrast to her adult-looking eyes.

Claire bent to kiss the cool cheek that was hardly offered. Still, her daughter didn't pull away.

"Are you going to come on the shopping trip to Riyadh? The van is leaving in half an hour." She smiled. "Katy is playing with Ricky today. I'd love to have you come along."

For just a moment she thought she saw something in the depths of those crystal eyes, something that opened to her, something that connected. But then it was gone and Sam was shaking her head. "I don't want to go."

Claire bit back the lecture that threatened, all about how Sam should get to know the country, all about what an opportunity she was missing here. "What will you do all day?" she asked instead.

Sam shrugged. "I don't know."

"But Sam, if you really have no other plans. . . ."

Sam turned, pulling the covers up over her shoulder. "I'm really tired, Mother."

Claire felt like she'd been slapped in the face. She knew that was exactly what Sam wanted her to feel, and she refused to give her the satisfaction of knowing she'd succeeded.

"You just sleep then, darling," she said, forcing herself to sound cheerful. "And when you wake up, you can wax the kitchen floor. Bye-bye."

She left the room without looking back, but once outside, she had to lean against the wall and close her eyes. This was awful. She couldn't stand living with her daughter as though they were in the middle of some sort of cold war. Something had to be done. If only she had a clue as to what.

The van was already almost full when Claire arrived, and she seemed to be the last to arrive. She'd put on a red shirtwaist with gold buttons and she was feeling rather spiffy. As she approached the van, Shareen called to her from a window, laughing.

"You're late, Claire. There are no seats left. You'll have to ride shotgun with the driver."

"Well, it is the proper place for her," Frances chimed in. "Being the director's wife and all."

Shareen made a face only Claire could see, so she was laughing as she climbed into the front seat. When she looked at the driver, the laughter evaporated, leaving her with the hiccups.

"Hello, Mrs. Montgomery." Peter grinned at her and touched his finger to his cap, playing the subservient retainer. "It's nice to see you again."

She sank into the seat and closed her eyes. Was she never going to get away from this man?

The van started off down the road, and she sat quietly, staring out the window, much too aware of Peter and his strong arms with the sleeves shoved back, driving beside her. She'd lain awake nights thinking about those arms, feeling them around her. Her body already knew what it wanted her to do. But her mind knew better.

The buzz of voices in the back of the van was constant, but as her hiccups died away, Claire became aware that some of the women were talking to Peter.

"You are just the cutest thing." It was Margo, of course. Who else? "If you were just a few years older, I'd cart you home and keep you for my own."

"Don't embarrass the poor man, Margo." Sally

Neels was batting her eyes like crazy. "You'll scare him away."

Peter threw a wide grin back at the women. "Don't worry about me. I don't scare too easily," he said. His eyes met Claire's as he turned back, but she looked out the side window.

She was blushing. She could feel it. She was no good at this. Didn't he know that? She was sure to say something or do something that would give her away.

As they raced along the empty road toward the city, she stared out at the endless desert, the shifting dunes, the distant mountains, trying to blot out the good-humored bantering between the women and the driver. But with Peter sitting right next to her, that was not easy to do.

"A girlfriend?" she heard him say. "Do I have a girlfriend?" He considered for a moment and Claire held her breath. Peter was likely to say almost anything.

"Well," he said at last. "I couldn't exactly call her a girlfriend. She's more like a prospective girlfriend."

Sally Neels squealed. "Don't tell me there's someone who's been turning you down?"

He smiled enigmatically and Claire prayed he wouldn't cast her a playful glance, a gesture that would be just like him to make. "Let's just say she's making me work for it."

Sally and Margo were both hanging over the seats in front of them, drooling over Peter in a way that turned Claire's stomach. Her head was beginning to pound and she wished she'd stayed home with Samantha.

"Who is she?" Margo was coaxing. "You can tell us. We won't tell anyone." They both giggled and Claire had to concentrate hard to keep from visibly shuddering. "Does she live in the compound?"

Peter laughed softly, teasing them. "You don't think I would actually tell you that, do you?"

"Why not? We're trustworthy. Ask anyone." More giggling.

"Okay." Peter's voice took on a serious tone. "Okay, I'll tell you all the truth."

Claire cringed inside. Not the truth! He was always telling the goddamned truth! Didn't this boy know how to lie?

"I'm crazy about this lady. I'm going to take her away from here if I can."

Claire froze, making her breathing soft and shallow, but getting in as much air as possible.

The women were silent for a moment, seemingly impressed by his earnest declaration.

"What do you mean?" Margo said at last. "Is she an Arab?"

"Don't be silly, Margo. They'd draw and quarter him. I'll bet she's married—a wife of one of the Draxon employees." Sally leaned forward. "Is she married?" she asked, obviously thrilled at the prospect.

"I can't tell you that. All I can say is, she's given me the cold shoulder—so far. But if I have my way, she'll be leaving with me when I go."

"God, that's so romantic. Are you going to ride up on a white horse . . ."

"And grab her, right in front of her husband . . ."

"Sling her up in front of you and ride off into the sunset?"

"If I have to." He grinned. "I'm hoping it won't have to get that melodramatic. But I'll tell you one thing. I won't leave her here with her husband. He's a bad actor."

Their eyes got very big as they tried to figure out whom he could possibly be talking about.

"Does he work on the rigs, or is he an executive?" Margo asked.

Peter shook his head. "I'm not giving you any more clues. That's all I'm going to tell you."

Taking the microphone in hand, he began pointing out landmarks to his passengers, and Margo leaned forward to whisper to Claire. "Girl, you ought to find yourself a guy like that."

Claire was trying to breathe normally. "Yes," she said weakly, then remembered where she was and added sarcasm to her tone. "Oh, absolutely, just what I need for my sagging marriage."

Margo laughed and said softly, right next to her ear, "The hell with your marriage," before sitting back again.

The hell with her marriage. Her marriage was hell. The road to hell was paved with bad marriages. Bad marriages were made in hell.

Her mind was beginning to go, she was sure. Would they never get to Riyadh?

Peter was on the speaker again. "On our right, we've got sand. On our left, we've got more sand. And straight ahead, ladies, we've got the Royal National Guardsmen."

Everyone surged to the side of the bus from where they could get the best view. Claire's vantage point was excellent, and she was impressed. Thirty to forty men were mounted on beautiful Arabian stallions, each one white with dark ears, mane and tail. The men wore white robes with colorful jackets, and red-and-white headdresses. Curved swords were strapped to their sides. They looked beautiful—and dangerous. Peter slowed as the van passed them, and the women didn't say another word until the guardsmen were well behind them.

Then the chattering reached ear-splitting levels, until Peter called out that the city was ahead.

And when they reached it, Claire took note of the sunlight gleaming on the windows of brand-new skyscrapers, office buildings, towers of industry. She saw construction cranes and bulldozers moving about like giant insects, and cars clogging the streets. As the van drew nearer the center of the city, she saw throngs of men in white robes with red-and-white head scarves, women in black robes with black veils hiding everything but their dark eyes.

Peter navigated the winding streets and threaded through traffic to take them to the *suq* near the Great Mosque. The passengers were quiet for there was so much to see. Now and then a camel appeared alongside one of the many late-model cars. The old and the new were jockeying for position in this city still in its youth.

Peter parked the van in the parking lot and turned to look at them. "How many of you have shopped here before?"

A few hands went up.

"Okay, I just want to remind you to remain as modest and as inconspicuous as possible. Whatever you do, try not to draw attention to yourselves. Once we get out there and you ladies start shopping, I know you're going to be breaking up into smaller groups and I'm going to lose track of some of you. Don't get too far away. Don't ever go off on your own, just one woman alone. Stay around the shops. If you see a bunch of men coming your way, go on into one run by a woman and ask to sit with her awhile. She'll be happy to serve you tea or fruit juice in the hope of making a sale, and you'll at least be out of harm's way. Meanwhile, I'll always be around in case you need me." He grinned at them cockily. "And ladies, don't forget, look out for the morals police!"

They laughed and began to file off the van, heading for the vegetable stands in the nearby open-air market. Claire purposely kept ahead of the group, taking Shareen with her on through to the stalls selling pots and pans, fabrics and jewelry.

"You don't have to run," Shareen complained. "Margo and Sally have him cornered. He'll never catch up with you."

Claire whirled to search her friend's eyes. "What are you talking about?" she tried tentatively.

Shareen took her hand and squeezed it comfortingly. "It's you, isn't it? The woman he was talking about. I saw you with him the night of the reception for Robert Camden, and the few things you've hinted at lately . . . I can put two and two together."

"Oh, Shareen!" Claire slumped against the counter of the small jewelry shop they'd slipped into. Relief warred with horror. It would be so good to talk to someone about this. But at the same time, if Shareen had figured it out, couldn't someone else? "I don't know what I'm going to do. Howard is being so horrible and Peter is always there, offering me everything that Howard is refusing me. . . ."

Shareen gave her a quick hug and smiled at her. "You'll do what's best for you and your family," she said firmly. "I know you. You'll take care of what's important." Her eyes were shadowed suddenly. "Just one piece of advice. What's best for you may not be what's best for Howard. At this point, I think it's up to him to provide direction there. If he can't bring himself to help you . . . well, you'll have to make that judgment on your own."

Claire wanted to ask Shareen how she was supposed to do that, but it was too late. Peter was entering the stall area. He had caught up with them after all. Shareen looked quickly at Claire, who whispered, "Whatever you do, don't you dare leave me alone with him!"

"Great," she whispered back, suppressing her grin. "I get to baby-sit Romeo and Juliet for the afternoon. Some shopping trip."

Actually, it didn't turn out badly. Peter did stick with them, but his jokes and casual asides as they made their way through the stalls and shops of the *suq* had them both laughing. At one point he left them to go into an electronics shop, and when he came out, he was carrying a box under his arm.

"What did you buy?" Claire asked.

He glanced at Shareen, who was off to the side, handling silk scarves. "A compact disk player," he said casually, avoiding meeting Claire's gaze. "It's a present for a friend."

She came to a stop beside a display of rugs, pretending intense interest in the designs. "I see." She knew he meant her. And she couldn't possibly accept such a gift. She reached out to trace an arabesque with her finger. "Are you going to mail it?"

"I don't have to mail it. I can give it to her in person anytime."

She turned to face him. "But perhaps she can't accept it. Did you think of that?"

"She has to accept it. When you're given a gift with true feeling, it would be an insult to give it back."

She hesitated, staring at the top button of his shirt. "Perhaps she would be afraid to take it, for fear the giver would read too much into her acceptance."

He leaned close, his voice a soft caress. "The giver isn't trying to buy anything. The giver just wants to give happiness. He asks for nothing in return."

She met his eyes, and for just a moment, she

believed him. An urge to melt against him swept over her and she reacted quickly, shaking it away. She remembered instead a bone she had to pick with him.

"I can't believe you did that on the bus," she whispered to him, turning and pretending to look at some Chinese rugs. "I wanted to stop you but I didn't know how."

"What? I never said your name or gave any hint as to who you were."

She threw him a baleful glance. "You don't think your hanging around with Shareen and me might give someone ideas?"

He shrugged lazily. "No. I could have picked any bunch to walk around with. They won't figure it out."

"I don't know why not. Shareen did."

"Did she? Well, more power to her. I don't really care who knows."

She turned to look at him earnestly. "But I do, Peter. That's just the point. Not only for myself, but for Howard. He's the director. I can't let them start to gossip about me."

The sound of a scuffle made them both turn. Shareen was being pulled by the arm by a tall man in a uniform. Peter reacted immediately, leaping forward to free her.

"Hey, whoa, wait a minute. What do you think you're doing here?"

The man shouted at him in Arabic and Peter immediately responded in the same language, speaking forcefully, pointing and gesticulating. The man's hold on Shareen loosened and she hurried to Claire's side, her face fearful, her eyes huge.

Claire drew her close. "What is it? What did he say? What's Peter doing?"

"It's the morals police. He was going to take me in for being in public without a veil. But Peter . . ." She leaned close to Claire's ear and whispered. "Peter is wonderful. He told the man that I was not an Arab at all, that I'm an American of Greek parentage, hence my coloring. Since I hadn't said anything I guess he fell for it."

Claire stared at her in horror. "You mean, he could have arrested you for not wearing a veil?"

"Oh, yes, if he thought I was a Saudi. The morals police keep strict tabs on everyone. They make sure boys and girls don't strike up conversations when they bump into each other if they're out shopping. They frown on taking pictures. They remind everyone of the rules this society lives by."

"Reminding is one thing," Claire said faintly, still aghast. "Arresting is something else."

The policeman left after throwing a few suspicious looks Shareen's way, and Peter came back to them with a jaunty grin.

"That was fun," he said. "These little confrontations keep the blood flowing."

"My blood flows very well without them, thank you very much," Shareen said, still looking pale. "I almost feel like going back and waiting in the van."

They dissuaded her from that. There was still so much to see. The abundance of wares was dizzying. They dallied near a display of necklaces with intricately forged links in a variety of shapes and sizes.

Claire was charmed by them all. "I want that one and that one and that one. . . ."

"Uh-oh," Peter returned with a laugh. "Excessive greed. I'll have to call the morals police."

While his attention was captivated by a coin collection, Claire came close to Shareen and whispered, "So what do you think of him now?"

Shareen glanced over at him and smiled. "He's a sweetheart. But I wouldn't call him husband material."

Claire laughed. "I've already got a husband. I don't think I'm ever going to want another one," she said.

"So she says now, in all her innocence." Her smile became wistful. "Just wait until you face a few of those lonely nights."

Curious, Claire turned and looked into her friend's dark eyes. "What do you know about it?"

Shareen hesitated, looking around as though she didn't want to be overheard.

"I lived it. I guess I haven't told you I was married before. He was an Arab—a Syrian. Very handsome, very wealthy, very powerful. But he treated me the way all Arabs treat their wives. Like a chattel. I couldn't take it. I thought, I'll never let any man treat me that way again. I'll never risk it. But then I met Larry." Her smile resonated with love. "And I knew it was worth the risk to try again."

Claire touched her shoulder. "You're so lucky," she said softly.

Shareen shook her head. "It's not just luck. I had to go through the bad before I got to the good. It took persistence—and a bit of courage, if I do say so myself." She paused. "You've got the courage, Claire. I have complete faith in your ability to find your way home, too."

They'd wandered out onto the street by this time. Something seemed to be going on. Police whistles and bullhorns could be heard all up and down the street. People were running toward the commotion.

"What do you think?" Peter looked at them, his eyes bright with anticipation. "Let's go see what's going on."

Shareen looked doubtful. "I'm not sure that would be such a good idea."

His grin was challenging. "Come on. What are we? Men or mice?"

"We're women, and we're not completely welcome on these streets, and you know it."

"I'll take care of you." He glanced back toward the uproar, obviously dying of curiosity. "Come with me. I'll park you at the outskirts and go on into the crowd to scout it out."

They went with him reluctantly, trying as best they could to look inconspicuous. Shareen was the target of some angry looks and a few angry-sounding comments from locals who didn't appreciate seeing a woman with Arabic features without her veil. Claire took her hand after one nasty encounter and found she was trembling.

"Peter, we should go back," she called.

But it was too late. The crowd moved forward suddenly, and they were caught up in the tide. Peter had disappeared. Shareen and Claire found themselves being pushed along toward the Grand Mosque, bodies pressed close all around them. At last the movement stopped and the crowd fell eerily quiet as the loudspeaker began to trumpet words Claire couldn't understand.

"Oh, my God!" Shareen clutched her arm and pressed close. "Claire . . ." She looked into eyes that stared back in bewilderment.

"What is it? What are they saying?"

"It's . . ." Shareen swallowed and went on in a hoarse voice, "It's an execution. They are now recounting the crimes. Robbery, embezzlement, drug dealing, murder." She listened for a moment. "Thieves will have their hands cut off," she repeated, her voice rasping now. "The others . . . will be beheaded."

Claire stared at her. "Right now?"

"Right now."

Without another word, they threw their arms about each other and clung. Claire closed her eyes and began to recite a prayer she remembered from her childhood. She could hear Shareen humming an unfamiliar tune. They held on to one another as though they would drown in this sea of humanity if they let go.

Claire was numb with horror. This was a culture, a country, where transgressions were dealt with harshly, where transgressors were made to pay for their crimes. No second chances. No appeal. If you did wrong, you paid for it.

She'd known that. She'd read enough about the country before coming here. And yet, knowing something with your head and feeling it, seeing it, hearing it—that was altogether different. And very frightening.

Suddenly Peter was back and ushering them away, carving a path for them between the silent men, and as they reached the outskirts of the crowd, some of the men began to call, "Al Hamdulillah! Al Hamdulillah!" and others began to applaud.

"It means, 'Praise God,'" Shareen explained as they hurried back to the shops. "As far as these people are concerned, this is a religious as much as a civil matter."

This time when they passed the morals police, no one felt much like joking.

It was after dark when Claire got home. Howard was sitting on the couch in the family room, watching a movie on the VCR. Katy was playing with her dolls on the dining-room table.

"Sorry I'm so late," Claire said as she breezed in, putting down her packages, including the large compact disk player, which made her feel guilty every time she looked at it. "The van had a flat and then the spare was no good. . . ."

"Just as long as you had a good time," Howard said.

She turned to look at him, unsure of how to take his words. He sounded so reasonable, she felt a spark of hope. But no, she realized with disappointment, his eyes told the true story. His words were laced with sarcasm. Why did he hate her so much?

"I'll get dinner ready as quickly as I can," she said, turning toward the kitchen. "Where's Sam?"

"Up in her room."

"Oh?" Claire paused. "Has she been out of that room at all today?"

"Not that I know of."

She hesitated, torn between getting dinner going and checking on her daughter. She looked at Howard. He seemed to be heavily engrossed in his movie. She slipped back across the room and went up the stairs, knocking softly on Sam's door.

"Sam, honey, may I come in?"

There was no answer.

She knocked again, more loudly, then tried the knob. The door was locked.

Suddenly her heart was in her throat. Hurrying into her own room, she rummaged for a certain slim screwdriver, then raced back to Sam's door. Her hand was shaking and it took a few tries, but she managed to unlock it. She stepped into the room and turned on the light.

The chiffon curtains billowed with the light breeze coming through the open window. The room was empty.

Claire stood very still, stunned. Where on earth could Sam have gone? She claimed she didn't have any friends. It wasn't as though she'd been confined to her room when there was some social function she wanted to go to. Why would she do something like this?

Claire went to the window and looked out. It was easy to see how Sam could have climbed out on the little roof over the window below and jumped to the ground. It was not as easy to see how she planned to get back without being seen. Or maybe she didn't care about that.

Claire knew she had to go out looking for her daughter, but she didn't want Howard to know. His reactions to things these days were so unpredictable. She had no idea what he would do about Sam's disappearance. And she didn't want to find out.

Moving quietly, she went back down the stairs and tried to sneak behind Howard into the kitchen. She was almost out of the room when he called, "Hey! I thought you were cooking."

She turned and smiled at him, her lips stretched painfully across her teeth. "I am. I just had to . . . go to the bathroom. I'll have dinner on the table in no time."

She went on into the kitchen, feeling like a criminal. "Katy, come on in here." She gave her youngest a hug and drew back. "Do you know where Sam is?" she asked.

Katy blinked. "In her room."

Claire nodded. "All right. Thank you, sweetheart." She turned, hand over her heart as though she could stop its wild beating that way. Her mind was racing, but the thoughts were very clear.

"Listen, would you help me out a little? You get the table set and start warming the spaghetti sauce." She filled a large pot with water as she talked. "And I'll start the water boiling for the noodles, okay?"

"Okay." Katy was helpfulness personified, but she looked up, surprised, as her mother started toward the back door. "Where are you going?"

"I . . . I have to go out for just a minute, honey. Can you hold the fort?" She didn't want Howard to know she was going out, but she couldn't bring herself to ask her little girl not to tell her father. She would just have to hope for the best. "I'll be right back."

She went out into the dark and stood on the sidewalk, not sure where to go next. Where could Samantha possibly have gone? Without a destination, she walked quickly toward Shareen's house, but one look into the front window showed her a happy family at dinner, with no sign of Sam. She didn't want to disturb them.

Where could Sam be? Claire's eyes were getting adjusted to the dark beyond the streetlights. She turned, looking back toward her own house, and something caught her eye. A shadow moved. There was someone behind the garage.

She began to walk in that direction, moving quietly, but completely alert. The sand crunched beneath her feet. She passed a patch of ice plant and turned the corner. There was a figure leaning back against the wall of the garage. No. It was two figures intertwined. She stood where she was and stared, her heart in her throat. Her baby, her little Samantha, was in the arms of Margo's son Jesse. They were plunged into a kiss that hardly looked sweet sixteen, much less sweet thirteen. The boy was devouring her daughter's mouth, obviously completely engrossed in exploring everything his young tongue could reach. And even worse, his hand was way up under her shirt, moving back and forth with a practiced technique—

A voice came out, a voice Claire didn't realize at once was her own. "Get your filthy hands off my daughter," the voice said, fury sizzling in every syllable.

The two figures broke apart and turned to face her.

"Mother!" Samantha backed away from the boy.

"Hi, Mrs. Montgomery," said Jesse, surprised, but in no way embarrassed. In fact, he produced an arrogant grin, as though he were rather proud of what he'd been up to. He was handsome in a punkish way, with the devil-may-care air so many girls found exciting.

"How old are you?" Claire demanded.

A flicker of unease crept into his face. "Uh, almost eighteen."

"Almost eighteen. Well, Samantha is only thirteen. Did you know that? Five years younger than you are. Don't you think you could be pawing someone a little more your own age?"

"Mother!" Samantha turned toward Jesse, but he was perfectly capable of taking care of himself.

"Don't talk to me, lady," he said, squaring his shoulders. "Talk to your sweet little girl. She's the one who asked me to teach her how to french." He shrugged grandly. "And who am I to turn down a cute little chick like her?" He wiped his mouth with the back of his hand. "And hey, you know what? She's a fast learner. She just about swallowed—"

"Get off my property," Claire hissed, hating the boy, sure he was lying, sure he was making things up to protect himself. "Get out of my sight. And don't you ever come back here."

He shrugged his unconcern and began a slow saunter through the backyard of their neighbor toward his own house. Trembling with rage, Claire watched him go. Then she turned back to her daughter, whose face was twisted with tragedy, tears sparkling in her eyes.

"Sam, darling—"

"Stay away from me, Mother," she cried, backing away, the tears beginning to stream down her face. "Don't touch me. You've ruined my life!"

"No, honey. You've got a lot of time. There'll be so many other boys—"

"No! Not anymore. He'll tell the others and no one will talk to me."

Claire wished she could think of the right words to reach the child. "Sam, sweetheart, that boy is nothing but—"

"How would you know?" Samantha spit out in fury. "You're just jealous, that's all. Just because Daddy won't sleep with you anymore, you don't want me to have a boyfriend, either."

Shock radiated through Claire. "Samantha!" The girl had never talked to her this way before. She could hardly believe those words had come from her daughter's mouth—or even that such thoughts could be in her head. For the first time, she wondered if Jesse hadn't been telling the truth after all. How could things possibly have deteriorated to this degree?

Samantha broke away and ran for the back door into the kitchen, her silver-blond hair waving behind her like a flag. Claire followed, dreading what Howard would say once he saw Sam's tear-stained face. But when she went into the family room, he merely looked up and said, "Is dinner ready yet? I'm starving," so she assumed Sam had got past him without his noticing.

She murmured something and went back into the kitchen. Katy was staring at her, round-eyed. She'd seen it all, of course, and was wondering what was going on. But she didn't say a thing.

The water was boiling and Claire put in the noodles. A part of her wanted to go up to the bedroom to try to talk to Samantha again. But she couldn't risk Samantha screaming out things for all to hear. She would have to save that chore until later.

She was moving in a fog. The picture of that boy's hand under her daughter's shirt kept flashing across her consciousness. And the sound of Sam's ugly accusation kept sounding in her head.

A part of her was mourning, too. Why did they have to grow up so fast? She remembered her own first experience with a groping boy, how shocked she'd been at the strange feelings her body had suddenly produced. How very, very frightened. But she had been sixteen, not thirteen. This was too soon. This was much too soon.

How had things come to this? The more she tried to bring her family together, the more they slipped away.

"Dinner's on," she told Howard a few moments later. "Katy, could you please call Samantha?"

Katy went upstairs and came back down almost immediately. "Sam says she's not hungry," she announced, looking from Howard to Claire and back again.

Howard swung around like a wounded bear. "You tell that girl to get her tail down here, now," he barked. "No excuses."

Samantha emerged, looking like Camille, and they all sat down to eat. Things went remarkably smoothly, Claire thought. It was very near a normal meal. She talked about what she'd seen in Riyadh and Howard had nothing caustic to say.

She looked at Sam. She was so pretty, her blond hair so straight and long and lovely. She was toying with her food in silence, but that was hardly unusual, and Howard didn't seem to notice anything out of the ordinary.

If only she could keep this from him she might be able to deal with it, Claire thought. She would talk to Samantha, figure out some way to get through to her. There had to be a way. All she had to do was find out what it was.

They all turned when they heard the tapping on the sliding glass door. Claire realized it must be Margo, but before she could do anything to save the situation, Katy was up out of her seat, crying,

"I'll get it," and running from the room. Then Margo was with them, pleading with Howard to forgive her son.

She looked thoroughly upset. "I came over to apologize. Jesse told me all about it. It shouldn't have happened. I'm so sorry, Mr. Montgomery, really I am. He's a good boy, but he likes girls a bit too much. He can't seem to resist them. So when your little beauty asked him to teach her how to kiss. . . ."

Howard had been staring at Margo as though she was speaking a foreign language and expected him to join in. But now he reacted.

"What?" he said softly. And then his eyes widened. "What?" he bellowed. "What the hell are you talking about, you crazy woman?"

Margo drew back, blinking rapidly. "I . . . Didn't they tell you?" She glanced at Claire, then Sam. "Claire found them out behind the garage, I guess, making out, and—"

"Get the hell out of my house." Howard's face was turning purple.

"I . . . you won't hold it against Joe, will you? I mean, he couldn't help it. He wasn't even home—"

"Out." Howard pointed toward the door, and after another pleading look at Claire, Margo left. Howard turned toward his wife, his eyes flat with fury. "Do you want to explain this?"

Claire told him quickly, omitting the hand under the shirt, as well as Sam's angry comments. She tried to make it sound like a typical teenage adventure, something to be aware of, but not taken terribly seriously, but Howard had heard every word that Margo had said, and Claire could tell by the look on his face that her ploy wasn't working. This was the first time he'd had to deal with the possibility that his little girl was turning into a woman. It was a prospect that did not please him.

Sam sat like a statue, staring straight ahead, as though oblivious to what was going on around her. Howard looked at her oddly and said, almost under his breath, "She's just like you, isn't she? Cool as a cucumber. Thinks she's better than the rest of us."

Claire's heart felt like a stone in her chest. She looked from Howard to his daughter and back again, his cold fury, Sam's supreme unconcern, and a premonition of disaster crept into her soul.

Howard seldom got involved in the disciplining of the children. For one thing, he was hardly ever home. And when he was around, he usually backed away from unpleasant situations like this, as though unsure how to punish young girls and reluctant to learn.

But this was something different. There was a look on his face and a tone in his voice that Claire didn't like.

"Katy, go to your room," she said softly.

Katy was an intelligent child and she could sense the storm brewing. She left without a word.

"You go too, Claire," Howard said evenly, staring at his blond daughter. "I want to talk to Samantha alone."

Claire hesitated. "Howard, I don't think—"

He turned steely eyes her way. "She's my daughter just as much as she is yours. I have a right to do this my way. I've left the disciplining up to you all these years, and look what it's got us. Our daughter is turning into a little tramp before our eyes. This sort of thing has got to be nipped in the bud."

Clair's mouth felt dry. "I agree it's not good, but—"

"I want to talk to her alone."

Claire looked at Sam's pale face. "You won't . . . hit her?" she whispered.

Howard made a sound of disgust. "I'm not an animal, Claire, no matter what you think of me. No, I won't hit her, though God knows she deserves a good beating. I just want to make clear to her how stupid she's been, that's all. I want a chance to do this without you and your anxiety hanging over my shoulder, okay?"

The agony of indecision kept her immobile. She couldn't help but think of how Howard had shattered her mirror and her compact disk player. How could she leave him alone with Samantha?

"Claire, go up with Katy."

She searched his eyes. He was angry. But was he irrational? No, she couldn't say there was any evidence of that. And he hadn't had too much to drink, either. She really had no leg to stand on here. He was Samantha's father. Slowly, reluctantly, she rose and started for the stairs.

"Samantha, move here, closer to me," she

heard Howard say in a perfectly reasonable voice as she left the room.

She felt a bit of relief. It was probably going to be just fine. Samantha deserved a good talking to. Howard would give it to her. Things would be fine.

She found Katy huddled at the top of the stairs and said to her, "Come on into my room. We can look through my jewelry case."

They went together into Claire's room. She got down the heavy jewelry case and put it on the bed, and they both crawled up and sprawled across the quilt, chattering softly as they began sifting through the rings and earrings.

Both the girls had always loved doing this. Claire had very few pieces that were worth anything. But to the girls, the costume jewelry was a treasure trove.

Katy pulled out her favorite, a silver charm bracelet Claire had worn in junior high. The chain was hung heavy with teddy bears, hearts and stars, intricately formed animals, a crystal ball with a mustard seed inside, a skateboard, a silver spoon and a tiny Corvette. Watching her daughter look through each charm brought back memories of a time so much simpler Claire could hardly believe it had ever existed.

Where had it gone? Where had those people gone? A feeling of loss swept over her, and she thought of all those wasted years when she should have known her father better.

A scream pierced the air. Claire was stunned

for only a moment, then she was up off the bed and running for the door.

"Stay here," she commanded Katy as she ran, but she didn't have time to look back to see if her order was being followed. She couldn't breathe, couldn't think. She only reacted, every instinct atuned to protecting her child.

She stumbled down the stairs and into the dining area. There was no one there. She turned toward the kitchen, but a sound spun her around and she ran for the downstairs bathroom instead. The door was ajar and she shoved it open.

The first thing she saw was Samantha, cowering on the floor in the corner of the room, her arms protecting her head. Moving like a robot, Claire swung around to look at Howard. He was standing by the sink, scissors in one hand, swaths of Sam's silver-blond hair in the other.

"What have you done?" she gasped, though she could see very well for herself.

"The little bitch deserved it," Howard said calmly. "She talked back to me."

Claire turned back toward her daughter. "Samantha, darling . . ."

Sam lowered her arms and looked up at her mother. Her hair was cropped in ugly tufts about her ears. Tears were streaming down her cheeks. "Mommy!" she cried, holding up her arms, like a toddler asking to be lifted.

Claire lifted her up and held her close. "Oh, my baby," she murmured, her own voice rough.

"Oh, my darling girl. We'll fix it. We'll make it better. Don't cry, sweetheart, we'll make it better."

She took her daughter up to her room, not giving a thought to what Howard might do, nor caring. He was a nonperson to her now. She settled Sam into her bed, taking off her shirt and jeans, leaving her in her bra and panties, murmuring to her all the time. Sam still wept, her shoulders heaving, her face red and swollen. But she responded to Claire in a way she hadn't in months. Claire tucked her in, turned off the light, and left her there.

Coming out of the room, she looked down the stairs and met Howard's gaze from where he was standing at the bottom. He didn't say a word, and neither did she.

But at that point she knew that any shred of hope for an affectionate relationship between the two of them was gone forever.

"Have you both got your passports? Let me see them. Okay, now the list of phone numbers in England. They should be picking you up at the train station, but just in case . . . Oh, and your airline tickets. Keep them in that special pocket in your travel bag. And—"

"Mother, come on. We've been over all this a hundred times. Katy and I will be fine. We've traveled alone before, you know."

Of course they had. Claire looked at them with pride. Dressed in plaid suits with square-cut jackets and short skirts, they both looked so grown-up. The airport terminal was crowded, but they didn't seem as intimidated as she would have been at their ages. They were world travelers. They knew what to expect.

"School in England is more structured than what you're used to," she told them again. "You'll have to be very careful to watch and listen and learn what is expected of you." Tears stung her eyes, but she held them back. "Oh, my babies," she sighed. "I'm going to miss you so much."

They both gave her looks of pure disgust, and she didn't dare pull them into a bear hug yet. But she knew she would before she let them get on the plane.

She couldn't help but wonder what they would look like when she saw them next. How much would she lose? How could she bear to let them go?

She remembered every stage of their development—Sam's first steps, Katy's first tooth. What stages would she miss? Those were things one could never get back again.

It was almost two weeks since the incident with the scissors. Claire had decided that very night that she would send the girls away to school. She couldn't risk what Howard might do next. It was one thing to put herself in the line of fire, but it was quite another to allow the same thing for her children.

"You should go, too," Peter had said from the first time she'd told him. She hadn't described to him exactly what had happened, but he had been able to fill in the blanks. "You shouldn't stay with him. If you can't trust him any longer, there's no reason for you to stay."

But she didn't quite see it that way. Howard was losing control, but that didn't mean she wanted to completely abandon him to his fate. She pitied him as much as she distrusted him. He needed help.

The marriage was over, but her responsibility wasn't wiped out so easily.

"I can't hang around here forever," Peter had warned her on the telephone just the day before. "I told the bosses I was going rig-crazy and needed some time in dry dock, and that's why they've been letting me stick around and do odd jobs for them, plus the occasional work on installations. But I'm starting to get the comments and nudges. They want me back on the line."

Claire had taken a deep breath and pretended to herself that she didn't care. "You should go, then," she advised him.

"I can't yet," he'd said. "I want to take you out on the desert. I want to take you to the Greek Islands. I want to take you to Paris in the springtime."

She had closed her eyes and let fantasy take her to those places for a moment, before she'd laughed ruefully and said, "Peter, you're crazy. We can't do any of those things."

"Yes we can. You just wait and see."

He was here now, leaning against a counter, watching them. She'd seen him when they'd first entered the terminal. He wouldn't approach while the girls were still here. They'd never met him, and there was no reason why they should now. But there was something comforting in having him nearby.

"Mom," Sam was saying, "did you hear it? I think that was the first call for our flight."

Relations between the two of them hadn't been perfect, but they had been a lot closer to normal these past two weeks. Sam had kept her distance from her father and had even seemed to look to Claire for protection of sorts. And Claire had done what she could for her hair.

Margo had come to the rescue there. She'd walked into the middle of a session where Claire was trying to trim Sam's hair and she'd taken over. It seemed she'd once been a hairdresser. She'd shaped the hair until it looked almost as though it were meant to be that short. And she'd done it without making any comments.

Although no one had actually told her why it had happened, the timing had been such that the cause was difficult to conceal.

"Second call, Mother. We'd better go."

Claire moved with them reluctantly to the gate. The girls were brimming with anticipation. They were going away. How could she stand it? This wasn't the same as leaving them in Atlanta for a couple of weeks in the summer. Here she was sending them away for months.

She felt sorry for herself, sorry for Howard, and sorry for the girls. This had hurt them all. She kept thinking if she could just get the girls away from the situation, so that she wouldn't have to worry about them, she might be able to think more clearly, get her head straight about what she should do.

They reached the gate, she drooping, the girls dancing with excitement.

"Bye, Mom. Don't forget to write!"

She caught hold of them and pulled them to her, squeezing her eyes tightly to hold back the tears. "I love you so," she whispered brokenly. "I'm going to miss you."

"Us, too." They showered her with kisses and laughed again. "Don't cry. We'll be good and have fun and get good grades. Just wait and see!"

As they dashed down the ramp, Claire dissolved into tears. Her babies were moving out of her reach. Someone else would be raising them now.

She felt an arm slide around her shoulders. She turned toward Peter, letting him take her against his chest as she sobbed her heart out.

"Déjà vu," he murmured. "We can't keep meeting like this."

She looked up at him and smiled through her tears. "We're not supposed to be meeting at all," she reminded him.

He grinned down at her, not caring a whit about *supposed to*. "Some women cry at weddings," he teased softly. "But Claire Montgomery cries at airports. What a gal."

"Claire Duvall Montgomery only seems to cry at airports when she finds your strong shoulders there to cry on," she said, sniffing and dabbing at her eyes with a handkerchief. "If you'd stay away, she would be perfectly fine."

"Would she?" His eyes changed as he stroked her hair. "I think she's perfectly fine already. The only thing missing . . ." He tilted her chin up with a finger beneath it. "The only thing missing is a trip to the desert."

She stared back at him, totally tempted. She

was so tired of the dismal atmosphere at home. And now it would be worse.

"Let's go to the desert. I'll show you the Bedouins. I've got the day off, I've got a Jeep, I've even got the duds. How about it?"

"I've got a driver out in the parking lot."

"I already paid him off and told him to go."

"Peter!"

"How about it?" he repeated, smiling at her.

She found herself smiling right back. "Why not?" she said simply.

He blinked. "Did you say . . . yes?" He was so used to her turning him down, he didn't know how to respond.

"Let's go," she repeated. "Why not?"

"Why not?" He grinned. "Okay. Great. Just wait right here. I've got something for you to wear."

"Oh, I can run home and change into slacks."

"Not good enough. Wait here." He was back in no time with a bundle wrapped in brown paper and tied with a string. He passed it to her slyly.

"Go into the women's room and change into this," he said out of the corner of his mouth, like a celluloid gangster making plans. "You'll never recognize yourself."

She took the bundle into the restroom and opened it. Inside were a black robe and veil, the *abaya* every Arab woman wore. "Oh, Peter," she whispered, "I couldn't."

But there was no one else in there. Why not try it? She slipped the robe on over her light dress, and then set the veil before looking in the mirror.

What she saw stunned her. That was not Claire Montgomery, for heaven's sake. That was an Arab woman. What a wonderful disguise.

She went out hesitantly, sure others would know immediately that she was an imposter. She looked around but didn't see Peter. There was an Arab man in a white robe and red-and-white headdress standing where she'd last seen him. It was only when she came close that she realized the Arab had blue eyes.

"Peter!"

His grin was definitely Western. "Hey baby. Want to join my harem?"

"Shh, someone will hear you." She laughed up at him. "Can we really get away with this?"

"Sure. And wearing clothes like this will allow us to move around with a lot more freedom. Come on. I've got a Jeep parked outside."

He started off through the terminal and she followed. She was amazed. He even walked with a new sense of purpose, his strides long and arrogant, while she found herself scuttling along behind him like the subservient woman she was supposed to be. Clothes did make the man—and the woman— didn't they?

※

The desert sand stretched out like a moonscape as they raced across it in the Jeep. With the wind whipping at her veil and sending the ends of her *abaya* streaming out behind her, Claire felt a sense of freedom she hadn't experienced in a long, long time. The loss of her girls, the ruins of her marriage, her father's death—all the elements of despair that had tugged at her for weeks blew away in the wind, leaving her free to lift her face to the sunshine, to exhilarate in the huge sky, the white sand, the distant mountains.

Peter called to her, pointing out elements on the landscape, and she laughed, nodding, not attempting to fight the wind to talk back. She wanted to drive on and on and never stop.

Now and then they passed someone else, and whenever that happened, they both sat very still in the moving Jeep, hoping not to raise suspicions.

"What would happen if they found out we really weren't Arabs?" she'd asked Peter when they started this wild ride.

"I really don't know," he replied. "And I'm pretty sure I don't want to find out."

Their gazes caught and they both knew they were thinking of the public execution of a few weeks ago. But neither spoke of it. The fact that this country took transgressions seriously had not been lost on either of them. They didn't want to think about getting caught.

It was still startling to see Cadillacs and Mercedes Benzs drive by with men at the wheel dressed in the same robes and headdresses as men who had traveled these same routes by camel only decades ago. Even more incongruous was the sight of a sporty Jaguar by the side of the road, its driver out on the desert floor, facing Mecca, chanting verses from the Koran as he touched his forehead to the sand.

But they dashed by, heading for the hills, and then the plateau. Peter slowed as they passed a Bedouin encampment. Great, low tents of dyed animal skins sewn together provided shelter. Women worked about a fire pit where a lamb was turning on a spit. They were black-veiled, just as women in town were, but their dresses were varied in color and style, and none of them wore the *abaya*. Children played nearby, and men lounged where camels were tied; it was a picture from another century. But parked behind the camp were three shiny new pickup trucks, one of them with a TV antenna attached to its battery.

Everyone turned, their faces expressionless, to watch the Jeep go by. Claire wondered what would happen if the Jeep broke down and they had to go to these people for help.

"Where are we going?" she called at last to Peter.

"You'll see," was his only response.

They came to another, smaller camp and he pulled the Jeep close to a small tent. When a young man came out of the tent and stared at them, Peter leaned out the window and called something in Arabic. The young man smiled and nodded, and Peter turned to Claire.

"That's Mack, one of our liaison men at the installation. I've got some business with him. You stay here until I get back."

"But . . . what if someone sees you?"

"Don't worry. I know Mack. Where do you

think I got these robes? I'll only be a couple of minutes."

Claire watched them meet, shake hands and talk. Mack glanced toward the Jeep, but Peter seemed to be drawing him away from where Claire was. Reaching into his pocket, he drew out some money, which Mack took and quickly stuffed into a pocket in his robe. They spoke again, and then Mack disappeared into the tent and Peter started back toward the Jeep.

"Sorry," he said, sliding back into the driver's seat. "Let's follow this dirt track for a while and see where it leads."

They turned off the main road and started through the sand, leaving a plume of dust behind them. When they stopped and the dust settled, Claire could see that they had come to an oasis, a small spring that nourished a miniature garden—a seeming miracle in the arid desert. There was no one else around, though there were plenty of signs that others had been here. They got out of the Jeep and went to the spring.

"How did you know this was here?" she asked him, watching the bubbling water in fascination.

"I've been here before."

"Oh?" She turned to look at him, wondering who he'd come with, then felt herself color and was glad for the concealing veil. "I see."

"You don't see anything," he teased, reaching out to take her hand. "I've been up here with a bunch of other roughnecks from time to time. You're the first woman I've ever come with." He pulled her around to meet his gaze. "Does that matter to you?"

She could no longer deny it. She nodded.

The blue of his eyes deepened and his free hand came up under her veil to touch her cheek. "Do you know how sexy you are, all covered up like this?" he said softly. "The mystery element adds a touch of spice, makes me wonder what else is beneath all this black cloth." He pulled her closer. "Arab women have to learn to make love with their eyes. I think you were born with the instincts for it."

She laughed, but his words warmed her.

"Come on," he said. "There's more to see." He led her on a gravely path up a hill and suddenly they were standing at the edge of a cliff that looked out over a vast stretch of desert. The white sand shimmered before them, looking as hot as the sun that burned down on it. The horizon seemed a world away, the sky was blue as infinity, the sand a shifting stage for forever. They stood side by side, not speaking.

"It reminds me of the sea," Peter said at last. "God, I love to sail."

"You love to sail, and you stick yourself out in the middle of the desert?"

He grinned. "Sure. Didn't you ever deny yourself something in order to sweeten the joy? Didn't you ever buy a luscious pastry and set it aside, watching it, anticipating it, until desire built up in you so much . . ."

She stared at him, hearing more than he was

saying, and her heart began to beat quickly. "Yes. I . . . I see. Is that what you're doing out here in the desert? Denying yourself sailing until you just can't stand it any longer?"

She stared into his eyes and he stared back, and then suddenly his smile was back. "No," he said shortly, amusement shimmering in his voice. "But it makes a good story, doesn't it?"

She caught her breath and looked away, never sure how seriously to take him. He was gazing at the view again, letting it affect him. "When you look at something like this," he said softly, "suddenly you understand things that were never clear before—like great love affairs or how great composers produce such stunning works of music, what fills their souls for those magic moments necessary to creation. Do you know what I mean?"

She nodded. "Yes, I think I do. Somehow this sort of scenery should inspire man to dream great dreams and make enormous sacrifices." She looked at him speculatively. "I wonder what it will inspire in us," she murmured.

He shrugged. "To be the best we can be," he said with certainty, but that answer didn't satisfy her. It was too pat, too cliched. She wanted more, something deeper and more profound, and she wanted him to say it. For just a moment, she ached to know. But Peter was turning away. He had obviously had enough philosophizing for now.

"Come on," he said, beginning to head back to the Jeep. "Are you hungry? I've got plans for lunch. And something else to show you."

Claire's stomach growled at the thought of food, and she followed him eagerly, climbing into the Jeep, expecting him to turn back toward the main road. Instead, he drove higher into the hills, and they bounced along the barely discernible dirt track until they reached a plateau.

There was no greenery here, but there was a tent of white canvas. Peter stopped the Jeep, turned off the engine, and reached out his hand. "Here we are."

Claire got out and looked around. "Where is here?" she asked.

"This—" he made a sweeping gesture with his hand that took in the tent "—is for us. I brought along the food." He reached in behind the driver's seat and pulled out a basket. "Come on. Let's go in and see what it's like."

Claire caught at his arm. "Wait! Who lives here? We can't just walk in and—"

He laughed, pulling her into the curve of his arm. "For this afternoon, we live here. I made arrangements with Mack. We've got the place to ourselves for a couple of hours."

She stared up at him, realizing what this meant, and he smiled. "Don't worry, Claire," he said. "I'm just tempting you to join my harem. I'm not abducting you."

She found herself smiling back, her heart beating just a bit faster. "Let's go in," she said. "I want to see what it looks like."

They pushed back the canvas doorway and entered another century. Gorgeous Persian rugs covered the floor and hung along the walls. Low couches and huge pillows lined the room, as well as stacks of folded prayer rugs. On the floor in the center of the room was a huge brass charcoal-burning samovar. The colors were brilliant, the deep red of the rugs, bright green and blue on the walls, and here and there, gold threads woven into the fabric.

"This is beautiful," Claire breathed.

"Beauty is forever," Peter paraphrased, "but hunger is here and now. Let's eat."

The food Peter had brought was a contrast to their surroundings—fried chicken and biscuits and apple cider. Claire laughed delightedly. In fact, the whole situation made her happy. She was enjoying her day of truancy. She didn't let herself worry about what it was leading up to.

"Don't you think it's time you removed the veil?" he asked as he set out the food.

She made no move to do so. "Now?" she asked.

He swung around and looked at her, reaching out to tug at a corner. "I want you to share."

She didn't move away, but she was flirting outrageously with her eyes. "I thought you said it was provocative, having me all covered up like this."

"Up to a point. And that point has been reached."

She put her head to the side, pretending to consider. "I don't know. I rather like it. I can look out at you and see your expressions, but I don't have to reveal my own."

He looked at her and shook his head. "Going native on me, huh? Have it your way. But I don't think you've had enough practice with it to know how to eat through it." He shrugged, teasing her with his eyes. "Still, if that's what you want . . ."

He won. She reached for the veil and took it off, turning back a bit shyly. "There you go. Happy?"

He studied her face for a long moment before he replied. "Yes," he said, his voice soft and low. "Yes, I'm very happy, thank you."

They ate and talked, and when they were finished, they leaned back against the pillows and talked some more.

"Do you remember when you accused me of being as dominated as an Arab woman in a harem?" Claire asked him at one point.

"I didn't accuse you of anything."

"Well, implied, then."

"That I remember."

"I've been thinking about what you said a lot ever since. And it seems to me you had a point."

"Of course I did. Words of wisdom come tumbling from my lips all the time."

She chuckled. "Not to mention the modesty that oozes from your every pore."

"Hey, no fair. I never claimed modesty. After all, if you got it, flaunt it, I always say."

She smiled. "Oh, so you're the one who said that."

"Damn right. I also said female mud wrestling

should be an Olympic sport, but nobody paid any attention to that one."

As she laughed, he turned toward her, his face serious again. "But you know something about that theory you mentioned? The difference is, in our society, you're only as dominated as you let yourself be. There's a whole world of freedom out there waiting for you. You can grab it if you want it."

She looked at him, seeing him again as she'd first seen him. His hands were hard and calloused, his shoulders wide and strong. But there was a fineness to his profile, an intelligence in his eyes, that belied the roughneck image.

"Is that what you did, Peter?" she asked him suddenly. "Did you grab for that world of freedom when you left home and came to the Middle East?"

For a moment, the guarded look hovered in his eyes. But then he relaxed and nodded. "That was pretty much it. I wanted more out of life than what my family had lined me up for. So I split."

"And broke your mother's heart," she guessed softly.

Annoyance flashed across his face, but he answered calmly, "By the time I left, my mother was glad to be rid of me. Believe me. As far as she was concerned, I had pretty near ruined her life by then, anyway."

She found that hard to believe. What mother wouldn't adore a son as handsome and manly as Peter was? "And how had you done that?" she asked skeptically.

He shifted restlessly. "She wanted another

doctor in the family. She wanted a son who hung around and did odd jobs for her and was always ready to be on display for her friends, someone who studied until midnight, never heard of wine, women and song, brought home every honor available, and had good table manners, too."

"And you weren't that type."

His grin seemed genuine enough, but she could detect a hint of bitterness.

"Not hardly. If I stayed up until midnight, it was more likely to be playing poker with my buddies. Or out at the river, drag racing. I had a reputation in our town, but it wasn't the one she wanted for me."

Claire felt a smile threatening. "I'll bet it was more the sort where mothers hid their daughters when you came down the street."

He laughed. "Sort of. Let's just say I was a major disappointment to my mother. And when she found out I was planning to try out for the roller derby instead of studying for med school, it was all over."

Claire shook her head, smiling for real now. "Sounds to me like you already had your freedom."

He considered for a moment, then disagreed. "Not at all. My mother found ways to make me pay for disappointing her. And she almost trapped me," he said softly, his eyes focusing somewhere beyond Claire's head. A slight smile twisted his mouth as he remembered. "You've got to hand it to my mother. When she wants something, she goes all out to get it."

"I guess you take after her, don't you?"

He stared at her, his eyes wide with surprise. "No way," he said vehemently. "I'm not like her at all."

Claire retreated, but she knew she had struck a nerve. "So you took a look at all your family's rules and expectations and took off for freedom," she said musingly, leaning back against the cushions and staring into space. "Well, I did just the opposite. I memorized the rules and I tried very hard to live by them."

"And that's where you went wrong," Peter informed her promptly. "You should never live by the rules made by others. Live by your own. It's the only way."

How easy that was for him to say, she thought, almost resentful. He had no one depending on him. He could come and go as he pleased. It was different for her. So very different.

She turned and examined his profile, his strong chin, his sensuous mouth. "Peter, why did you bring me here?"

He looked up. He had taken off the Arab robe when they'd first arrived and now he stretched back, his shirt tight against his muscular chest.

"Because I wanted to show you the Bedouin, I wanted to show you the camels, I wanted to show you the desert and make you love it like I do." His voice lowered. "But most of all," he said simply, "I brought you here so we could make love."

She stared at him for a moment, then smiled, not at all shocked. After all, he'd made his intentions clear long ago. If she had no interest in him sexually, why would she be here? Even though she hadn't allowed herself to think of it that way on the surface, underneath, she'd known it all along.

Was it right? Of course not. It was totally wrong, and she wasn't sure she could go through with it. But she was excited, not afraid. And so she decided to keep things light.

"I'll bet you say that to all the girls in your harem," she teased him. "Tell me something I don't already know."

"Oh, you want to hear something you don't already know, do you? Well, how's this?" He moved closer, touching her hair. "Making love in an Arab tent in the middle of the day will bring seven years good luck, cure pattern baldness, and guarantee peace in our time. Is that good enough for you?"

"I don't know. What happens if you don't make love in an Arab tent in the middle of the day?"

He leaned closer still, breathing against her cheek. "War will break out, you'll go bald, and you'll be bitten by a black cat. We'd better not risk it."

"Sounds dangerous," she agreed.

His eyes were gleaming in the muted light. "We got rid of the veil. Now how about the *abaya?*"

She sighed. "I don't know. It's so comfortable. . . ."

He reached for her and she laughed, pulling away playfully. Catching her, he tossed her gently back against the pillows, holding her prisoner with the weight of his body, as his hand slipped beneath the *abaya*, looking for the fastening.

Claire tensed. She could feel his strength, and she longed to luxuriate in it, but the inhibitions of a lifetime held her back. She was going to make love with Peter. They both knew it. But was she going to be able to enjoy it?

The black fabric of the robe slid away, leaving her vulnerable. She looked almost longingly at where it lay in a heap on the crimson Persian rug. But Peter was holding her, his mouth hot as he dropped slow kisses along the line of her neck, and she tried to force herself to relax.

His fingers were working on the buttons of her shirtwaist dress. For just a moment, panic flared in her chest. It was the middle of the day and there was no light to turn off. He was going to see her as she really was, skinny and bony and flat. Peter Pan. That was what Howard had called her.

Oh, God, why had she thought of that? She cringed and writhed and closed her eyes, not wanting to see if he was disappointed in her body, not wanting to see regret mirrored in his eyes as the cool air hitting her skin told her that her last defenses were gone.

She was going to go through with this, she told herself grimly, if it killed her. There was absolutely no way to avoid it.

"Claire." His voice was soft, close to her ear. "Claire, don't shut me out. Look at me."

Slowly and with total reluctance, she opened her eyes and met his gaze, so close to hers.

"Do you hate this?" he asked her, searching her face for clues. "Do you want me to stop?"

A wave of affection for him broke over her. Howard had never stopped. In fact, Howard had usually been in such a hurry, he forgot to take her along with him. But Peter was waiting for her, checking to see if she was ready, willing to rest for a while if that was what she needed. She felt as though he had picked her up in the palm of his hand and brought her to his heart. Smiling, she reached up and encircled his neck with her arms, digging her fingers into his thick hair.

"Don't you dare stop," she whispered hoarsely.

She forgot about her body. She forgot about how wrong this was. She forgot everything but the joy of his touch and the fire it built inside her, a fire he coaxed into a roaring blaze before he quenched it with an authority that left her clinging to him, making small, sobbing noises deep in her throat, her legs wrapped around him as though she would never let go, her fingers digging into his back.

As sanity slowly seeped back into her sated body, she gazed at him in wonder. The ecstasy had never been quite like this before, so full, so long, so deep. She wasn't sure if it was his expertise or her appreciation of his consideration that had done it. She only knew she'd liked it. And she wanted it again.

But before she could say a word to Peter, a sound brought her head around, and she listened intently.

"Horses," she whispered.

Peter's head came up, too. "You're right." Jumping up, he reached for his clothes, swearing softly. "Damn Mack, I told him two hours at least. . . ."

The hoofbeats were coming closer. Claire's heartbeat echoed the sound as she stumbled to her feet and began to pull her own clothes on with shaking fingers. She could hear them arriving, hear the shouts as men pulled horses to a stop.

"Stay here," Peter ordered, still buttoning his shirt as he started for the entrance. "I'll go out and see what's going on." He pulled on the Arab robe, then looked out, called out something in Arabic, and was gone.

She pulled on the *abaya* and fastened the veil, feeling a strange relief when she had the two garments in place. But she didn't dare look out for fear someone would see her and want to know what she was doing here. So she waited, trying to calm her pulse, and listened.

Peter was back shortly, leaning in through the entrance and motioning for her to come out and join him. Outside, she could hear the horses galloping off.

"It's Prince Ihbrahim and his entourage," he said. "They're on their way to the camel races and they want us to join them there."

She stopped dead and stared at him from behind her veil. "They want you, you mean."

He shrugged. "They know I have someone with me. Come on. It will be fun."

He had that same light in his eyes he'd had in Riyadh the day of the execution. She was beginning to recognize this trait in him, this urgency to see what was beyond the next horizon. Still, there were other things to consider.

"Do you know them? Don't they find it odd that you're dressed like an Arab?"

"I met the prince when I first came to Saudi. They've seen me dressed like this before. They won't say anything."

Always the optimist. What if he was wrong? She felt a strong desire to go home. "Won't they wonder about your having an Arab girlfriend?"

He answered quite reasonably, "You're not an Arab girl."

Claire sighed. He wasn't going to give in, was he? "No, but I'm dressed like one, and they may not realize the difference."

At last a frown of thoughtfulness appeared on his handsome face. "That does present a bit of a problem." His face cleared. "But I don't think anything will happen as long as you stay quiet and in the background."

"Where I belong," she said with a bit of sarcasm, walking slowly toward him.

He grinned. "Hey, you said it, not me. Just don't try to talk to anyone out there. Okay?"

What she could possibly have to say to a bunch of men watching camels lurch across the desert was more than she could imagine. They got into the Jeep and Peter headed for the highway. Claire loved racing along like a slice of wind, but she dreaded getting to their destination. She had a feeling all was not going to go as swimmingly as Peter hoped.

It was soon in sight. Pickup trucks, Jeeps, Cadillacs and stretch limousines were pulled up against pens made of pieces of wood leaned together, giving the scene the look of a Gypsy camp. And in the background were the camels, huge, ungainly beasts milling about, each with a turbanned boy hanging onto a rope tied around the animal's muzzle. Perched high on some camel humps were small boys with long sticks.

Peter parked and turned to look at her. "Maybe you'd better stay here," he said. "I'll check things out and come back."

She nodded, watching him go. It occurred to her that he hadn't said a thing about what they'd done in the tent together. Making love had been just one more adventure to him, it seemed. Like fighting off the morals police. Or watching an execution. Where was the tenderness, the bond strengthening and growing firm? Was it asking too much that he treat their intimacy as a bigger deal than a camel race?

Perhaps. He was a man, after all. They said that men didn't look at lovemaking quite the same way women did, and on the evidence of the men she'd known, she could believe it.

Well, what the hell did she want? Perfection? The man was wonderful to her—loving, gentle, considerate. Just because he didn't want to hold hands and go over every detail of the past hour or so didn't mean he was an ogre. He was a man, that was all.

She watched the shifting scene and let her mind drift, and then realized Peter had been gone for some time. She couldn't spot him in the milling crowd. It was mostly men, but there were some women on the fringes, mostly sitting on mats around tents toward the side of the clearing. Claire was getting restless. If Peter didn't come back in five more minutes . . .

Time was up and she was slipping from the Jeep, walking quickly, head and eyes down, to find a place from where she could watch the action and not be observed herself.

She made a wide detour around a group of shouting men and then found herself confronted with the longest, widest limousine she'd ever seen. There were people inside, but she couldn't make out their features behind the dark-tinted windows. She walked quickly toward the front of the car intending to get around it. She was careful not to make eye contact. As she rounded the right fender, a near collision made her head come up. Suddenly she was staring into the fierce, dark eyes of a man in a white headdress, a man who'd stepped purposely in her path and lifted the AK 47 he held into position, staring at her coldly.

"Oops," she said, backing away. "I . . . I'm sorry."

Too late she realized what she had done. He was looking at her strangely, as though unsure of the language she was speaking, and she thanked God for that small blessing.

She hurried out of his sight and, she hoped, out of his mind, moving toward the tents where she'd seen the women. But they were gone now. The mats were empty. She looked around and found they had taken up a position farther back from which to watch the race.

A gun sounded, and the air was full of shouts.

The camels were off. All around, men were jumping into Jeeps and pickups to give chase to the racers. Claire watched as they roared away, and she wondered if Peter was in one of those vehicles. Surely he hadn't left her here!

But no, there he was. She finally picked him out, walking along the far side of the corrallike fencing, talking to someone who was walking next to him. Someone in a Western-style business suit. Someone . . . Oh my God, it was Robert Camden.

Heart in her throat, she shrank back among the tents. What now? She couldn't let Robert Camden see her. How could she explain being here with a roughneck? He would assume she was having an affair. And he would assume right.

She tried to clear her mind, tried to think. If she hid, maybe he would go away and she could eventually come out and meet Peter. On the other hand, if she made her way back to the Jeep and waited for Peter there . . . but what if Robert Camden came back to the Jeep with him? What could she possibly do? Pretend she really was an Arab woman and didn't speak English? That would still get Peter into trouble.

A shadow fell into her line of vision and she whirled to find the tall Arab with the AK 47 coming toward her. She hardly had time to feel afraid. He said something in Arabic, gesturing toward her with the rifle, and she began to back away. He yelled something, and she turned and began to run, holding up the hem of her *abaya* so that she wouldn't trip, racing back and forth between tents, desperately trying to find a way out of this nightmare.

She couldn't let him catch her. God only knew what he might do. Saying a little prayer, she half-ran, half-stumbled into one of the tents and rolled to the ground, looking around and saying another prayer of thanks at finding the area empty. She lay very still, holding her breath. Heavy footsteps sounded outside. A man, most likely the one with the rifle, was running past. But the footsteps faded and then there was nothing but the sound of her own heart beating like a drum in her ears.

Moving very slowly, she made her way back to the opening of the tent and pulled the dyed animal skin back enough to make a small crack to see out through. There was no one nearby. She widened the crack and looked out into the clearing. There were still men strolling about, though most of them seemed to have gone off to see the end of the race.

About a hundred yards away, she could see Peter talking to Robert Camden. Robert seemed to be angry. He was talking quickly and jabbing at Peter's chest with his index finger. She couldn't make out the words. Peter looked worried and was glancing about, obviously looking for her. She wanted to call his attention, but how could she do that without alerting Camden?

She watched anxiously, trying to decide. But all she could think of to do was wait it out and hope that Robert Camden left before the occupants of the tent returned from the race.

Peter turned, suddenly, saying something to

Robert as he stepped away, and Robert lunged forward, grabbing him by the arm.

Peter's words came to her clearly for once. "I can't," he said. "I have something I have to do."

But Robert was jabbing at his chest again, and from the looks of it, he was making threats. Peter looked around the clearing again, shrugged, and started toward the Jeep, with Robert Camden and another man in Western dress Claire hadn't noticed before walking alongside him. Toward the Jeep. Claire's heart stopped. Surely he wouldn't leave her here.

She stumbled out of the tent, adjusting her veil, and ran around the tents, keeping as much out of sight as possible, but still following them. Robert Camden and the other man got into a limousine with an Arab driver, and Peter swung up into the driver's seat of the Jeep.

He was leaving. He couldn't leave. She ran forward and stopped at the side of the road, and finally Peter saw her. He drove up beside her and paused, looking down at her and shaking his head, then glancing to where Robert Camden's car was waiting for him. He looked back at her, shrugged and said something she couldn't hear over the roar of the engine. And then he drove off, leaving her standing there at the side of the road.

For a moment, she was stunned, unbelieving, sure that he would turn around and come back for her. She watched as the two vehicles kicked up rooster tails of dust and disappeared around a hill. He was gone. What was she supposed to do now?

She looked back at the tents, at the few people still milling about the clearing. There was no way she could go up to any one of them and ask for help. Not only was she doing something they would frown upon, she had been brought out here by a man who was not her husband. For all she knew, they might decide to behead her right here and now. Or sell her into slavery. Or . . .

No, her imagination was running away with her. She had to think clearly. There had to be a way. Now, what would she do if she were at home? Catch a bus. That wasn't going to work out here in the desert. Call for a cab. No telephone. And there was no way she could possibly hitchhike.

She turned nervously, looking back toward the tents, wondering if she should go back to her hiding place. And then suddenly, there he was again, the man with the rifle. Only this time he was too quick for her, and when she turned to run, he threw one strong arm around her waist and picked her up, leaving her feet to dangle in the air.

She shrieked, but he clamped a hand over her mouth and began to carry her off, speaking in low, angry Arabic. She didn't even try to struggle. He was much too strong for that. Instead, she tried desperately to keep her head clear and watch for an opportunity to escape. The smell of his sweat was overpowering, and his hands were rough. And all the while, a part of her was sure this couldn't possibly be happening. It must be a dream. Things like this just didn't happen to people like her.

Couldn't anyone see what was happening? She

tried to twist her head to look around, but he said something that sounded mean and jerked her head back again, then yanked her closer to him. When her face hit his chest, she opened her mouth and bit as hard as she could. Even through her veil and his shirt, she could tell she'd made contact.

He screamed, but instead of dropping her as she'd hoped, he shook her as he walked, yelling in Arabic, his anger now directed only at her.

She was afraid she would be killed. And the way he held her, she couldn't see where they were going or what he was doing. She heard what sounded like a car door opening, and suddenly she was dumped unceremoniously into a luxurious car seat and the man was closing the door on her, still yelling at her, shaking his fist at her through the glass before he turned away.

She blinked, trying to catch her breath and right herself in the seat at the same time, her hands sinking into soft leather. She was in the stretch limousine. Across from her in two facing seats sat two veiled women, both staring at her with huge dark eyes and chattering in Arabic.

Claire tried her voice and was surprised to find it worked fine. "What . . . what is this all about?" she demanded. "Why did that man bring me here?"

"He brought you here because I told him to," the younger of the two women said in perfect English. "I knew from the first moment I saw you that you were a foreigner. I wanted to prove to my cousin that I was right."

Claire stared for a moment, outrage spreading

through her. "Do you mean to tell me you ordered that giant to manhandle me that way for no other reason than to prove a point? I . . . you . . . How dare you? I have certain rights, even in this country. You can't just grab people and carry them off!"

The young woman's head rose regally. "I am Princess Nadia, and this is my cousin Meme. My father is Prince Ihbrahim. My dear American woman, I may do what I wish."

The outrage began to ebb as Claire realized this encounter might be a blessing in disguise. After all, here was a car. And here were two women she could talk to.

"What is your name?" the princess demanded.

"Claire."

"Now tell me," she demanded, "how did you come to be in this place?"

"It . . . it's a long story." She took a deep breath and ran a shaking hand over her forehead. What could she tell them? Surely not the truth. Arab women lived such sheltered lives—how could they ever understand? "A man brought me," she began, tentatively.

Nadia cried out. "Ah! A lover!" she said blissfully. "I love stories like this."

Her cousin frowned disapprovingly and turned her face away as though she were determined to listen to no more of this nonsense.

But Nadia was another matter entirely. "Tell me, tell me, is he handsome? Is he very strong? Do you feel weak when you see him?"

Claire wasn't sure how to proceed. She crossed

her ankles delicately and cleared her throat. "It's not exactly like that," she began.

"Oh, do not tell me that he is not your lover, because then I will not listen to you. I love romance stories. When I am in London I read all the romance stories. I know how these things are done in the Western world." She glanced at Meme, then back at Claire, lowering her voice conspiratorially. "I will tell you about something very daring I did once."

Claire hesitated. "Oh. Well, all right."

"Meme will turn her face away so she will not hear me because she hates to hear of this." True enough, her cousin did just that, sniffing loudly. Nadia giggled. "It happened many months ago. I went to the shopping area and there I saw a very handsome young man. He looked at me—you know—with the eyes?"

Claire nodded in understanding.

"So I went again the next day. And he was there again. Day after day. And finally, one day—" she looked around as though afraid of being overheard, and leaned closer, lowering her voice "—I walked very close to him and pretended to knock against him by mistake, and when he reached out to steady me, I put a piece of paper in his hand. A piece of paper with my telephone number on it."

Claire could see how this was something very daring, indeed. "You didn't."

Her eyes sparkled. "Yes. I did."

"Did he call you?"

"Of course." She sighed melodramatically, obviously seeing no irony in her tale. "He said such things to me. I cannot tell you how excited I was. My heart was beating so hard I thought I would die. It was beautiful, so beautiful." She sighed again, her hands over her heart. "I wish I had thought to use my tape recorder, so that I could listen to him again and again."

Did that mean it had been a one-time experience? "He never called again?" Claire asked.

Nadia looked at her as though she were slightly addled. "Of course not. I had Mama change my telephone number right away." She shrugged grandly. "What if he had found out who I was? We couldn't have had that."

Claire was slightly bewildered. "But . . . who was he?"

She spread her arms wide. "Who knows? But I will always have the memory of that telephone call. Always."

They were all three quiet for a moment, each with her own thoughts on the subject, and then Nadia brightened again. "Anyway, tell me now. What did you do with your young man? Why did he bring you here?"

"Well, he's not exactly my young man—"

"A-a-ah!" She shook her finger at Claire. "Tell me, now."

Claire gave in to the inevitable. If Nadia wanted a romance, she supposed she would have to supply her with one, especially if she wanted her help. "He brought me here to watch the races and we got separated and . . . and he left me."

Nadia was scandalized. "He left you here?"

"Well, you see, it wasn't his fault. He was forced to leave."

"Ah! They grabbed him? At knife point, no doubt. Kidnapped at the races!"

Kidnapped by Robert Camden and the threat of exposure. "S-sort of."

"How exciting. Do you suppose you will ever see him alive again?"

That gave her a start. "I certainly hope so." She looked from one veiled face to the other. "Now that I've told you my story, do you think you can help me?"

"Help you? Help you in what way?"

"I need to get back home, to the Draxon Oil compound outside of Riyadh. Can you take me there? I would be happy to pay you for your time and gas. . . ."

"Oooh. You would like us to drive you?"

"Yes, please."

But the princess was shaking her head. "Impossible. My father would never allow it."

Claire's heart sank, but anger surfaced, as well. This was ridiculous. She was stuck out in the middle of the desert with no way home. A society that put these kinds of constraints on a woman could use some reordering.

"Where is your father?" she asked brightly. "I will ask him myself."

Both women gasped. "You would not dare!"

"Of course I would dare. Don't you understand? I don't have much to lose here. I have to get home. I need a ride." She gathered the skirts of her robe in her hands, preparing to depart. "Just tell me where he is. I'll tell him how we've talked, that we've become good friends. Surely he won't leave a friend of his daughter's stranded in the desert."

She glared at Nadia, and Nadia glared back, fully aware of the implications in Claire's little speech. There was no way she wanted Claire anywhere near her father.

Letting out a sigh of exasperation, the princess knocked on the window of the car, summoning the man who had carted Claire to the limo. He opened the door and snarled at Claire, then turned to hear Nadia's wish.

She spoke quickly in Arabic, and Meme cried out in protest at part of her speech, but she brushed her cousin aside. When the man had gone, she turned to Claire.

"I have sent word to my father that I am bored with the races. I want to go to where they are flying the falcons today. I shall be back before sunset." She glared at Claire again. "So we are off for a long ride. Thanks to you."

They left in a caravan of five cars. Claire assumed the cars in the front and the cars behind them were filled with bodyguards for the two women. Once they were under way, Nadia was friendly again, chattering away in English to her, in Arabic to Meme. Claire found herself enjoying the ride.

It was interesting that the princess never questioned why Claire was wearing Arab clothes. Of course, to her, it was quite normal. And the only safe way for a woman to travel.

As if there was any safety anywhere. Being stranded had a way of shaking one's confidence a bit. She thought of her children, winging their way to England, of Howard, likely wondering where she was, of Peter . . . Peter! Just wait until she got her hands on him. How could he have left her like that? It made her furious to think of it.

She tried to think of other things, noticing the beautiful gold braiding on Nadia's *abaya* and mentioning it to her.

"Oh, yes. We all get this done now." She sniffed a bit contemptuously at Claire's plain model. "It's the lastest thing."

That led to a discussion of the Arab woman's place in the world, and the princess became quite heated in defense of her nation's customs.

"We are a people of honor and tradition. The Koran proscribes a woman's place in society, and she tries to live her life according to these teachings. Don't you know that there are many ways women can have power without running around half-naked in the world and bossing men around?"

"Of course, but—"

"Besides, we have many women who work now. I myself have a degree from the university. My sister is an artist and she sells her paintings. I have a friend who has a jewelry store, a very elegant one, with a chandelier in the lobby. My mother's cousin runs her own construction company—of course, she cannot go on the site when the men are working, but she has others who do it for her."

"But she can't even drive herself to work, I'll bet."

"Why would she need to drive herself? She has a driver."

Why, indeed? But Claire didn't give up, and neither did Nadia, so they had a spirited disagreement until the compound appeared in the distance.

And then a new problem presented itself. How was Claire going to get into her own house, still preserving the aura of Arabic womanhood, and yet convincing the compound guard she belonged there?

"Tell the driver to say we are visiting Mrs. Howard Montgomery," she told Nadia.

They pulled in next to the guard shack and the driver did just that, but Claire could hear the guard's skepticism. "I'll have to call the Montgomerys and ask," he said.

No one answered at the Montgomery house. Claire could have predicted that. Then she thought of Shareen. "Change it to Mrs. Jim Hunter," Claire whispered to Nadia, who told the driver quickly.

Claire watched as the guard returned to the telephone and dialed Shareen's number. What on earth would Shareen make of this? Would she be curious enough to let them in?

Yes! The guard was signaling for them to go on through. Claire directed the driver to Shareen's house instead of her own, just in case they were being watched, and there was Shareen on the sidewalk, waiting for them.

She smiled as the cars came to a stop before her, but her eyes went from one car to another, searching for a clue as to why this entourage was visiting her.

The princess got out and nodded to her, and then Meme did the same. Finally, Claire was allowed to leave the confines of the car and step to the ground.

"Thanks for letting us in, Shareen," she said from behind her veil. "Do you mind if I just go into your house and—"

She didn't get any further. Shareen let out a screech and grabbed her by the shoulders. "Is that really you? Claire! What on earth are you doing in that robe? Where have you been? Howard couldn't find you anywhere. Where are you going? What are you—"

"Perhaps we should go into the house," Nadia said in her regal way. "She can explain all about it inside, away from prying eyes."

"Prying eyes." Shareen glanced up and down the street and nodded. "Yes, of course." Giving Claire another look full of helpless bewilderment and suppressed laughter, she led the way into her house.

"Is this a women's room?" the princess asked as soon as they were inside.

"It will be if you have your guards make sure no men enter," Shareen told her. As Nadia hurried out to do just that, she turned to Claire and whispered, "Won't Larry be surprised if he comes home early and they won't let him into his own house?"

"Surprised," warned Claire, "may not be the word for it."

"But what on earth . . . ?"

"Sit down." Claire took off her veil with a sigh and watched as the others did so, as well, revealing their attractive faces. When they slipped out of their robes, the two Arab woman were wearing filmy Western sundresses, which showed a lot of back. "I'll try to explain as best I can."

Shareen served tea and cookies and Claire told an abbreviated story, calling Peter "a friend," though of course Shareen knew exactly who it was, and not detailing why he had to leave. Nadia jumped in often, refining the tale into something much more romantic and adventurous.

Finally the two Arab women left, after much waving and promising to get together again. The entourage took off down the street looking for all the world like a circus procession.

Claire sighed, feeling drained, and gathered up the Arab clothing to take home with her. "I'd better call Howard—"

"Don't bother," Shareen interjected. "He's gone."

Claire stood stock still. "Gone?" she echoed softly.

Shareen looked at her face and reached out to touch her reassuringly. "Oh, no, dear. Only on a business trip. There's a meeting in Jiddah he had to attend. He was looking all over for you. He seemed so helpless I finally went over and helped him pack." She hesitated, searching Claire's face. "I . . . I hope you don't mind."

Mind? Mind that she had seen the sleeping arrangements, mind that she knew for certain now that the Montgomery marriage was in trouble? If it had been anyone else, Claire would have been furious. But Shareen was learning more and more about the real life of Claire Duvall Montgomery. Why not this, too?

"Of course I don't mind. Thank you for doing it. I appreciate it." With a smile, she started for the door.

"Claire." Shareen followed her. "Please be careful."

Claire looked back and nodded. "Don't worry, Shareen. I intend to be."

Howard's absence was a blessing. Claire was too exhausted to do much more than take a long, hot bath and pull on her nightgown. What a day. She wasn't sure she'd be ready to face another one like that for a good long while.

She could hardly believe the things she'd been through. As she lay back against the pillows in her big empty bed, she let her thoughts drift slowly over the events of the day—the girls leaving, her aching loneliness for them, the ride in the desert, the Bedouin, the camel races, Nadia's bodyguard, the ride back home. Only vaguely did she allow herself to realize she was neglecting one major event, ignoring it, in fact. She had made love with Peter.

She shivered and turned to her other side, trying to push it away. But the facts wouldn't die. She had made love with Peter. And it had been wonderful.

A part of her was still shocked. He was the only man other than Howard with whom she had been intimate. It had been unlike anything she could have imagined. But it must never happen again.

Why not? Her mind was confused on that point. But she knew right from wrong, and sleeping with Peter was definitely wrong. It went against everything she'd ever been taught, everything she believed. And yet, she couldn't say she was sorry.

She sighed and shelved those thoughts and let her mind dwell on her daughters again, how grown-up they had looked boarding the plane. Tears rose and choked her and she gave way to a compulsion to go to their rooms, as if that would somehow bring them closer.

Slipping out of bed, she glided soundlessly down the hallway and into Katy's room. She switched on the little ballerina lamp next to Katy's bed. Turning slowly, she looked at the room with its white-and-pink-frosting decor, the posters on the walls, the one of toe shoes, laces dangling negligently, the next of a famous soccer player, the last of a rock star with hair half way down his back. Katy, her eclectic darling.

Something was sticking out from beneath the bed. She bent down and pulled out a sock with an embroidered cuff, and suddenly, tears were choking in her throat, tearing at her heart, streaming down her face. Her baby. She couldn't bear that she was gone. Would she be the same little girl when next she saw her? How could she be? She was in a new place, experiencing all sorts of new things without her mother to turn to for comfort, advice, guidance of any sort.

It was the middle of the night, and the "midnight terror" struck Claire, tingeing everything with doom. What kind of a mother was she to send her children off like that? How could she live with herself?

Dabbing at her eyes with the sock, she stumbled out of Katy's room and turned toward Samantha's. For just a moment, she thought she heard something, a sort of bumping noise, coming from her own bedroom. But she hardly paid any attention to it. She was immersed in self-flagellation, and she went on into her oldest daughter's room without giving it a second thought.

Samantha. It was a completely different story here. In some ways she felt as though Sam was already lost to her. She turned on the overhead light and gazed about, noting how different this room was from Katy's. The only picture adorning the wall was an anonymous print of abstract art. Sam's colors were gray and black. Everything she owned was methodically put away, or in a neat stack. There was none of Katy's exuberance, none of her careless revelation. Everything in Sam's room was controlled.

Claire's tears dried as she stood there, thinking. What would happen to her silent child? Would she always be so closed? Would she ever find the kind of joy that would unlock her soul and set it free? Claire's heart wept for Sam, and those tears were the most painful of all.

She turned off all the lights and made her way back to her own room, feeling her way in the dark, finding the end of the bed with her knee and sliding forward to sprawl across it. She slipped into place—and right up against a hard male body.

She stiffened in shock and a scream began to claw its way up her throat, but a large hand covered her mouth before it could escape, and Peter's voice was warm in her ear.

"Hush, now. It's me."

"Peter!" Panic transformed into outrage. She turned in his arms. "What are you doing here? You left me all alone! You—"

"Hush." His hands felt huge and hot through the silky fabric of her nightgown. "No explanations now," he whispered, his lips against her neck. "Just kiss me."

Just kiss this stranger in her bed—but of course. She knew she should be demanding explanations, but instead, she found herself lifting her face to his, feeling her body lose its tension as his lips touched hers. He wanted her again. That alone was enough to thrill her.

His touch was molten gold and she arched into his hand, glad for the darkness that made her feel free. He was so sure, so right. She didn't have to think. She only had to feel. And Peter could make her feel like no one else ever had.

He came to her quickly this time, as though he was hungry, as though his need was urgent, and she found her own growing passion matching his, impatient ecstasy.

When it was over, she lay beside him, catching her breath, holding on to the last delicious remnants of the sensations.

Peter was the first to speak. "Is Howard downstairs?" he asked.

"Howard?" She turned and looked at him, though she could make out little more than his silhouette in the dark. "Do you mean to tell me you came into my bed when you actually thought my husband was downstairs?"

"Isn't he?"

She let her breath out very slowly, not sure she liked this. "No," she said. "He's in Jiddah on business." She rose on her elbow. "And you! You left me in the middle of the desert—"

"I know. I'm sorry. There was nothing I could do that wouldn't jeopardize your reputation." He shrugged. "I couldn't very well tell Robert Camden I had the director's wife with me, could I? He was upset enough that I was out there. Seemed to think I was going to screw up some deal he was making with the prince."

"So that was why he insisted you leave with him?"

"Yup. And he followed me all the way into town, too. Just to make sure I didn't double back."

"And what did you think I was going to do out there all alone?" She managed to hold on to her indignation a little longer. He deserved it.

He chuckled softly, reaching for her. "I had no idea. But knowing you, I was pretty sure you would come up with something."

"So you just relied on luck?"

"And pluck." He pulled her into the circle of his arms. "I went back out there, Claire, as soon as I could." His voice lowered to a husky rasp. "I was almost out of my mind when I couldn't find you, and no one seemed to know what had happened to you."

Her hair was loose, full and flowing, and he buried his face in it. She smiled in the dark. That was better. All she'd wanted was a healthy dose of concern.

"What did happen to you, anyway? When I got back, it was all over the compound that you arrived in a stretch limo with a couple of Arab women."

She described her encounter with Princess Nadia and her bodyguard.

"Actually, it turned out to be very interesting. In the last twenty-four hours, I think I've learned more about this country than I learned in all the other months of living here put together."

"Great." His lips skimmed her bare shoulder. "Since you know Saudi so well now, you should be ready to move on. How about coming with me to Greece?"

His last words seemed to stay suspended in the air as she took a long, long moment to comprehend the full meaning.

"To Greece?" she echoed. "But . . . why are you going back to Greece?"

"I've got a friend there with a little yacht he says I can use. We could sail from one island to another. . . ."

"What about your job?"

He seemed to hesitate, then said almost too forcefully, "To hell with my job. Who needs it? I've got better things to do." His fingers raked her hair. "And I want you to come with me."

Confusion put Claire off balance. "I can't. How can I?"

"Why not? Your girls are in boarding school. There's nothing to keep you here."

She was tempted. She held the idea close for a moment and smiled in the darkness. To sail away from this hellish mess with this gorgeous man— what could be more delicious? But she couldn't.

"I have to be here for Howard."

His voice was tight. "You don't love Howard. Give it up."

"I don't give up things as easily as you do." The words were out before she could stop them. She could feel his fingers tighten in her hair.

"What is that supposed to mean?"

"I . . . I'm sorry. I didn't mean it like it sounded. It's just that, well, how can you throw your job away so carelessly?"

His laugh was short and harsh. "I didn't throw my job away, Claire. I got fired. I got fired because I refused to follow Robert Camden's orders and stay in the bachelor barracks tonight. I had to go back out into the desert to look for you. So Camden canned me on the spot. I'm out of here, whether I want to be or not."

A rush of shame filled Claire. "Oh, Peter, I'm sorry, I thought—"

"I know what you thought. I know what you think. I'm not like you, Claire. Or the men you're used to. I'm not a college graduate. I don't have goals and a career and a split-level future in mind. I turned my back on all that when I left home looking for adventure. And I've never regretted it." He shrugged grandly. "Take it or leave it. That's what I am."

Exactly. That was what he was, and she knew she liked him that way. "Do you want me to try to talk to Robert Camden?"

"Be serious, Claire. What could you say?"

"I'd think of something. I could say you were my cousin. . . ."

He laughed softly and some of the hardness melted away. "Forget it. It's time to move on." His long fingers stroked her cheek. "I just don't want to go alone this time," he added softly.

She didn't say another word. But when he reached for her, she went to him willingly. In his arms, she could forget Howard, and almost forget how far away her babies were. Her mouth opened to his kiss, reaching eagerly for the hot sensations he was so good at producing. She wanted to smother thought, smother reality. At least for one night.

~

"Ah, so you're a great chef, too, I suppose?"

Peter looked up to see Claire framed in the doorway of her kitchen. He brandished the fork with which he had just been turning bacon and wiggled his eyebrows. *Mais oui, madame.*

She came in, still smiling. "May I help?"

"*Mais, non!*" He gestured imperiously toward the kitchen table where he obviously expected her to take a chair. "Sit, *s'il vous plait.*"

She sat and watched him. There was a new warmth where her heart resided. She'd been lucky to have Peter drop into her life.

She had woken at the first light of dawn to find him still beside her, cradling her in his arms, and she'd sighed with contentment and closed her eyes, drifting off, and when she'd opened them again, he'd been gone.

She'd sat up quickly, her hand over her heart, but the noises coming from downstairs had reassured her, and she'd slipped on her robe and gone out on the landing. From there she could smell the bacon cooking. He was being domestic in her kitchen. It made her laugh, and the smile still lingered.

"How do you like your eggs?" he asked.

"With a French accent," she answered, teasing him. "What happened to yours?"

"I can change my nationality at will," he boasted. "Name a country, and I can be from it."

"I'll settle for plain old American, if you serve it sunny-side-up."

"It's a deal." He pulled open the bread box and frowned. "No bread? No toast."

"I can live without it."

"No, no. Impossible. We must find something to go with the eggs." He pulled open the refrigerator and began to rummage. "Got any tortillas? Left-over rice? Chocolate cake?"

"Chocolate cake?" She shuddered. "That would be against the rules."

"Rules?" He looked at her from over the re-frigerator door. "What rules?"

"The breakfast rules. You know. Bacon and eggs and toast. Those're the rules."

He shook his head sorrowfully. "Claire, Claire, haven't you understood a thing I've tried to teach you?" He reached out and chucked her under the chin. "There are no more rules, darling. You're free to play without them. Just like me."

She ate her eggs with only bacon to enhance them. He ate his, too, and told her stories and made her laugh. And all the time he was watching her, wondering.

She wasn't going to go with him to Greece. It wasn't just the words she'd used when she'd re-fused. There was something in her eyes that told him. She wasn't ready to take that step yet, and he couldn't think of anything short of kidnapping that he could do to change her mind.

What was he going to do? He couldn't stay. He'd burned his bridges when he'd landed a right hook on Robert Camden's jaw the night before, when the man had tried to bar his way from going out to find Claire again. It had been one thing when Camden had acted like an overbearing potentate at the camel races. When he'd ordered Peter to go back to the compound, Peter had felt he had to comply or risk revealing that Claire was with him.

It had been in his mind to go to the bachelor quarters, wait until Camden was out of sight, and then head back to the desert. Unfortunately, Camden had been suspicious enough to keep tabs on him, even going so far as to follow him to his room, and then try to order Peter to accompany him to dinner. By then, Peter had run out of patience.

As a result, Camden had lost some dignity. And Peter had lost his job. Not to mention the fact that the security force was probably looking for him right now.

The front doorbell rang and they both jumped. Claire shot to her feet, looking around the kitchen in panic.

"I have no idea who this is," she whispered. "Stay here, whatever you do."

Clutching her robe around her, she walked swiftly to the door, pulling it open only a crack. Frances was on the doorstep.

"Oh." She smiled through the crack. "Good morning, Frances. Listen, I'm not really up yet. Could you come back a little later?"

"Not up yet?" Frances made a show of looking at the time on her watch. "Good gracious. Well, of course, dear, if you don't have time for me now." She glanced at Claire's robe. "But I do need to come in for just a moment. I stopped at the gas pump to fill up my car and I got gasoline all over my hands. Just let me in to wash it off, won't you?"

She was already pushing her way in and Claire could hardly refuse such a request. "The bathroom is this way," she said, beginning to lead Frances across the room.

"Never mind. I'll just go on into the kitchen."

"No!" Claire threw herself in the way. "Don't go in there."

Frances laughed. "I've seen messy kitchens before, Claire. Don't be silly." She already had the advantage in body weight, and unless Claire wanted to tackle her to the ground, the woman was going into the kitchen. Claire closed her eyes, waiting for the inevitable, as Frances's spike heels tapped across her floor.

She waited. But all she heard was the water turned on at the sink. Breathing once again, she hurried in to find the kitchen empty except for Frances.

"It's not so bad," Frances said smugly, looking around. "But who have you been having breakfast with? There are two settings here. I thought Howard was in Jiddah."

Claire's mouth was so dry she was afraid she might not be able to get out the words. "I . . . Shareen came over earlier. . . ."

"Oh, I see." Frances looked hurt. "You have time for her, but not for me." Her nose rose six inches into the air. "Never mind, Claire. I can take a hint." She started for the door and Claire didn't even bother to follow. She did hold her breath until she heard the front door slam shut, then turned and whispered, "Peter?"

There was no answer. Heart in her throat, she ran out into the living room, then into the den and on into the family room, where she ran right into his open arms.

"Oh." Relief flooded her as she laughed up into his face. "That was a close call."

"Wasn't it?" His arms tightened around her. "I think we ought to celebrate." He bent close and began depositing tiny kisses along the lines of her neck. "Don't you?"

"Mmm." She dropped her head back and let herself melt against him. "I think that's a marvelous idea," she whispered.

Pushing back her robe, and then the strap of her nightgown, he exposed her shoulder and buried his face there, while she arched back, eyes closed. He was murmuring something sweet and sinful against her skin, and that was probably why she didn't hear the sliding glass door open until Margo was all the way into the room.

"Hi, Claire, I—"

The words died in Margo's throat as she stared at the two of them, caught like deer in the headlights of an oncoming truck. The color drained from her cheeks. "Oh, my God," she whimpered, her hands going to her face.

Claire was the first of the three to come to her senses. Straightening her robe, she pulled away from Peter's embrace and started toward the woman. "I'm afraid you really are interrupting, Margo," she said crisply. "And I must say that in the future, I would appreciate it if you would knock like everyone else before you come into my home."

In retrospect she realized she should have

done this months ago. What had seemed like a silly thing to complain about at the time had turned into a menace.

Margo was backing toward the door. "Oh, my God," she said again. Her eyes were huge, stunned, as though for all her talk, she had never imagined that Claire would have a lover.

"Margo." Claire took hold of her arm. She didn't want to have to beg the woman to keep quiet about this. But perhaps if she asked Margo to think it through, if she understood the background, there might be hope.

"I'm sorry you had to see this. But after all your advice, surely you can understand—"

"Understand?" Margo stared at her bleerily. "I . . . no, that's all talk. I would never . . . I mean . . ." She yanked her arm out of Claire's grasp and looked at her with disgust. "You're married. How could you?"

Claire's hand dropped to her side. She felt wounded, vulnerable, even close to tears. Yes, Margo was right. How could she? What kind of a woman was she? All the moral training of a lifetime flooded back and filled her with self-loathing. For just a moment, she agreed with Margo.

Then she got a grip on herself and held her head high. "This is really none of your business, Margo," she said. "No one can know what goes on inside another person's marriage. It's not for you to judge me."

"Oh, yeah? With you judging my boy all over the place? Are you the only one with the right?"

Margo's resentment was clear on her face. "I'll judge you all I want, lady. And so will everyone else in the compound."

She turned and was gone. Claire closed the sliding door with a firm hand and locked it with a snap.

Turning back to Peter, she sighed. "It was inevitable, I suppose," she said as he took her hands in his. "I just wish it didn't seem so . . . tacky." She shuddered.

"Claire, my elegant lady, nothing about you could ever be tacky."

She smiled her thanks for his support. She needed that right now. And then she closed her eyes and moaned. "But why did it have to be Margo of all people? It will be all over the compound by lunchtime."

"So you might as well come with me to Greece."

She opened her eyes and laughed. "You're like a dog with a bone, aren't you? Go on up and take a shower, before we get more company. Whatever happened to the good old days when nobody ever visited me?"

He went, and she stayed in the family room, leaning against the wall, wondering what she was going to do next. Her head was throbbing. When Howard came home . . . oh, Lord, what was she going to say to him? Would he be hurt? She hadn't meant to hurt him, didn't want to bother him in any way. But then again, maybe he was beyond being hurt by her.

She was glad the girls were in England, far away from this mess. Claire Duvall Montgomery with a messy situation on her hands. Who would ever have believed it?

Suddenly she remembered what Peter had said earlier. He might be right. There might not be any rules to the game. But you still had to pay if you wanted to play. That would never change.

❦

"I'm going to the Greek Islands. Sailing."

"With . . . some kind of tour or something?" Shareen's lovely dark eyes were suspicious. She poured Claire a cup of coffee and handed it to her across the kitchen table, with its yellow cloth and pot of daisys.

Claire smiled and shook her head. "I'm meeting Peter. I know, I know, I'm horrible, morally bankrupt, unclean. But I'm going anyway."

Shareen didn't look surprised. She pretended to find some crumbs to pick off the table.

Claire watched her, knowing she was groping for words. She hoped Shareen didn't hate her. She needed all the friends she could get right now.

It had been three days since she and Peter had been caught red-handed by Margo. Now everyone knew. She could see it in their eyes when she met them on the street. And they all had their own little opinions of her behavior. But everyone, as far as she was concerned, could take a flying leap. She wasn't about to hang her head and beg forgiveness.

"You've thought this through?" Shareen was

trying hard to be a friend. "You know this will probably destroy your marriage?"

Claire nodded. "I think you know me well enough to know the marriage is a sham. It has been for a while. I just wouldn't face it before."

Coffee sloshed over the rim of her cup, and she put it down with a thump. She tucked her hands into her lap so that their shaking couldn't be seen. "I feel awful about my daughters, though. There's no way to spare them heartbreak over this, and I hate myself for having put them in this position. And Howard, even. But . . ." Her voice cracked. "I . . . I . . . oh, Shareen, Peter makes me so happy. Can you understand that? He makes me feel beautiful and worth something. No man has ever made me feel like that before, and I can't let go of it. Not yet."

Shareen reached across the table and for her friend's hands, lifting them from her lap and covering them with her own. "You do what you have to do," she advised her softly. "And Claire . . . just one thing I think you ought to know. Just so you don't feel so guilty where Howard is concerned."

As Claire stared at her curiously, she hesitated, then rushed ahead. "Claire, this is the sort of thing I usually don't believe in telling a woman. But I think this case is special. And I'm going to tell you. I . . . I'm sorry if you really don't want to know." She took a deep breath and let it out, the words tumbling over one another. "Howard is sleeping with Kim Striper, the secretary. He took her to Jiddah with him. And before her, he was sleeping with that other secretary that was here, Georgia Mac-Donald."

A wave of numbness crept over Claire. She nodded, more in nervous habit than in agreement. "I suppose . . . everyone knew about it? I was the only one who didn't?"

Shareen nodded, her face a mask of misery. "I'm so sorry, Claire. I was hoping you would never have to know. But now, with you feeling so guilty . . ."

Claire managed a smile and squeezed Shareen's hand. "I think I did know. In my heart of hearts." She frowned, shaking her head. "Isn't it silly how much it hurts? I . . . I don't love Howard. I don't want him. I would give anything just to be rid of him. And yet—" her smile wobbled "—it still hurts. The rejection. Did he ever want me?" Tears filled her eyes. "I could have been a good wife, Shareen. Really, I know I could have. If he had only given me a chance."

Shareen nodded, tears in her own eyes. "I know, Claire. Don't blame yourself. Use this little vacation to think over your options, decide what will be best for you and the girls. And then, do it. Get this behind you. Get on with your life."

"And cut out the self-pity," Claire advised herself, half-laughing as she dabbed at her wet eyes with a napkin. "Talk about a dog-in-the-manger attitude. I don't want him, but I can't stand that he doesn't want me."

"It's only natural. You've been married. That's not an easy tie to break."

They talked in soft voices for a time, and then Shareen had an announcement of her own.

"I'm going away, too."

Claire frowned. "Back to Beirut to see your grandmother?"

"Yes. She's been having dizzy spells."

"So you're going to go help her guard the gates against the barbarians."

"You might put it that way."

Claire sighed. "I wish you wouldn't go. I was just reading in the paper about another kidnapping in Beirut. It's so dangerous there."

Shareen smiled. "Life is full of dangers." She waved her cup in the air. "Everything you eat or drink could kill you."

"I know, I know. Life is hazardous to your health. It will kill you every time. Eventually."

"Exactly."

"Are you taking Kevin?"

"No. He'll stay with his father. They like that. They eat ice cream for dinner and stay up all night watching horror movies together."

A father who actually enjoyed being with his child. Why hadn't she married one of those? She thought of her own father, of Howard. Was there a man out there for her, someone who might have the same values, want the same things? Or was she living in a never-never land? She squared her shoulders. "Well, I'd better be off." She leaned over and hugged her friend, then rose. "I've got to pack. Peter has already left."

"Does he know you're coming?"

"Not yet. He's in Crete right now, but he'll be at this other little island by the end of the week. He told me the name of the hotel. I'm going to surprise him there."

"Claire." Shareen touched her arm. "Have you thought about how you're going to get out of the country?"

"Out of the country?" Claire looked at her questioningly, then realized what she meant. "Oh, my God. I need my husband's permission, don't I? Do you suppose I could forge it?"

Shareen shook her head. "Larry will do it. And he'll come with you to the airport, too, just to make sure all goes smoothly."

"Your husband? Oh, no, Shareen. He might be jeopardizing his job if he does that. I couldn't let him—"

Shareen gave her a push out the door. "Don't give it a thought. He'll do it. He won't even think twice."

Claire was suddenly overcome with emotion. "Then he's just as wonderful a person as you are," she said, tears back in her eyes as she hugged her friend again. "Goodbye Shareen. And thank you— for always being there."

"You, too, Claire. And don't worry. You'll find a way."

It wasn't until she was on an airplane headed for Greece that she remembered Shareen's last words and remembered where she'd heard them before. She shuddered. She wasn't sure why, but it worried her that Shareen had said them. Was it a bad omen? She felt like calling Shareen from the Athens airport to warn her. But then she stopped herself. It was all just silly superstition anyway.

Claire stepped from the hydrofoil and looked up at the whitewashed houses scattered about the hillside above the bay. Dusk was falling and the air was light and sweet. Was that lemon blossoms she smelled? She walked quickly, enjoying the swing of her hair against her bare shoulders, the swish of the full skirt of her yellow sundress against her knees. Excitement fluttered in her chest. She felt free!

Hotel Paradissos, Peter had told her. That was where he would stay. She stopped and asked a woman selling the day's catch from a rickety table set up along the side of the cobblestone street, and received a quick set of directions that had her walking briskly along the waterfront.

And then, there it was. Hotel Paradissos. It was fronted by a terrace, overlooking the sea. A girl in a white dress was lighting cheery lights hung from the edges of the blue awning, and the delicious smell of barbecued chicken filled the evening air.

Claire shifted her cases and went closer, searching the faces at the tables. It was almost too much to ask that he might be sitting out here right now. But no. There he was.

She dropped the heavier of her bags and raised her hand to wave at him, about to call out his name, when she noticed his companion—a beautiful woman in a low-cut dress, a woman who was leaning much too close to be a casual acquaintance.

She stopped, her greeting still in her throat, her hand fluttering back down to her side, and watched as the lovely blonde reached out and took the back of Peter's head in her hand, pulling him close, and kissed him full on the lips. When he drew back he was laughing, and the feeling between the two of them seemed sensual and flirtatious.

They were talking all the while, saying words Claire couldn't hear. But even if she'd been close enough she still wouldn't have heard them, not with this horrible buzzing in her ears.

She shouldn't have come. What had she been thinking of? Peter was a playboy. He didn't need her to have himself a good time. He had plenty of resources, as he had told her when they had first met. After all, what was there really between them? A little sex, a little fun, nothing more. What had she expected?

Maybe she should go off on her own. She could stay in a seaside hotel, sunbathe all day, drink little cups of dark coffee in the cafés at night, and think her situation through—without a man around.

Yes. That was it. No man around. She bit her lip and started to turn away.

But before she'd quite turned, she saw a man joined Peter's table. Claire lingered for a moment to see what would happen. The woman immediately straightened in her chair, and the man put his arm around her shoulders as he sat very close to her side. He and Peter laughed about something. It was evident this man was also entranced with this woman.

A threesome? Did that mean she could change it to a foursome?

She felt pulled in both directions. Should she go? Or should she at least stay to find out how the land lay?

Claire stood where she was, undecided, and suddenly Peter looked up and saw her.

There was no denying the look of joy on his face at the sight of her. "Claire!" he called, jumping up so fast his chair tumbled behind him. "My God, I can't believe it. You made it!"

He was kissing her and hugging her and grabbing her bags, then ushering her to the table with laughter and loving looks and little jokes; and before she knew it, the incident with the blonde had been pushed away, shoved back into the recesses of her mind, an unimportant thing worthy only of discarding.

He was happy to have her here. And that was what she had come for.

"This is Tony de Marco," he said, introducing the dark man, "and this is Karen Saunders."

The blonde's welcome was a wide, jaunty grin, and Tony's was an appreciative wink. She felt included from the moment she took her seat among them.

"Claire, honey," Karen told her with a rich twang that surely hailed from Texas, "this boy has been yakkin' about you till we near wanted to tie him up and gag him. I thought he was going to break out in hives at any moment." She grimaced dramatically and threw her arms out. "So she's gorgeous. So she's smart. So she's perfect. So all right already!"

Claire was blushing. She could sense the heat filling her cheeks and she laughed, feeling sixteen again. "That's very flattering, but—"

Karen made a comical face. "Flattering! Honey, he's gone ga-ga over you." She leaned close and spoke in a stage whisper. "Take my advice and enjoy it while it lasts. You know how men are. If you're looking for faithful companionship, you better get yourself a dog."

Her last words hung in the air as Tony leaned his head against her shoulder and began to make puppy noises. They all laughed, but Peter reached out and took Claire's hand in his and gave it a good squeeze.

"I'm glad you came," he whispered. "We're going to have a great time."

She searched his eyes for reassurance, and it was there. Perhaps it was silly to keep needing to test for support every step she took. But right now, she had to.

Karen was taking care of her other needs. "Yoo-hoo!" she was calling out to a waiter, waving her hand in the air. "Can you bring us over some more stuff? We've got another mouth to feed."

The woman was loud, the woman was brash—but she was also so good-natured no one seemed to take offense. The waiter arrived with a smile on his face and soon Claire was sitting before a mountain of steaming food, and feeling hungry enough to pack it all away.

"Tony and Karen are the ones who own the yacht," Peter told her as she ate. "We'll take it out tomorrow. Just a short sail over to Delos to see the Terrace of the Lions and all that."

"But won't Tony and Karen be using it?" She looked at them questioningly.

"Not really." Peter seemed to feel free to answer for them. "They have a . . . project they're working on." He hesitated, looking from Tony to Karen and back again, and Claire had the distinct impression he was looking for permission of some kind. But then he was talking again as though nothing had happened.

"I think Claire and I will move onto the boat tomorrow. We can keep our bigger things here in the hotel room."

Tony shrugged. "That's fine with me," he said. He turned and fixed Claire with a steady gaze and said, like a man about to uncover important information, "We'd better get a few things straight. Claire, are you prone to motion sickness?"

Claire blinked. His stern aspect reminded her of certain unpopular teachers she had endured as a child. "I don't think so."

"Are you in any way allergic to the sun?"

She bit back a smile, feeling a little giddy. "Sunscreen is my second skin."

He raised an eyebrow and nodded. "Good. Good." Frowning again, he made another thrust. "Can you swim?"

She held up a hand like a scout taking a pledge, her eyes sparkling. "Like a fish."

"Ah. Very good." He seemed pleased with her so far. "Now, last but not least—" his voice lowered an octave "—*do you know how to sail?*"

"Not really." She was tempted to add, But hum a few bars and I'll see if I can fake it.

She was glad she hadn't given in to temptation when he leaned forward quite seriously and said, "Sailing a boat is like making love to a woman."

"Well, I've never done that, either," she said lightly. "But I think I'll stick to learning how to sail."

He looked startled, but when Peter and Karen laughed, he chuckled, too, if belatedly. "You joke, but this is quite serious. When a man goes out onto the sea, he is challenging God himself. He is facing Nature and saying he is ready to struggle to the death, if need be. There is an art to sailing." He shrugged. "But Peter is a good sailor. I will leave the teaching to him."

Karen had just about had enough. "Oh, sugar, do hush up and leave Claire alone." She gave her friend an affectionate pat. "Don't mind Tony. He tends to get carried away."

"I think he's charming," Claire said, trying to make up for having teased him.

Tony was impressed. His eyes warmed, and he took Claire's hand and kissed her fingers. "And you, lovely lady, you look like a queen," he said, his words flowing beautifully. "You hold your head so high and your hair floats about your shoulders. . . ."

"Yeah, yeah, yeah." Peter pulled her hand away from Tony's and closed his own around it, but his tone and his face were good-natured, even amused. "Enough of that, old man. You can't possibly steal her away from me on the very first night she's arrived. We haven't even said a proper hello yet."

Tony pretended to scowl. "Then take her up to the room and get it done so that I can get on with it," he said. "I'm not a patient man."

Everyone laughed and Claire felt almost light-headed, as though the air were thin or she'd just had a glass of champagne. Peter rose and pulled her up alongside him, and they said good night to the others. He led her into the hotel, his arm firmly about her waist, his voice whispering into her ear, and she giggled and was glad she had come.

The room was small and almost bare, with only a single bed and a small table and chair. The bathroom was down the hall, and it had no shower. Still, the lack didn't throw her as it might have a few months before, when all she had been used to was the best Conrad Hilton had to offer. She'd done some traveling since then, and she'd learned you didn't need nearly as much as you thought.

Besides, she had Peter—Peter showing off the room as though it were an exclusive condo, Peter unzipping the back of her dress while explaining the intricacies of Greek customs, Peter giving the bed the bounce test and declaring it noiseless, contrary to all evidence, Peter kissing her as though she tasted like well-aged brandy, Peter holding her, touching her, taking her to the edge of insanity and then restoring her soul.

And when it was done, they lay in the dark and talked for hours.

"I'm so happy you came," he told her at one point. "Don't ever go back. Stay with me."

It would have been easy to let such talk carry her away, but Claire knew better than to take him seriously. After all, this was the man who prized freedom above all else. "I have two daughters to think about, you know," she reminded him.

He was silent for a moment. "But they're in school now, aren't they?" he said. "I mean, they're taken care of. I know you'll want to go and visit them from time to time, but—"

"You don't understand, Peter. I sent them away because I felt I had to. It's a temporary solution. As soon as I can decide what I'm going to do, I'll get them back again. No matter what."

He was quiet for a moment, then he touched her. "Never mind," he said huskily. "That's for the future. I want to live in the present with you. Okay?"

She found his lips in the dark. "Okay," she whispered.

Her body responded to his touch as though it had been made for exactly that purpose and no other. He had but to brush his hand between her legs and her hips would begin to move of their own accord. The charge between them seemed to get more powerful every time they made love, rather than diminishing. She wasn't sure how long they could go on like this, but it was heady stuff while it lasted.

Would he be amused to know he was the only man who had touched her besides her husband? Probably. But that was something she would keep to herself. This was definitely not the start of a trend. Her time here with Peter was special, a cleansing. She was on vacation from being Claire Duvall Montgomery. For just a few days, she would be someone else entirely.

❧

The yacht was lovely, a thirty-four-foot ketch, a slice of graceful lines and angles that swept across the water like an agent of the wind, her sail rainbow-colored, billowing with the gusts. Peter did most of the work with the ropes while Claire sat with her face into the breeze, letting the spray from the ocean curl her hair as it flew out behind her.

"When are you going to take it off?" Peter called to her, nodding at the bright blue bikini she wore.

She stared down, then folded her arms across her chest protectively. It had taken all her courage to come out in the open in the skimpy suit, with her hip bones jutting out and her skinny legs dangling beneath the strip of blue cloth. And now he wanted her to jettison even this tiny bit of protection to her dignity? Forget it.

"Everyone else goes topless, at least," he told her, and she knew it was true. They had already passed boats full of women sunbathing sans tops, their breasts lined up like clay pigeons in a shooting gallery. To Claire it all looked rather silly.

"Maybe tomorrow," she lied. "I have to ease into these things."

How odd the world was. One day she was living in a land where women wouldn't go out in public unless they were covered from head to foot in black cloth. The next, she was seeing everything from nipples to pubic hair, flaunted as though there were nothing special about it. Surely there was a happy medium to all this.

Peter looked quite tasty himself, in a small electric-orange men's bikini, with all his tanned muscles showing. She felt like taunting him about getting rid of his suit as well, but she held her tongue, knowing he would probably shimmy right out of it and throw it overboard. And then where would she be?

In the middle of the Aegean with a naked man, that was where. It made her laugh to think of it. Mother, if you could only see me now!

The "holy island" of Delos was ahead. Claire shaded her eyes as they approached the harbor.

"This is a neat place," Peter told her as they prepared to dock. "Lots of old ruins and things. The best stuff was stolen by other countries years ago, and some of it is now in the National Museum in Athens. But there are still lots of painted walls and artifacts to gawk at."

"Shall I take my camera?"

"Absolutely. This is a famous place. Full of ancient gods. Legend has it that this was a floating island until Poseidon used a column of diamonds to anchor it so that Leto would have a place where she could give birth to Artemis and Apollo."

The paths were dry and dusty, no diamonds in sight, but the pervading sense of antiquity made the visit worthwhile. They spent a couple of hours wandering about the ruins, then climbed to the top of Mount Kynthos where they could view the surrounding islands. Tired and hungry, they went back to the boat and pulled out a basket packed with lunch, which Peter had ordered from the hotel restaurant the night before.

The wine was good, the bread hard and the cheese sharp and crumbly.

"Goat cheese," Peter informed her.

"Oh." She smiled and tried to pretend that didn't bother her at all. After all, she wasn't a naive Atlanta girl any longer. She was a world traveler. But her appetite seemed to dwindle after that, and she had more wine.

"Do you believe in God?" she asked Peter a bit

later. Still drinking wine, she was lying on her stomach and trailing her fingers in the water, letting the gentle sway of the boat cast its drowsy spell. "Do you think we're judged for what we do?"

"Ah, now don't start getting religious on me."

"I'm serious."

"Why? Do you think you've done something that ought to be judged?"

"Of course I have." She propped her head up on her hand so she could look at his face. "I've left my husband and gone off with a lover. How much worse could I get?"

Peter's look dismissed her contention out of hand. It was obvious he wasn't one to mull over morals, or feelings of mortality. "Don't go off on a guilt trip. Just relax and enjoy it."

Claire cocked her head and gazed dreamily out at the sunshine sparkling on the water. It would be nice to be like Peter, without guilt, without recriminations. Could she manage it? It was difficult with a background like hers. Guilt was bred into her. There seemed to be no escaping, no matter how she tried. But maybe, just for the space of a week or two . . .

"You know, when I was growing up, music was just about the only thing I was really allowed to enjoy. Everything else was either bad for my teeth or would keep me up too late or . . . might make my father angry."

If she'd only known how much of that don't-bother-your-father-now had been her mother's generalizing from her husband's annoyance with her, assuming it applied to Claire, too. If she'd only run, just once, into her father's study and leapt into his arms and said, "Daddy, I want *you* to read me my story tonight." Would he have smiled? Would he have cradled her closer and whispered jokes into her ear? She was sure he would have. All those wasted years. If only she'd known . . .

"Hey, come on." Peter was beside her, his hand in her hair. "Your father will never be angry again, and I don't care how late you stay up." He smiled at her. "The teeth, though, you've got to take responsibility for them yourself, I'm afraid. I don't want to get involved in that."

Claire laughed and reached up to kiss him. Maybe, if she stayed with him long enough, she could learn to take life at face value, too, the way he did. "Peter, you're so good for me," she sighed.

"We're good for each other," he countered. "Now help me get this leftover lunch packed away again and I'll take you around the island to a secluded cove I know."

The cove turned out to be so secluded that Claire, aided and abetted by the effects of the wine, actually did release the ties on the top of her bikini to do some sunbathing, and felt pretty daring at that. But she still didn't feel comfortable making love in the open, so they went below deck. Still, it was in daylight, with the water all around them and the sunshine streaming in through the open hatch, and she had a warm, loving man in her arms and felt about as close to heaven as she ever expected to get.

They got back late and went straight to the café on the terrace for dinner. A guitarist was playing, and they drank more wine and sang folk songs with the crowd until after midnight. They went to bed and slept in the next morning, so it was almost noon before they were out on the sea again.

This time they sailed to Paros to visit its old church and see the white marble quarries and some of the more recent archeological finds. And this time, Claire stayed away from wine and kept her top on, and they made it home before dark.

"There's a party tonight," Peter told her as they walked back up the hill to the hotel. "Some rich guy, one of those Greek shipping magnates, I think, is throwing it. He's built a replica of the Parthenon up in the hills somewhere. They used it as a movie set, and now he's using it to throw this bash."

"And we're invited?"

"Well—" his grin was jaunty "—we're going. He doesn't know me from Adam, but I know people who are invited. It'll be fun."

Claire wasn't so sure about that. Her proper background rebelled against such rude behavior as crashing parties. But she kept her doubts to herself. She was in Peter's territory now, and she would follow his rules.

"Oh." She stopped in the street. "I don't think I brought anything fancy enough for a party."

"Don't worry. Karen promised to set you up with something. She knows everyone on the island. She'll come up with something great."

Claire hadn't seen Karen and Tony since that first night, and she wondered when Peter had found all this out, but it turned out he was right. When they got to the room, they found Karen had left an entire outfit for Claire at the front desk.

The dress was a dream of white lace with a tight bodice and a full, flowing skirt. Feeling inspired, Claire piled her hair atop her head and used her iron to turn the loose strands into bewitching curls. A bit of makeup and she was more than pleased with what she saw in the mirror. Her cheeks were slightly sunburned, her shoulders tanned, and the white dress set her off dazzlingly. For the first time in a very long time, she felt almost beautiful.

That view was echoed by the long, low whistle Peter made when he saw her. "My God, you could be the Delphic Oracle herself."

She pretended to cast him a jaundiced eye. "She's not the one with all the snakes coming out of her head, is she?"

"Hardly." He looked pretty nifty himself in a white dinner jacket and dark slacks with razor-sharp creases.

It was dark by the time they left for the party. As the cab made its way up the winding road to their destination, the reconstructed Parthenon came into view. With lighting set to highlight the columns, it was a stunning sight that took Claire's breath away.

She didn't know what Peter said to the uniformed man at the entrance, but he ushered them in without comment and soon they were mingling with men in tuxedos and women in designer gowns and extravagant jewelry. Peter whispered the name of a film star, and when Claire looked up, sure enough, it was really her. A few minutes later a shaggy-haired rock-and-roll star walked by. Claire recognized him from one of Katy's posters. But for the most part, the party-goers looked rich, but not famous.

Claire found Karen and thanked her for providing the gown.

"You look truly elegant," Karen said, looking her over with a practiced eye. She herself was in gold lamé, low-cut, tight and strapless. "I thought the historic touch would be just your style." She grinned. "And I knew Peter would go for it."

Claire felt a bit awkward. There was something about the relationship between Karen and Peter that she hadn't got straight yet. Karen was whisked away by the crowd, and when Claire turned, she found Peter coming back toward her with a distinguished-looking, silver-haired gentleman in tow.

"This is Milos Constantine, the director," he told her. "Milos, my friend Claire Montgomery."

Claire was impressed. This man, she knew, had been nominated for at least one Oscar, and was idolized by many in the industry. She held out her hand. Milos took it, his dark eyes glittering as they ran over her.

"You're right," he said charmingly. "She looks perfect. I shall have to cast her in my next period piece." He moved closer, smiling down at her. "Tell me, what are some of your credits?"

"Credits?" For a moment she couldn't think what he meant, and then she realized he was asking for her acting experience. "Oh, I've never acted."

"You see," said Peter, his eyes sparkling wickedly, "she's new, fresh, an innovation. Untried talent."

"Peter!" She turned back to the famous director. "Don't listen to him," she began, but he stopped her, throwing out his arm dramatically and taking her chin in his hand.

"He's quite right, my dear. I can see the talent burning inside you." With his free hand, he pulled a gold case out of his pocket and deftly extracted an embossed card. "Here is where I am staying. Please feel free to come by and see me anytime. We can discuss this further."

Withdrawing his arm, he gave her cheek a patronizing pat and moved on, melting into the crowd. Peter started to laugh.

"Why, the old lecher," he said.

Claire turned on him indignantly. In fact, she found the situation amusing too, but she wasn't sure if she should admit it. So she stuck out her chin. "How do you know he doesn't really want to cast me in something?"

"Yeah, like into his bed." He stopped laughing when he saw the look on her face. "Hey, I'm sure he might want to cast you in a film. Who knows? But that's not all he wants, believe me." He was laughing again. "That was pretty funny. Now let's see if we can find a writer for one of the tabloids to tell it to."

"We won't do any such thing."

"I suppose not," he said with real regret. "It would be fun, though, wouldn't it?"

He looked so disappointed, she had to laugh. "Don't worry," she soothed with a grin. "I'm sure you'll find some other mischief to get into."

"You're right. I usually do." He brightened, put an arm around her shoulders and began to lead her through the crowd. Champagne was flowing like water, sparkling in glasses all around. A magician, hired for the evening, was wandering from group to group, making watches disappear and appear again, changing coins into bills and back again, making handkerchiefs rise from pockets. A mime was twisting balloons into animal shapes. A ballerina was doing impromtu pirouettes. A gymnast performed on a bar high above the crowd. A Punch-and-Judy-style puppet show with adult themes was making people laugh in one corner. In another, a solitary guitarist pretended to be Segovia. Candles seemed to float around the area at will, making soft, intriguing light, creating interesting shadows on faces.

"What a party," Claire whispered to Peter. "It's fabulous."

"There's dancing downstairs."

Karen and Tony had come up behind them and Karen was angling for a partner.

"Mood music, perfect for slow, romantic snuggling." She took Peter's arm and smiled up at him. "Come on, honey. These feet were made for dancin'."

Claire followed on Tony's arm, feeling just a little resentful that Karen had taken Peter away. But it was impossible to be angry with the woman. She was laughing and calling out raucous, amusing greetings to people as they made their way through the crowd. The party-goers parted for them, turning and smiling, and Claire began to smile, too. She had a feeling Karen could turn a root canal into a celebration if she had a mind to.

The music was perfect and the dance floor was crowded. Peter and Karen were swallowed up by the other dancers right away, leaving Claire in Tony's rather stiff arms.

He didn't say anything and neither did she. Turn, step, step, turn, step, step. Tony's head was constantly turning, too, and she realized he was looking for Peter and Karen on the dance floor. Turn, step, step. And his head went back and forth, back and forth, searching the crowd. Poor thing. Obviously he was worried about his girl in Peter's arms.

The silence was getting oppressive. She had to say something. She cleared her throat. "So, Tony, what do you do?"

He looked startled and lost a step. "Do? What do you mean?"

"For a living. What is your business, your profession?"

His gaze moved away from hers and she could almost see the wheels rotating in his head as he tried to think up something to tell her.

"Uh . . . Peter didn't tell you?"

"No."

"Uh . . . I rent the boat out sometimes."

"Oh." Hardly a full-time career. Perhaps it would be better to move on to another topic. "Have you and Karen been together long?"

"Long?" He blinked at her. "Oh. No. You have the wrong idea. Karen and I are business partners. That is all."

Partners in sometimes renting the boat out? How interesting.

"She seems like a . . . really nice person."

His face took on a look of reverence and his feet completely lost the time of the music. "She's . . . she's . . ." He shrugged with European expressiveness. "She's the reincarnation of Aphrodite," he said solemnly. "Where she steps, flowers grow. When she passes, birds begin to sing."

Claire forced back the urge to grin, but she couldn't resist muttering softly, "Disney, circa 1935."

"What?"

"Nothing. Karen is a wonderful woman."

"I'm in love with her."

"I can tell."

"Can you?" He looked stricken. "Don't say anything to her. She doesn't know."

Claire could have answered, "You want to bet?" but Peter and Karen were back and Peter was ready to change partners, a move Claire seconded on the spot.

"Come dance with me," Peter coaxed, sliding an arm around her.

This time there was no need for conversation. The music seemed to wrap around them as they swayed. Peter's body was hard and smooth and vital, and she pressed against him, drawing in his vitality. His breath was warm on her neck, tickling her ear, and the brush of his cheek was slightly rough, tantalizing her senses. Looking up, she could see the stars, bright silver sparks in the deep purple sky. The air was as soft as the darkness, warm as the music, and filled with the rise and fall of murmuring voices. A slight breeze ruffled her hair, bringing again the scent of lemon blossoms. It was almost too perfect. If she closed her eyes, she could imagine herself in some ancient Greek paradise, living with the gods.

"Don't pinch me," she whispered to Peter as they danced. "I don't want to wake up."

"I won't pinch you," he said, his voice a low growl near her ear. "But I will kiss you all over. And that is a promise."

They danced and drank champagne and laughed and met people—and didn't see Tony and Karen again that evening. But late that night, as they lay side by side in the tiny cabin on the boat, drifting off to sleep in the happy afterglow of the evening, she prodded Peter with questions.

"How long have you known Tony and Karen?"

"Hmm?" Peter stretched. "Forever. Almost."

"What does he do?"

Peter seemed to become more alert. "Do?"

"Do. As in, what line of work."

"Tony is, well, Tony is kind of a . . ."

"Con man?" Claire supplied, running on instinct but sure, once she'd actually said the words, that she'd guessed right.

Peter laughed softly, taking her in his arms. "I guess you could call it that. He's had his share of trouble. But he's okay. And Karen is a doll."

"Oh, yes. I can see that."

And the funny thing was, she could. She wasn't jealous of Karen, even though she could see how attractive she was to men. Karen wasn't bitchy and she wasn't mean. In fact, she was all too open and accepting.

Claire lay very still in Peter's arms, listening to the water lap against the boat, and wondered at herself. It was a lovely existence she had here, dancing through each day, and never stopping to let herself think things through. Most of life was so full of planning and decision making. Still, one of her reasons for coming had been to give herself time to sort things out. And if she never thought about what she'd done, what lay ahead, how could she do that?

Much as she tried, she couldn't completely forget Katy and Sam in England, or the mess she'd left behind in Saudi. What was Howard doing right now? And what would she herself have been doing if she hadn't come to Greece?

Here in the quiet, her mind threatened to take over again, to begin thinking, worrying. But she wasn't going to let it. Sorting things out was one thing; letting it take over her existence was another.

The next day, Karen and Tony came sailing with them, guaranteeing that Claire would remain fully clothed once again. Even the bikini stayed hidden, covered with a light blouse, as she sat on the sea-sprayed deck.

"I got too much sun yesterday," she told the others. "I don't want to get sunburned and have to spend hours moaning in my room."

Tony teased her and Karen tried giving advice on suntanning, but Claire wouldn't budge.

"I will not go around half-naked in front of other people," she explained to Peter when they were alone.

"Tony and Karen? Oh, come on. They're friends. And you might as well know, Karen takes going nude as a matter of course."

She did, did she? Great. That meant Claire was going to feel like someone's maiden aunt.

Unless she could manage to . . . No. It was no use. She'd come to Greece to meet Peter so that she could be free. She'd wanted to sluff off the old, narrow way of thinking and open herself to a new life. But she wasn't sure yet how far she could go. Or how much of this new life was preferable to the old. Going nude in front of others was too far for her as yet.

The four of them got along fine, though, talking and joking as they skimmed across the water. A couple of times Claire heard some reference to "the project," but each time, the person who had said the words quickly changed the subject after a quick glance at Claire. She was beginning to feel paranoid. Just what was it they didn't want her to know?

They found a lovely sand beach and Karen immediately stripped off her tiny bikini.

"Look at this, y'all," she cried, patting her rounded belly, displaying everything she had without a trace of self-consciousness. "I'm getting fat!"

Claire watched her enviously. "Fat" had never looked better on anyone she'd ever seen. Karen's breasts were tanned a golden brown. They stood out with a lovely arrogance, full and round. Her bottom was firm and brown, her waist neatly slender, her belly a comfortable protrusion under a tiny navel. Her brown thighs were covered with golden hair, natural and lovely. Claire couldn't imagine any man being able to resist a body like this. She looked at Peter, expecting to see admiration for Karen shining in his eyes, maybe even the same dopey awe and lust she could see in Tony's face.

But no. Peter wasn't looking at Karen at all. He was looking at her, his gaze warm and appreciative, and her jaw nearly dropped. He couldn't possibly prefer her, could he?

"Last one in is a rotten egg!" Karen called, leaping over the side of the boat with a splash.

Tony followed quickly, still in his stretchy briefs, but Peter moved to Claire and cupped her face with his hands.

"Would you like to swim?" he asked.

At that moment, she would have done anything he asked. Her heart was soaring.

"I'd love to," she replied, undoing her cover-up. She stopped short of removing her swimsuit, but so did he, and they dove together and played like a pair of children in the crystal-blue water, splashing each other, making raids on Karen and Tony, and laughing all the while.

They finally started back for the boat, and Tony was just climbing the ladder when Karen called to him from where she was floating in the water. "Hey, you! The Italian one. What do you say we go up on shore and roll around in the grass a little?"

Tony was inarticulate with delight, but he dove back into the water, and the two of them paddled toward shore. Claire and Peter climbed onto the deck to dry in the sunshine, talking softly. They were alone in the little harbor, and the feeling of being deliciously isolated was making them want to touch, to hold, to feel.

Peter kissed her and Claire sighed, leaning back in his arms and shading her eyes to look for the other couple on shore. "Where did they go?" she asked.

Peter looked toward the shore and grinned. "Up there, in the brush along that ledge."

Claire looked more closely and gasped. There was Tony, disappearing into the greenery, but not before Claire saw a flash of white bare buttocks.

"Look at them." Peter chortled. "Both as naked as jaybirds. Ouch. Think of the thorns from those bushes."

"Peter!"

He pulled her closer. "How about you and me?" he murmured, kissing her neck. "We could do that, too. Do you want to?"

She always wanted to lately. She'd never really thought of herself as such a sexual being before. But this wasn't the kind of sex she'd always known. This wasn't a duty thing, another chore in a long line of daily activities. This was fun.

They went below deck and made love on the tiny bed, laughing all the while about the contrast between their setting and the scratchy surface Karen and Tony were enduring. When the other two returned, Peter joined them in the water again, while Claire stayed on board and read a paperback she'd brought along. After a time, the men went for a hike around the island while Karen kept Claire company. She rummaged through supplies and found a package of crackers, which she devoured cheerfully, then turned to Claire for conversation.

"I'm real glad you're with us this year, Claire. We're going to have a lot of fun together, I can tell."

Claire looked up, torn between her book and basic good manners. At least Karen had put her swimsuit back on. But she still looked like the Greek goddess Tony saw her as. Claire was getting more confident of her own attractiveness, but having Karen around was still daunting.

Smiling, she asked, "Do you ever not have fun, Karen?"

The blonde threw her a significant look. "Oh, I've had my ups and downs, honey."

Claire put her book away, ready to get to know this woman better. "What brought you to Greece?" she asked, genuinely curious.

"Ambition." Karen grinned and popped another cracker in her mouth. "When I first came, I was looking for one of those millionaire types. You know, the kind you read about in the society pages, with the big yachts and lots of change to throw around. I was looking for my pot of gold." She sighed and offered the box of crackers to Claire. "I had some near misses. But I learned a thing or two, I'll tell you—the most important being the secret of life for all women."

"And what was that?"

"Here it is, honey, in a nutshell. You can't count on some man to make your life wonderful. You gotta do it for yourself."

"Hear, hear." Claire took a cracker and munched on it. "We all have to come to that conclusion at some point, don't we?" She hesitated, then plowed on. "And how did you and Peter . . . When did you meet?"

"Oh, years and years ago. He comes out whenever he can to go sailing, usually when he's between jobs. And we've done little things for each other over the years. He gave me some money once when I was really broke. And one time when I was in a relationship that was going nowhere fast—meaning the guy was beating me—he came in and gave him a taste of his own medicine and helped me get out of there. He's been just about my best friend ever since I came to this part of the world."

Her gaze sharpened as it met Claire's. "But that's not what you really want to know, is it?" Karen grinned. "You want to know just how deep the relationship between me and Peter goes, don't you? Right?"

Claire smiled at her frankness. "Actually, you hit the nail on the head," she admitted.

Karen waved a hand airily. "Peter and I are real good friends. We've been lovers in the past, but that's over."

Claire's heart gave a lurch, but she managed a casual smile. After all, Karen had been here long before she'd arrived, and she would be here after Claire was gone. What right did she have to feel jealous? "I thought so."

"Peter and I had our time last summer. Boy, did we have fun. But we weren't ever serious or anything like that. I mean, does that boy look like millionaire material to you?"

They laughed.

"Are you still holding out for a wealthy man?" Claire asked.

Karen squinted into the sun, not answering right away. "I'm still looking for that pot of gold," she said softly.

"What about Tony?"

"Tony?" She swung around and stared at Claire. "What about him?"

"He's crazy about you."

"You think so?" Karen smiled, then laughed. "Like I said, I've learned I've got to stand on my own two feet now. Maybe *I'll* have to become the millionaire myself. Then I can pick and choose the man of my dreams for other qualities."

Claire thought of the "project" they all had been so secretive about. "Do you have a plan?" she prodded.

Karen nodded slowly. "Claire, I grew up in a sharecroppers' shanty. I worked four hours a day before I left for school and eight more hours once I got home. I know about focusing on what you want and going for it. I'm not one to whine about Lady Luck passing me by. I'm going to go out and catch that sucker, tackle her around the knees if I have to." She grinned and made her hand into a gun, snapping off a shot at the horizon. "Lady Luck, you are in my sights. You're mine, honey!"

Claire was convinced that there was something to this "project," and that it was pretty likely the factor that brought these three people together now. She wondered why Peter hadn't told her about it. It obviously had nothing to do with her, but still, it would be nice to be included in the secret. Maybe she would come right out and ask him about it. Maybe tonight.

But she didn't get a chance. When they got back to the hotel, Karen and Tony didn't disappear, and so they were still a foursome, going from tavern to tavern, enjoying the music, the dancing, the wine, the other people they met.

Claire had a great time. She felt like a child going from one birthday party to another. She didn't listen to the little nagging voice at the back of her head telling her it couldn't last. She knew that. She just didn't want to be reminded right now.

That night they slept on the boat again, and Claire waited until morning to bring up the subject of the project.

They lay side by side in streaks of sunlight, and she turned to trail a finger through the hair on his chest.

"Tell me about the project," she whispered. "What are you and Tony and Karen cooking up?"

She could see his eyes glittering through the thick veil of his dark eyelashes, and she knew he was awake, but he didn't move.

"Hey, you." She tickled him along his sides, but though she could see the corners of his mouth twitch the tiniest bit, he still pretended to be asleep.

"You're not going to get away with this," she murmured, kissing his bare skin. "I want to know."

And then she tickled him in a much more private place and got an instant response.

"Hey!" he cried out as he jerked back and leapt up to pin her beneath his beautiful body. "Want to play rough, do you?"

She laughed up at him but she wouldn't let the subject go. "Tell me," she demanded.

He frowned in seeming confusion. "Wait a minute," he said. "I've got you pinned. Why are you the one making demands?"

"Because morally, I'm the one with the upper hand," she announced against all logic. "So tell me. What is this project?"

He gave her a long, slow kiss and whispered, "You promise not to laugh?"

She grinned impudently. "No."

He sighed and rolled off her. "Okay, okay. Here it is. But remember, it's a big secret. We're diving for buried treasure."

She didn't laugh. But she did smile. "Buried treasure? You mean at sea?"

He nodded, watching her eyes. "There's a fortune down there," he told her earnestly. "We're going to find it."

She lay back and licked her lips. "But, Peter, if there's a fortune at the bottom of the sea, why aren't other people going after it? How do you know about it?"

"We've got a map."

"Right. What cereal was it in?"

He kissed her soundly. "I told you not to laugh."

"Could I at least chuckle?"

"No." He kissed her again. "Now you see why I didn't want to tell you."

"Oh, Peter." She dug her fingers into his hair and tugged. "You can tell me anything. I'm not laughing. I think it's exciting and romantic. Go for your buried treasure. I hope you find it."

❧

Buried treasure was something different to everyone who found it, she told herself the next day. She'd found hers when Peter had tossed a ball and stepped into her life. And now she was spending it like a drunken sailor.

She left Peter puttering about with the sails and went into town, strolling slowly through the streets, enjoying the noise, the happy commotion. A young man said something to her in a language she didn't recognize, and she smiled at him, tossed back her hair and walked on. He called after her and she laughed, but kept walking. Her stride was long and languorous. She felt free, a little wild, and very much alive.

Stopping in at the hotel, she went up to the room to get some things from her bags. She knelt down to rummage through the clothes and pulled out a pair of shorts and two tank tops before standing again.

Turning, she gasped, startled. There was a strange woman in the room.

But no. It wasn't a stranger at all. It was her own reflection in the mirror against the far wall.

She laughed, then slowly walked toward the

mirror. That was certainly her, but it was a different version than any she'd ever seen before. Twisting her body this way and that, she surveyed every part of herself. Her hair was full and long, her sundress soft and full around her knees, her feet in delicate sandals. She touched her face, her breasts, her hips and thighs. She looked fuller, somehow, less angular. Her skin had a golden tan, her shoulders were straight and relaxed. In fact, if she did say so herself, she looked darn good.

She thought of the night she'd sat and stared at herself in the mirror in the bedroom she'd shared with Howard. She looked ten years younger now. And a hundred percent happier.

"Thanks to Peter," she said aloud. And she meant it. But at the same time, she knew there was a lot more to it. Peter had been a catalyst of sorts. But most of the change had come from within her. As Karen said, you had to stand on your own two feet.

She threw an extravagant wink at the image in the mirror, gathered up the clothes and left the room, deciding to go down and sit by the water before she went back to find Peter. There was so much of Greece to enjoy. She didn't want to miss a thing.

That afternoon, she and Peter went out in the ketch alone, sailing from one island to another, until they anchored off the south end of a larger island, a series of three hills, lightly covered with small trees and brush, and dotted here and there with small white houses. Flocks of sheep and goats could be seen, their plaintive bleats drifting across the water as they made their way to and fro.

"Here it is," Peter said, nodding toward the sea. "This is it."

"The site of the sunken treasure?" She leaned out over the side and stared hard into the clear water. "Are you sure?"

He threw his arms wide. "This is where it all happened. In 546 B.C., when Croesus was deposed by the Persians, his son gathered all the gold the good old king had left, put it in a boat manned by a huge crew of slaves, and came crashing through here, looking for an island where he could hide."

Claire looked out at the sea, at the islands that hovered all around, at the blue sky, and in spite of everything, she could see it just as Peter was describing it.

"He never made that safe harbor," Peter continued. "A storm came up and overturned his boat. He went down, and the gold went with him."

She could accept the story, though she would have liked to see some proof that it was something more than myth. "How do you know this is the place?" she asked.

"We have the charts. They tell everything."

"Uh-huh. And where did you get the charts?"

"Karen got them from some old rich guy in Athens."

"What? He just handed them to her as an afterthought? 'I had a real nice evening, Karen. Oh, by the way, would you like these charts? You can use them to go out and find yourself a little sunken treasure.' "

Peter laughed softly. "I don't know the details, and I've never asked. I do know she was contemplating marrying this guy at one point, but she backed out at the last minute. How she ended up with the charts is anybody's guess. But she's sure they're authentic."

"I see." Her smile was loving but skeptical. "If everything on that boat went down to a watery grave, how did the charts survive?"

He stared at her, eyes narrowing. "You don't believe in the charts?" he asked, as though she'd said she had her doubts about the importance of oxygen to the human system.

"I believe, I believe." She touched his cheek with the palm of her hand. "Tell me. I just want to know."

He gave her a mock-sulky look, but went on, "They floated away and were washed up on a nearby shore, I guess."

"Two and a half centuries ago. They must have made those old documents out of pretty sturdy stuff. What is it? Parchment? Papyrus? Vellum?"

He caught her up in his arms and growled, nose to nose. "Okay, skeptic, no laughing. Remember?"

"I'm not laughing. I'm just . . . concerned."

But it wasn't really any of her business, and therefore nothing to be concerned about, was it? She pushed away her natural caution and asked, "Who's going to do the diving?"

"All three of us are certified. We'll do it ourselves." He held her closer. "We've been talking about this for three years now. And since I'm not working on the rigs anymore, we can go ahead and put our plans into operation."

Releasing her, he looked out to where he believed the treasure was waiting. She watched, touched by the eagerness she saw in his face. She knew in a flash that it wasn't the money or the jewels that drove him. It was the adventure.

"And once you find the treasure," she said softly, "what next?"

He flashed her a quick smile. "I'll find some new treasure to go after," he said, confirming her thoughts.

She stood watching him, fingering the golden heart she wore at her throat all the time now, and she thought of the woman who had given it to her, the woman who stayed at home with a shotgun across her lap to protect the family home, and traditions, values, togetherness. And then she thought of Karen tackling Lady Luck at the knees.

Which way did she herself want to go? It was her choice.

Reaching behind her back, she unhooked the top of her bikini and let it fall to the deck of the boat, leaving her naked except for the tiny strip of bright blue at her hips. The sea breeze tightened her nipples and ruffled her hair. She looked up at Peter, her chin high.

"Well?" she said, hardly sure what she was asking.

His eyes were laughing. "What do you want, a medal for bravery?"

"Not right now," she retorted. "There's nowhere to pin it."

A sultry smoke filled his eyes and he reached out and touched her, making her shiver with delight. "Would you settle for some other award?" he asked.

She nodded. "You bet," she said softly, and then she melted into his arms, dropping with him to the smooth surface of the deck. . . .

Now that Claire was in on the secret, the others talked openly in front of her, and that evening was spent in a smoky café, leaning over a table, talking earnestly about weight belts and ocean currents and oxygen tanks. Their excitement almost made Claire want to go take lessons in scuba diving. Almost, but not quite.

It all sounded like such fun. Not that she really believed in the treasure for a moment. But that sort of doubt was for the real world. She was living in a fantasy here, and hidden treasures fit right in.

The next few days skimmed by without anything marring their tranquility. Karen and Tony were around in the evenings, but during the day Claire and Peter were on the water. For Claire, time had an unreal, floating quality to it, as though she were waiting for something, some resolution, something to happen. Peter taught her the fundamentals of sailing and she was getting a beautiful tan. He petted and stroked her until she purred most of the day, and she let him, luxuriating in the unusual attention and care. But she knew time was running short. She couldn't stay forever.

One day he set their itinerary to the south, rather than to the north or east, as they usually went. A long, thrilling sail took them to a lonely island with a strange-looking structure at the top of a steep hill. From the bay, they could see a series of hairpin turns, which wound their way up to the ruin. A cluster of white columns struck a jagged pose against the blue sky. There were no houses, no signs of human habitation, other than the relic at the top of the hill.

"What is it?" Claire asked, shading her eyes against the sun as she gazed at it.

"A shrine," Peter answered, looking up from tying the ketch to the dock. "A secular shrine. I'll take you up there soon. But first—" He opened a bottle of wine and filled two glasses "—a toast. To you, my beautiful Claire, to the woman you have always been, and to the woman you have become in these last few days here in Greece."

She laughed and accepted the toast. "And to you," she added, holding her glass high so that the sunlight sparkled in the golden liquid. "To the joy of knowing you, Peter Arnold. It's been an education."

They drank down their wine and he kissed her lingeringly.

"Do you remember that first time we met?" he asked her, his voice husky. "I thought you were made of ice."

"Thanks a lot."

His fingers spread across the open back of her sundress. "The minute I saw you, I knew I could melt that reserve if you'd only give me half a chance."

"You melted it all right," she murmured, laughing softly. "There's not much more than a puddle left."

He kissed her, pressing her close, and then a sound drew his attention and he looked up. Other boats were arriving in the bay.

"The tourists are coming," he said, grinning down at her. "Time for us to go." He held her hand to his heart. "Are you game?"

She had no idea what he was talking about, but she trusted him so completely at this point that she merely nodded and smiled back. "Of course I'm game. Lead on, MacDuff."

"Come on."

Taking her by the hand, he led her off the boat, down the dock and toward the path to the relic at the top of the hill.

"Hurry," he urged, looking back at where the others were beginning to disembark from their boats.

"Do we have to run?" Claire puffed, glad she'd worn low-heeled sandals.

"Yes," Peter answered. "Come on. Hurry. Faster."

They raced up the path. Claire's heart was beating wildly in her chest. From the urgency in

Peter's voice, she almost felt as though they were being chased.

Higher and higher, back and forth on the hair- pin turns, they went as fast as they could, until they finally reached the top and entered the small, col- umned building, where they collapsed against the ravaged walls.

To Claire's surprise, Peter reached for her.

"Wait until I catch my breath," she gasped.

"Can't wait," he told her, his hands moving down her body as he began dropping kisses on the bare skin of her shoulders. "We have to do it quick. Before they get here."

"Do it?" Claire jerked her head back in shock. "You mean . . . ?"

He grinned down at her. "Yes. It's a tradition. This is supposedly the house where Aphrodite first made love to Adonis. To celebrate that, visitors have to make love themselves. The challenge is to beat the others up here and do it before they arrive at the door."

Claire's mind was spinning and she could hardly think straight. "You're kidding."

Instead of answering, he hung out the open window space and looked down at the path. "Hurry," he urged again. "The first group is half- way up and moving fast. We can just make it if we . . ."

Claire was laughing and at the same time shiv- ering from the adrenaline coursing through her veins. She quickly looked about the small space. "There's no place to lie down!"

"Who needs to lie down?"

He was holding her again, his hard body pressing her back against the wall, his eyes darkening with growing excitement. "Come on, Claire," he urged softly. "Come on. We can do it."

This was crazy. This was utterly insane. There were people coming, for God's sake! But Claire found herself responding to Peter with a surging speed that startled her.

"Come on, come on," he murmured, slipping up the skirt of her sundress as he pressed her back against the wall.

She blocked out everything else and wrapped her legs around him and then she was saying, "Now, Peter. Oh, now, now!" and they were doing it and she was crying out and he was whispering something in her hair, and then they were pulling away and straightening their clothes and they could hear the clatter of footsteps right outside the door. They looked at each other and began to laugh.

Claire knew her face was beet red and she was sure every one of the Danish tourists who came in and stared at the two of them knew exactly what they had been doing. She grabbed Peter's arm and forced him to go outside with her.

"I can't believe we did that," she kept repeating, and he laughed and hugged her.

"Come on," he said at last. "I'll race you back down. We need a swim."

The water felt cool on her flushed skin. She still couldn't believe it. What had happened to Claire Duvall Montgomery? Where had she gone?

CHAPTER

❧

16

Two days later Claire and Peter were having breakfast on the hotel terrace. The day was lovely, with the white sails in the blue water, the sun riding high in a cloudless sky. But Claire sensed a subtle change. Some of the glow had worn thin for her. She was beginning to feel as though it might be time to wind this vacation down.

"I think I'll stay here today," she told Peter.

He looked up, his eyes suddenly wary. "Are you getting bored with me already?" His words were light, but she detected a deeper thread.

She smiled and reached out to cover his hand with her own. "I just need some time to myself. I want to rest, relax, read, think, maybe do a little shopping."

"Okay," he said. "I'm going to go out with Karen and Tony. We're going to make a pass near the site for the—" his voice lowered and he glanced around to make sure they weren't being overheard "—the treasure," he finished dramatically.

She laughed. "I wish you luck with your treasure, Peter." She sobered, thinking of something. "But I do hope you don't sink all your money into the search. After all, it's such a long shot."

"Long shot?" He looked at her quizzically. "Of course it's a long shot. It wouldn't be any fun if it wasn't. It's a gamble. Claire, life is a gamble. That's what makes our blood flow."

A gamble. Well, maybe she simply wasn't ready to throw her dice quite that far.

"You all have a good time," she said dryly.

Peter looked at her searchingly. Reaching out, he took her hand in his, lacing fingers. "Are you sure you'll be all right here all by yourself?"

She nodded, loving his concern. "I'll be fine."

His fingers tightened. "You'll be here when I get back?"

That startled her just a bit. Did he really think there was a chance she would sneak away the moment his back was turned? What kind of women was he used to?

"Of course. I'll wait right here on this terrace."

She watched as the three went off together, ready to search for buried treasure, and she breathed a sigh of relief.

A whole day to herself.

She took a long walk into the hills, following a white bird that flew from one green area to another, searching for a waterfall. And when she finally found the stream, she sat beside it and took off her shoes so that she could dangle her feet in the icy water.

She tried to think, which was one thing she hadn't done much of lately. But her mind was still too full of such a jumble of things that she couldn't seem to pull her thoughts together in a coherent fashion and figure out where she was going.

After a while she put her shoes back on and returned to town to browse through the shops. She looked over some leather belts, tried to decide if pounded brass earrings got lost against her hair, then stopped for lunch in a small outdoor café that served delicious thin sandwiches.

A couple at another table caught her attention. The man was handsome, with steel-gray hair and a tanned face. The woman was beautiful, elegant, her hair tied back with a fashionable scarf, her dress chic but appropriate for her mature age. They were an attractive couple and seemed well-matched, their heads together as they chatted over coffees. She felt a low, twisting pang of jealousy. That was the way she and Howard should have ended up. What she saw at that table was very close to the fantasy she'd had of how life would be when the girls were grown and gone—she and Howard, traveling, sharing, enjoying the world together. She realized now it was a fantasy based on nothing at all. But the knowledge that the dream would never be realized didn't make it hurt any less.

The couple rose and Claire saw that they would have to pass by her table to the exit. She watched them coming her way, taking pleasure in the perfection of the picture they made. As they came close, she couldn't help but overhear a couple of phrases.

He was pulling a pipe out of his pocket and muttering, ". . . because they can't tolerate stupid idiot women like . . ." while his companion walked very firmly, her chin high, and snarled back, ". . . if you had only acted like a man instead of the sniveling little coward . . ."

They were gone and Claire sat very still, her eyes wide, her mouth clamped shut. The perfect picture had cracked. Appearances were, after all, deceiving. They had looked so good, and at the same time, the words coming out of their mouths were hateful, spiteful. Maybe there wasn't any hope. Maybe there weren't any good marriages left in the world. Maybe there never had been any.

She paid for her meal and went down to the beach, walking past the picnickers to the rocks, then on to the next beach, taking off her shoes and making her way through the warm white sand. She watched a volleyball game in progress for a few minutes, tempted to join in. But the players were all so young, boys and girls in the midst of doing as much flirting as they were playing volleyball, that she decided against intruding.

Turning inland again, she found a bench and sat with her legs drawn up to her chest, her arms around her knees. She could still see the ocean, and she stared out at it, mesmerized by the dazzling reflections that danced on every wave. It was so lovely here. It had been a wonderful vacation.

But had it done her any good? She was here

to renew herself, to forget, to wipe the slate clean, to start again. To a large extent, that had been accomplished.

But she was also here to get a handle on her problems. That hadn't happened. And had she just created new ones by coming? "Claire and Peter." Was that a problem? What was she doing here with him? Did she really know?

Fun. That was what it had come down to. Peter had taught her how to have fun.

Peter did not want to marry her. Peter didn't even want her to stay forever, no matter what he might say. And she'd never been under any illusions about loving him.

She was "in love" with him, but not in that forever way. No, "Claire and Peter" was not going to be a problem.

She shivered and drew her knees up even closer.

"Kyri-eerie," said a young voice nearby, and she jumped, startled, and looked down to see a very small child staring up at her. "Hello," Claire said, and then she couldn't help but smile.

The little girl appeared to be about two. Her head was covered with silky brown curls, and her beautiful face was smeared with chocolate that hadn't quite made it into her rosy little mouth. She wore a white sunsuit and her chubby legs were slightly bowed beneath her pudgy baby weight.

"Eerie . . . eerie," the child chanted, thrusting her little arm out and pointing at Claire. "Mama."

Claire looked around, expecting to see the

child's mother nearby. But all that met her gaze were a couple walking by arm in arm, and a trio of sailors, jostling one another and laughing as they went. "Where is your mama, sweetheart?" Claire asked with a frown. "I don't see her."

"Mama." Fat tears popped out into her huge dark eyes. Her fist went to her face and a sob emerged. "Mama."

"Now then, don't cry. We'll find your mama." Claire stood and looked quickly around, her hand shading her eyes from the late-afternoon sun. There was no one in sight who was in any way a candidate for parenthood of this child. She felt little arms coming around her leg, and when she looked down, she found the child clinging to her, sobbing softly. "Oh, baby . . ." Reaching down, she lifted the little girl into her arms and rocked her, holding her tightly, trying to convey security.

For some silly reason, tears were burning her own eyes. Empathy was unavoidable. She'd been lost before. And she'd lost her own children in crowds, at the beach. Lord, what the mother of this one must be going through!

"Which way, sweetheart?" she whispered to the sobbing child in her arms. "Which way shall we go to look for Mama?"

But the girl only clung more tightly, her eyes squeezed shut as if to blot out the reality of her situation.

Claire started walking quickly. The child had on clothing that looked appropriate for the beach, so it made sense to head in that direction. Surely the parents couldn't be far away.

She passed an open-air café, slowing so that the occupants would have a chance to notice a woman carrying their missing child in her arms. But no one said a word, so she hurried on, her feet slipping on the cobblestones as she made her way toward the sandy shore.

The little girl was heavy, and yet she felt so right in Claire's arms. Holding her this way brought back the days when Sam and Katy were young. How precious they had been. How precious they were now.

The yellow and pink umbrellas of the beach were in sight. And so was a young woman, running toward them, her hair flying out behind her.

"Marie?" she shrieked as she came near. Words flew from her, Greek words that Claire didn't know, but understood anyway. What mother hasn't felt that horrible, pit-of-the-stomach terror when a child was missing in a public place? She didn't have to ask if Marie was the child she held.

The curly head rose. "Mama?"

Claire smiled and held out Marie, and the mother grabbed her, clutching her child to her heart, feeling her all over just to be sure she was in one piece, as she chattered on, tears of relief and joy flowing down her cheeks.

Claire started to back away, but suddenly there were a father and grandparents and sisters and brothers who all wanted to shake her hand and invite her, in their minimal English and lots of Greek, to come and join their picnic. She found herself being carried along like flotsam in a strong tide, and then she was sitting beneath one of those gaily colored umbrellas and food was being thrust into her hand and now she was being patted on the back and given teary hugs, and she almost felt like the heroine they obviously thought her.

She stayed with the family for over an hour, eating and nodding and smiling and hardly understanding a word that was said, but understanding very well the love and closeness. It was a family that seemed to work. It was a family where everyone seemed to care, from the oldest grandparent to little Marie. So it was possible, was it? Claire felt as though she was the one who should be grateful.

She left feeling restored and hurried back to get a table on the terrace and wait for Peter's return. It wasn't long before she saw him coming up the hill from the marina. He came to the table and held out a fistful of wildflowers.

"For me?" They were beautiful, all lavenders and yellows, with tiny white flowers among the others like a sprinkling of snowflakes. She took them and looked up into his eyes.

"Claire," he said earnestly, "I know you're going to leave soon. I want you to know I wish you would stay."

"Peter." Reaching up, she touched his face. What could she say?

But he didn't seem to need any more answer than that. He took a chair happily and began to tell her about the events of the day, and she watched him, hardly listening to his words, but feeling an overwhelming affection. He was really very dear to her. She couldn't have asked for a better friend these past two weeks.

Still, the outside world was beginning to tug at her. The episode with Marie had made her think of her own daughters, and suddenly she was anxious to talk to them.

It was the next morning before she got the chance to call the girls in England. She rose early, with Peter still asleep, dressed quickly and went into the town to find a telephone. She'd been meaning to call the girls ever since she'd arrived. Now she felt as though she had to talk to them immediately.

Luckily she caught them between classes and was able to talk to them both. Samantha sounded very cool and grown-up. She was enjoying her classes, she had made many new friends, and oh, by the way, was it all right if she went home with her new friend, Melissa, for the weekend? Melissa's father was an American importer and they had a country estate with horses and hunting. It all sounded very Victorian and Claire gave permission readily enough, but there was a lump in her throat at the ever-widening distance between her and her older daughter.

Katy was a different story. Katy was upset.

"Mommy, they don't have Thanksgiving here."

"They don't?" Claire thought quickly and realized that was true. "But I'm sure they have other holidays of their own that—"

"I don't care about those holidays." Katy's voice was teary. "I want Thanksgiving."

Claire could hear Samantha's voice in the background, saying, "Oh, who cares about old Thanksgiving? You're just being a baby."

"Mommy." Katy was sobbing now, and Claire's heart was breaking. "I want Thanksgiving. Could you talk to them? Could you make them have it?"

"It's still over a month away, darling. We'll think of something. Maybe I'll come to England and we'll celebrate it together."

"Really?" The sobs subsided. "Really, Mommy?"

"Yes, darling. Of course I'll come." She hadn't planned to see them again until Christmas, but suddenly she knew nothing would keep her away from her babies in the end of November. "Put Sam back on, will you?"

"Samantha," Claire began when her older daughter was back on the line, "I want you to be more supportive. Katy is so young. She needs you."

"She's being ridiculous, Mother. She cries every day."

Claire's heart twisted. "Then you must comfort her every day until she gets used to the place."

"I don't have time for that. I have so much work—"

"Samantha Montgomery. You listen to me. Either you take the time to be nice to your sister, or you can forget about things like weekends in the country. Is that clear?''

There was a moment of silence on the other end of the line. When Sam spoke again, she sounded suitably demur. "All right, Mother. I'll try."

Claire softened. "Thank you, darling. Just keep in mind how young she is. She doesn't have me there. All she has is you."

"Yeah?" Samantha came back, her voice brittle as spring ice. "And who do I have?"

❧

The floating feeling had ended. It was time to come to some decision, make some plan. Claire wasn't sure where her life was going, but it was time to get back on the road to the future. No more floating for her.

Peter, Karen and Tony were getting more and more excited about the treasure. They had hired a couple of divers and were planning to go into Athens to buy provisions and machinery that would be needed for the search.

"How long will it take?" Claire had asked at one point. "What do you foresee?"

Peter had shrugged. "It could take weeks, or years. We'll search until we find it."

"Or until your money runs out," she said softly.

They spent hours hovering over a table on the terrace, sipping thick black coffee and going over maps and equipment lists. She couldn't keep her mind on their plans any longer. Their lives and hers were about to diverge.

Suddenly it was all so very clear. Her heart felt light again. She could see her future like a vision on the horizon. She was anxious to get going, get started on the rest of her life.

It was going to be difficult leaving Peter. He'd been wonderful to her. He'd nurtured her through a rough period of her life. She owed him a lot.

She went to the hotel and made her travel arrangements, and then went to find Peter. He was doing maintenance work on the boat, painting the wood along the railing. She stopped behind him and tried to think of how to tell him.

He turned and looked at her, and he read it all in her eyes. Slowly, he shook his head. "Do you have to go?"

She tried to smile. "Yes."

He put down the brush and rose to his feet, wiping his hands on a rag. "I wish you would stay. You know you're welcome to stay as long as you want."

"I know that, Peter. It's been wonderful. But I really have to get back to the real world." She met his gaze and suddenly there were tears in her eyes. He took a step forward and she fell into his arms. "Oh Peter. I can't thank you enough for what you've done for me."

"It's been a two-way street." He kissed her soundly through her tears. "I'm going to miss you, Claire." His grin was crooked. "I tell you what.

When we find that treasure, I'm going to come looking for you. I can't think of anyone else I'd rather celebrate with."

"Do that. I'll be waiting."

She flew out of Athens the next day with a sense of relief. She had been so glad to get out of the desert, and now she was so glad to be going back, not because of any intrinsic appeal of the area, but because it represented the next step, a rung in the ladder she was going to have to climb to get on with her life.

It was late afternoon when she landed. She hadn't let anyone know she was coming back, so there was no one to meet her. She called home, then when there was no answer, tried Howard at the office.

Gregory answered. "Claire, dear, so good to have you back. Howard . . . isn't in."

"He is in town?"

"Oh, yes. But he isn't in the office right now."

She could tell by his tone that Howard was off

somewhere with his secretary. Despite everything, she began to fume.

"Shall I try to find him for you?" Gregory's oily voice did nothing to improve her mood.

"Never mind that. Please send someone out to the airport to take me home."

"Of course. I'll send one of the men out momentarily."

The young man Gregory sent was someone she'd never seen before. He was extremely handsome and she couldn't help but think Gregory had sent him with an ulterior motive—as if to tempt her with another one. But perhaps she was being paranoid.

Just to be sure, she treated him with chilly courtesy. Refusing his offer to help with her things, she had him drop her at the house and she carried in her own luggage. She could tell immediately that there was someone there.

"Howard?" she called, going on into the living room.

There was no answer, but she could hear water running in the upstairs bathroom. He was taking a shower. She dropped the bags with a sigh and put down her purse. And then her gaze fell on the dining-room table.

Two yellow mats had been laid out, and the bright green napkins. Her best sterling shone beside her new microwave-proof dinnerware. Cascading white carnations made a lovely centerpiece. Howard was expecting a dinner-guest.

Claire's jaw dropped. She couldn't imagine

Howard fixing the table that way. It had to be. . . .
It had to be that damn secretary. Her eyes rose to
where the sound of the shower was coming from.
He couldn't. Could he? If he had that little slut
here, now, and in Claire's shower . . .

Visions of the two of them together in her bed,
in her bathroom, hit her like a physical blow, wiping
all logic from her brain. It never entered her mind
to remember that she herself had brought Peter
into this house. Howard bringing in the secretary
seemed so much worse.

She was boiling now, and she had to steady
herself before she could take the stairs, one at a
time, up to the second story. She peeked into her
bedroom, but nothing had been touched there.
Turning, she steeled herself to deal with Howard.

She approached the bathroom. Howard was
humming. Funny. He'd never hummed in the
shower before. She relaxed a little, realizing this
meant he was probably alone. At least she wouldn't
have to confront the woman.

She opened the bathroom door. The place was
full of steam, and that was odd, too, because Howard was usually one to jump in, soap down, rinse,
and be out again in about thirty seconds. She could
make out the outline of his body behind the steamy
glass, happily washing away.

"Surprise!" she called gaily. "I'm back. I guess
you didn't expect me tonight, did you?"

The humming came to an abrupt halt and the
figure behind the glass went as still as a statue.

"Sorry if I'm ruining a planned night of revelry

with your little floozy," she went on, letting her own words egg her on. "But you know, wives are prone to doing things like that."

There was nothing but stunned silence, and then Howard cleared his throat. His reticence was making her even more angry.

"Will you say something?" she demanded, and then, hardly giving him time to get a word in, she marched up to the shower door. "Oh, come on, Howard, come out here and face me like a man," she cried as she yanked the door open and stared straight into the eyes of a complete stranger.

"Oh, my God," she gasped, and then—she went back over this moment a hundred times, later, and she never could quite believe that she had done this—instead of turning away immediately, instead of whispering apologies and beating a hasty retreat, instead of closing her eyes and feeling her way to the door, she looked the man up and down and took in every inch of his wet nakedness, from his wide, tanned shoulders to his lovely flat navel to his strong feet, and everything in between.

"Oh, my God," she breathed again. "I . . . I thought you were . . ."

"Well, I'm not," he said at last, moving a bit uncomfortably. "Now, if you don't mind, I'd like to finish my shower."

"Oh. Of course. I'm so sorry."

She left then, but she was still in shock. She'd never dreamed she would find a stranger . . . But wait a minute. That was no stranger. She'd seen him before, heard that voice. Who was that man, and what was he doing in her shower?

She waited, pacing the living-room floor, until he came down, dressed, now, in a polo shirt and slacks. She looked at him, suppressing the embarrassment she couldn't help but feel over their recent meeting in the bathroom, and her response to it, and nodded. She knew this man all right.

"Matt Stevens," she dredged out of her memory bank. "You're the one with the great library cards and credit rating. You gave me a ride home after the concert that night in Atlanta."

His intelligent blue eyes were full of awareness. "Bingo," he said softly, smiling.

Claire had a sudden thought. "Don't tell me Laura sent you?"

He stared at her blankly for a moment, then made the connection. "Oh." He laughed shortly. "No, nothing like that. I came as a consultant to Draxon Oil. I'm here on short-term lease from the university."

That was a relief. She looked at him and decided she didn't have to worry about being embarrassed. There was something calmly reassuring about the man. He wouldn't rattle easily. She felt something deep inside her begin to relax.

"That explains what you're doing in Saudi Arabia. I still don't quite get why you were in my shower."

"There was very little room in the bachelor quarters when I arrived, so Howard invited me here. He was all alone, and he's hardly ever home anyway. . . ."

She nodded wearily. "This is a story I know well." She glanced at the table. "So the place settings are yours, aren't they? Are you expecting company?"

"Not really. I was hoping Howard would be home in time to join me for dinner. I'm broiling lamb chops and tossing a nice green salad."

"Great." She looked at him cockily. "I'm famished."

His eyes sparkled with mocking amusement. "Sit down," he offered. "I'd be happy to have you join me."

He turned to go into the kitchen and she hesitated. "Would you like some help?" she asked, and then wanted to kick herself.

He turned and gazed at her. "You don't think I can handle this on my own?" he asked.

"I . . ." She gestured helplessly.

"Sit down," he repeated. "Talk to me while I get dinner."

She did sit down, watching as he began to work in the kitchen. There was some advantage, she mused, to letting men live on their own for a while. Some of them actually learned how to do more than supply basic rations fit for animal survival and not much else. This one seemed to know what he was doing.

"Why are you here?" she asked. "I mean, you of all people."

He smiled, and she suddenly realized she liked

his eyes. They were so blue, and his prematurely silver-gray hair only made them stand out more.

"What would you say if I told you I came out to Saudi because of you?"

She blinked. "Because of me?"

He grinned. "Well, partly. Meeting you that night piqued my curiosity, and when some Draxon officials came to the university for some core tests, I began asking questions. One thing led to another, and I was offered this job on a contract basis. Since I was on sabbatical, I decided to come on out and see what the rest of the world was all about."

"You teach?"

"Teach and research."

"What is your area of expertise?"

He looked up from the bowl into which he was shredding lettuce. "I'm a geologist and a petroleum engineer. I'm doing some technical evaluations, mainly checking work other engineers have done."

She thought that over for a moment, then said, "Is Howard in trouble?"

His hands stopped, but he didn't look up. "I understand that you and Howard . . ."

"That our marriage is headed for oblivion. That's right. But that doesn't mean I don't care what happens to him any longer. If nothing else, he's the father of my children, you know."

He turned and popped the chops under the broiler. "Still, I don't know—"

"Oh, come on. I'm not trying to build a case against him to use in divorce court."

He turned to look at her. "Aren't you?"

She stared at him, aghast. "What has he told you?"

"He hasn't told me anything. But the rest of the neighborhood has gotten a few licks in." He smiled. "Florence Barberry made damn sure I heard exactly what was going on."

Claire nodded. "I'm sure she did." She waited, but he did not amplify. "Well," she prompted impatiently, "what, in the opinion of Florence and the rest of the neighborhood, is going on?"

He hesitated, and from the look on his face, she could tell he was sorry he had taken this road. "It's a little brutal," he said dismissively. "And probably only partly true."

"Tell me."

"Claire—"

"I have to live here. I might as well be prepared for what they're going to use against me out there. Shoot."

He came out and leaned against the doorjamb, hands shoved deep into the pockets of his slacks. "Okay, the gossip, according to the Draxon compound employees." He took a deep breath. "Howard is shacking up with one of the secretaries. I take it you knew about it—from the shower scene we had together." He raised an eyebrow, remembering. "I don't think I've ever been quite so thoroughly at a loss for words before."

Well, she'd promised herself she wasn't going to be embarrassed by what she'd done, but he'd caught her off guard. To her amazement, she found herself blushing. "Words were hardly necessary," she murmured, then blushed all the harder as she realized how he might take that.

But he was laughing. "Where's a damn fig leaf when you really need one?"

"Precisely." She met his gaze and was laughing, too. Looking away, she sobered. "Come on. Let's hear the rest."

"Right." He stared off into space. "The word here is that Howard's lovely wife Claire has been spending her days off in the Greek Islands with her teenage boyfriend."

Claire gasped. "Teenage boyfriend?"

He was looking at her again, studying her reaction. "That's the way the story goes."

"He's not a teenager."

His eyes darkened. "Is he a boyfriend?"

She opened her mouth to protest, then shut it again without saying anything, and something seemed to close off behind his eyes. He turned back to his salad. "This is hardly the picture of the happy marriage you gave me just a few months ago in Atlanta."

"I was dreaming in Atlanta. I was hoping I could do something to salvage things, but it was too late. I think it had been too late for a long, long time, but I just hadn't been able to face it before."

He came out with a bottle of wine and two glasses. "So your marriage to Howard is over?" His tone was casual, but he was glancing at her sharply.

"Yes," she said in a very small voice. "I'm afraid it is."

He poured wine into her glass, then into his own. "Does Howard know this?"

"Not in so many words."

"Oh, brother." He raised his glass and she met it in a silent toast. "I'll move out immediately," he promised.

"No, don't do that."

His smile was lopsided. "I rather like the idea of getting off the battlefield before the shooting begins."

She bit her lip to keep from smiling. "And I rather like the idea of keeping you around as a nice big shield." She shook her head. "But really, I'm sure Howard knows what's coming. I think we'll both be very civilized. Please stay."

He made no promises, but went back to cooking and soon emerged with nicely browned chops and a wonderful salad, as well as a basket of warm rolls. They had a pleasant meal and a long talk. Claire was surprised at how personal they had become so quickly. But then, she mused to herself, there wasn't much use in artificial niceties once one had said hello naked. Besides, he was someone from home, and she felt as if she could talk to him. He seemed to feel the same way about her.

She probed for more information about his reason for coming to Saudi Arabia. "Tell me about Howard. What is the problem with the company?"

Matt hesitated. "What makes you think there's a problem?"

"The fact that you're holding something back."

He smiled. "I think you'd better ask Howard. He'll tell you anything you want to know."

"Or whatever he thinks is good for me," she countered with just a touch of sarcasm. "Thanks a lot."

When Howard did come home, he barely nodded to her. It was amazing how little they had in common now. They looked at one another as strangers, with almost no feeling between them, not even hatred. The years of living as husband and wife seemed to have vanished. How could she have been with him for so long, telling herself that she loved him, and now—nothing.

He seemed to be happily ensconced in the den, with his papers and his computer. He'd given Matt Sam's room, and Claire still had the master bedroom. There was no problem there.

The three of them chatted for a while, fairly cordially, and Claire could see Matt looking from one of them to the other, speculating on their relationship. She might have saved him the trouble. There *was* no relationship.

When Howard started in with Matt about some football game that had happened thousands of miles away and three days before, she gave up and went to bed. Lying there in the dark, she thought of her daughters, whom she would call in the morning to inform of her return, and of Peter.

Peter. Dear, sweet Peter. As she began to drift off to sleep, Peter and Greece and the treasure all began to blur and blend into a dream, and they

were sailing in a high wind, but there was a knocking, knocking . . .

And then she realized the knocking was on her
bedroom door.

She froze, wide awake. Could it be Howard?
But no, he wouldn't knock; he would come right in.
She slipped out of bed, shrugging into her robe,
and padded softly to the door. "Yes? Who is it?"

"It's Matt. Can I talk to you for a minute?"

Her heart sank. Had he taken that story about
the teenage boyfriend a bit too seriously? Did he
think she was up for grabs at any time? That was
what happened when you got a bad reputation, just
like her mother had always told her when she was
a girl. Well, if that was the case, it was time to set
him straight.

She whipped open the door and stood squarely
in front of him, her hand on her hip. "Yes?" she
challenged.

"Howard just left," he said quietly.

"Oh?"

"I don't know where he's going, but I thought
it might give us a chance to talk for a bit. I have
something I want to say to you."

"You want to talk?"

The corners of his wide mouth twitched.
"Yeah. Talk. What did you think I wanted?"

"It's hard to know what to expect from a knock
on the door in the middle of the night."

His grin widened. "With me, it's all talk. Believe me."

For the moment, she did. "Come on in." She

stepped back and he came into the room, sitting down casually on the corner of her bed as though they'd been best friends since childhood.

"You wanted to know what kind of trouble Howard might be in, and I was going to let you hear it from him. But I can see by the way you two are talking past each other, that isn't likely to happen. And I think you deserve to know."

She sat down beside him, tucking her legs under her. "Thank you," she said simply.

"I'll be honest with you, Claire. I'm here to help save his ass."

Claire found, to her surprise, that she was trembling. Howard's problems still affected her, no matter how she tried to pretend otherwise.

"The bottom line is," said Matt, "he screwed up royally. The Saudi Arabian government is so angry at him, they want to nationalize Draxon Oil."

"What?"

"It wasn't totally unexpected. They've struck deals with the other oil companies, taken over at least partial ownership. Aramco is wholly Saudi owned now. But Draxon thought they were immune. Those fools in San Francisco thought they had special dispensation from some prince or other.

"What did Howard do?"

"Stepped on toes. Acted like an arrogant bully. Tried to push the wrong people around. Of course, it wasn't all his fault. San Francisco was blind to some things that had been going wrong for years. And then, there was Robert Camden."

Claire looked up in surprise. "What does he have to do with this?"

"He came in and tried to cut his own deal with the Saudis."

"Do you mean he was working behind Howard's back?"

"It seems so. He was offering to act as a front, buying up shares in Draxon for Saudi interests."

That jogged Claire's memory. "You know, I saw him once, up at a Bedouin camp. There were all these members of the royal family having camel races and there was Robert Camden, moving among them as though it were a perfectly normal role for him."

Matt nodded. "He was probably negotiating a deal there on the spot. I don't imagine he was too pleased to see you."

She couldn't avoid the guilty look. "I . . . he didn't exactly see me."

"He didn't?" Matt looked at her curiously, but she decided to forgo explaining that one. There was enough in her life that needed sorting out, and that incident was still in the think-this-over-at-your-leisure pile.

Matt waited, but when she didn't expand on her statement, he went on, "Well, Robert Camden has been fired. And the best we can do now is try to salvage as much as we can."

"You mean, San Francisco is losing the company?" It was a concept almost beyond belief. There had always been Draxon Oil; it was a monolith, a structure for the ages. That it should crumble in a matter of months . . . That sort of shook the foundations, she thought, made everything look just that much less secure.

"No doubt about it. Draxon Oil as we have known it will be no more. We only hope we can swing a deal so that the shareholders—and the employees—don't come out of this with nothing at all."

The prospect of Draxon changing hands didn't really bother her once she got over the novelty, but she did hope Howard managed to save some face.

"I understand how it is between the two of you," Matt was saying. "Your marriage is over. You might just as well abandon the sinking ship, get out while the gettin's good." His silvery gaze ran over her face, as though he sought her innermost thoughts. "Certainly no one would fault you for it. I thought you ought to know the whole picture so you could make plans."

He left her then, and she went back to bed, but she lay awake for hours, thinking about Howard and how he must feel like a failure, and betrayed by the company to whom he had given so much loyalty. Despite everything, it hurt to see him torn apart this way. Abandon the sinking ship? No way. She would stay as long as he needed her.

The next few days passed peacefully enough. She called the girls in England and cleaned house and took over the cooking from Matt. She was coolly cordial to Howard, but never antagonistic, and he was much the same to her.

She managed to avoid Frances and Margo was

studiously avoiding her. She wished she could see Shareen, but her friend was still in Beirut.

"Her grandmother has the flu," Shareen's husband, Larry, told her when she dropped by. "She wants to stay there with her until the old lady feels well enough to get around by herself."

"Of course." Claire smiled as ten-year-old Kevin shot through the room on a pretend spaceship for which he was making very loud sound effects. "And how are you holding up?"

"Taking care of Kevin?" Larry laughed along with her at his son's antics. "I don't mind at all, actually. They're getting a bit testy at the office because I've been taking so much time off to be with him. But he comes first, as far as I'm concerned. I love it."

"You should send him over sometime," Claire offered. "He could play with Katy's old Lego sets."

"I'll do that," Larry promised. "And I'll tell Shareen you asked about her."

She was disappointed in not being able to talk things over with Shareen. For short-time friends, they had become very close, and she trusted Shareen's special insights.

But Claire was busy, filling her days with organizing the house, preparing to pack up everything to be shipped to the States. Though Howard had said nothing directly, she was sure such a move was coming soon. And then she would collect her daughters and go home to Atlanta.

CHAPTER

Matt was as comfortable to have around as any guest could be. He picked up after himself and made himself useful. She was getting used to his wry comments and subtle sense of humor. He made her laugh, and that was a valuable asset in her relatively gloomy life.

She'd been out working in the yard one afternoon a few days after her return from Greece when Matt met her at the door with a surprise.

"You've got a call. The teenage boyfriend."

Claire's eyes widened and she looked at him quickly to make sure he wasn't teasing her. "Peter?"

He nodded, his eyes strangely clouded.

But she hardly noticed. A smile lit her face. Peter. Just the thought of him brought back Greece and the wonderful time she'd had. "Thanks," she said happily as she raced inside to take the call in the kitchen.

"Peter. How are you?"

"Missing you."

She laughed. "You mean you haven't replaced me yet with a new love?"

His voice was soft with humor. "Darling, you know you're irreplaceable. I don't think I'll ever find another woman to take up to Aphrodite's shrine. The memory of that day will live—"

"In infamy," she interjected, choking back laughter. "Don't remind me!"

"Did you have a good time?"

"You know I did."

"Then come on back, Claire. I mean it. I really do miss you."

For just a moment a tempting picture of white sails on blue water, of islands scattered in a calm sea, of breezes through lemon groves, filled her mind and she sighed. But then she caught sight of Matt through the kitchen window and the dream broke apart like a bubble bursting in the air.

"That would be wonderful, Peter. But I can't."

He groaned. "I was afraid you'd say that. I only wish I could go to Saudi and make you change your mind. But you know I can't do that anymore—not without a job waiting for me there."

She smiled. He was such a dear. "Peter, you have to understand, I have other things going on in my life. The time with you was something I'll never forget. But it's over now."

"I know that. I was just . . . hoping." He

laughed, then added, "Hey, who was that man who answered? It wasn't Howard."

"No. It's Matt Stevens. He . . . a consultant who's staying with us for a while."

"Uh-huh." After a moment Peter said softly, "Don't forget me, Claire."

Something in his tone brought a lump to her throat. "I could never do that, Peter. You're a part of me. I'll never lose you."

He hung up, but she stayed in the kitchen, leaning on the counter with her eyes closed, holding the receiver, holding on to Peter for another moment or two. She owed him so much. When Howard's rejection was beginning to destroy her self-esteem, Peter had given her his natural, open sense of love and affection and rebuilt her, piece by piece. She could never repay him for that. And soon she would be leaving this part of the world. Would she ever see him again?

For just a moment, she felt panic. She couldn't lose Peter, not that way. And yet, what could she do? She wasn't about to go live on a Greek island and search for sunken treasure for the rest of her life.

Hearing a noise, she looked up and found Matt watching her silently from the doorway. "Bad news?" he asked, his eyes still clouded in that distant way.

She managed a smile. "No. Not at all." She replaced the receiver in its cradle and began briskly to clean off the kitchen counter. "Just an old friend saying hello."

Matt didn't say anything else, and for that entire evening was unusually uncommunicative. But she had a feeling he was very much aware of her, even when he was sitting on the couch reading a magazine and not looking up at all. This new tension between them disturbed her, but it seemed to vanish in the next morning's sunshine, and she forgot all about it.

She called her mother and the two of them had a pleasant chat. Her mother seemed in good spirits. But it wasn't until she put in a call to Laura that she found out what was really going on.

"Mom's gone crazy," Laura announced. "She's opened up her home to exchange students at the university—you know, those kids who come over here for a semester or two? And they sent her six— count 'em, honey, six!—Swedish girls."

"Six?" It did seem excessive. "I wonder why she didn't tell me?"

"She didn't tell you because she's embarrassed. She wanted to do something that would fill the emptiness since Daddy died but, Claire, this is ridiculous."

"Well, Laura, if it's making her happy, I don't really think it's any of our business."

"Oh, yeah? Just wait until you see these girls— or maybe I should say women, because these are fully grown. Jim's eyes nearly popped out when he saw them. And all of a sudden he was offering to do any odd jobs Mom might have around for him. He wants to go over there all the time."

So that was Laura's problem. Claire had to

laugh. But she was happy her mother had found something to keep her busy.

The time flew by. Howard was spending day after day in Riyadh, and Matt was going out into the desert to look at sites all over the country. She hardly knew when to expect either one of them. One day, just as she was wondering where in the world Matt was, she got a call from the compound gate guard.

"There's a Princess Nadia to see you, Mrs. Montgomery. She's got this whole train of five or six cars and I don't know what all else."

"Princess Nadia? Let her in."

She couldn't imagine what the lively princess had come for, but she went out onto the sidewalk to meet her. An entourage of stretch limos drove up and parked, and the door to one opened, revealing a giggling, veiled Nadia inside.

Claire bent to see her. "Princess Nadia, it's so good to see you. To what do I owe the honor?"

The princess waved a finger at her as though she had been very naughty. "I have something for you. I found him out on the desert, stuck in the sand. Another one of your men." She giggled some more.

"What?" Claire was bewildered.

"This one is so handsome. I like his silver hair. I found him—his Jeep was stuck in the sand. I had my man ask where he belonged, and he gave your address. I couldn't believe it. 'Another romance for Claire!' I told my cousin on the car phone. She told me to leave him there, let him die in the sun like a dog, but I didn't pay any attention to her. Not when one of Claire's men is involved!"

By now Claire had figured out that Nadia had found Matt broken down in the desert, and had rescued him and brought him home. But where was he? Not in the car with Nadia. She straightened and looked up and down the caravan, but no other doors were being opened.

"When he said he lived with you, I thought, not another one!" Nadia was chattering on. "Please, may I come to visit you in America sometime? Then I will find out how you do it. You can show me the ropes of romance. Okay?"

"I'd love to have you." It wasn't until later, thinking this incident over, that Claire wondered how Nadia knew the Montgomerys would be leaving soon. Perhaps the princess knew more about the workings of the oil industry than one might expect of a woman who spent her days cruising the desert highways looking for strays. "Where is he?"

"Oh." She snapped her fingers at her driver. "We will bring him out for you. I hope you are happy to have him back."

Three cars back, a door opened and Matt was shoved from the car. His hands were tied behind his back. Claire gasped. One of the bodyguards cut the rope around his wrists and he pulled his hands apart, rubbing where the binding had been and looking back at his "rescuers" with disbelief.

"Thank you so much, Princess Nadia," Claire said doubtfully. "You've done me another favor and I'm grateful."

"It is nothing," the princess answered happily. "Just remember, I will be coming to visit you in America. Goodbye!"

When the cars drove off, Claire turned to Matt. He looked shell-shocked.

"Who was that masked madam?" he muttered.

Claire suppressed a giggle. "Princess Nadia. She's a friend of mine."

"What does she have? Her own private army?" He rubbed his neck as though it were sore. "They held me at knife-point all the way home. Apparently they were protecting the princess's virtue—as if I could do anything about that from three cars away."

"You might have caught a glimpse of her face or something. Count your blessings. If that had happened, they would probably have had to put you to death."

Matt groaned. "And as if that weren't enough, my Jeep is still out there in the dunes. I guess I'll have to get someone to go out and help me dig it out and bring it back."

Claire nodded her sympathy. "Just keep an eye out for Princess Nadia and her guys. It might be best not to hitch a ride with them again. They might begin to wonder if you're trying to get to know her."

Matt groaned again. "And life seemed so simple when I got up this morning."

"It's still simple," she told him cheerfully. "You're the one who's getting complicated."

Within the next week it became common

knowledge that the American Draxon employees were going to pull out of Saudi Arabia. People were clustered on street corners, hanging over backyard fences, burning up the telephone wires. Margo even came over to wail about their fate, and Frances took the next flight to Paris, loath to stay around for the burial of her own particular dream.

Howard never said a word to Claire, assuming, she supposed, she was getting her news from others. And, in fact, Matt was keeping her up-to-date.

"We're getting out with our tail between our legs," he told her one evening. Howard was out and they were sitting on the back steps in semidarkness, enjoying the warm desert evening breeze. "But we're leaving with our gold collar intact."

"Then it's not a total disaster?"

"No, and Howard is coming out of it okay, I think. He's not being blamed in the official version. He'll be able to get a job with another oil company, maybe in South America, maybe even in the States."

"Good." She looked up at the stars, brilliant as scattered diamonds. It was a relief to know Howard hadn't lost everything. She still cared about him in an odd, detached way. "I've contacted an attorney in Atlanta to begin divorce proceedings."

Matt's head swung around and he looked at her in the moonlight. "Did you tell Howard?" he asked softly.

She nodded. "Last night. He barely looked up from the work he was doing on his computer.

'Whatever you think is best,' he said. So I guess that's that."

Matt reached out and took her hand in his. "I guess it's got to be done."

"Yes." Her shoulders drooped. Matt was so understanding, such a comfort. It wasn't that he always agreed with her, but he managed to see her point of view even when he didn't. Was that just respect? Or plain old self-confidence, something that let him give other people space, because he knew he had enough of his own?

She looked at him but couldn't read his eyes in the dark. "It all seems like such a waste, just throwing out all those years, all we did together."

"It can't be a waste. You learned from each other. You grew. And there are those two girls you made together."

She smiled. "Yes. You haven't met Katy and Sam yet. I think you'll like them."

"How could I help but?" he murmured. "And then, you'll have to start thinking about remarrying."

"Oh, no." She shook her head vigorously. "Not on your life."

"No? Not even the teenage boyfriend?"

She yanked her hand away. "Please, Matt. Peter is not a teenager. He's in his late twenties. And . . ."

She hesitated, then charged ahead. If anyone would be able to understand what Peter had been to her, it would be Matt. "Let me try to explain to you about Peter. He was very kind to me at a time

when I was really down. He was there when I
needed him. When my world seemed to be falling
apart, he acted as though I was worth something,
which was something I'd begun to doubt." She
threw out her hands in supplication. "I can never
repay what he did for me. Do you have the slightest
idea of what I'm talking about?"

Matt was nodding slowly. "Yes," he said. "I
think I understand better than you know."

Claire smiled. She believed him. "How did you
get so nice?" she asked, only half-joking.

"Nice?" He winced. "As in 'boring'? Maybe
I'm not as nice as you think, Claire," he said huskily.
"Maybe I ought to bring out my mean streak and
show it off."

She gave his statement the laugh it deserved,
but he sobered more quickly. "You really don't
think you'll marry again?" he asked.

She shrugged. "You haven't, have you?"

That set him back for a moment. "No, well . . .
but it would be pretty difficult to replace Blair."

She knew she was treading on dangerous
ground, but they had become close friends lately,
and she thought it wouldn't be out of line to ask.
"Tell me about her."

His voice almost jerky, he said, "You don't
want to hear that ancient history."

"But I do." She was sure he only needed a bit
of prodding.

"Okay." He sighed, leaning back against the
railing. "Blair played viola in the city orchestra. She
played like an angel. She danced like one, too. She

was always smiling, always moving. She brought sunshine into my life, more sunshine than I could ever have believed might exist. She made me laugh, she made me cry, she made me live life more fully than I ever had."

He was trying to keep his voice even, matter-of-fact, but she could feel the emotion behind every word. He wasn't in the habit of talking about Blair, she could tell. It would probably be good for him to do so.

"She sounds like a lovely person," Claire said softly. "What happened?"

"Cancer."

She reached out a hand and placed it on his forearm. "I'm so sorry."

He stiffened at her touch. "Everyone was so sorry." There was bitterness in his voice, which she'd never heard before. "I . . . I thought I'd kill myself when she died. I didn't think I could go on without her." He looked toward Claire and smiled. "But you do, you know. One day at a time."

Tears were stinging her eyes and she waited a moment to speak, not sure she could control her voice. "You never did marry again," she reminded him.

"No one ever touched my heart and soul the way Blair did."

"Do you think anyone ever will?"

"There was a time when I didn't think so. But lately . . ." He smiled at her quickly. "What about you? No matter what you say now, I'm sure you'll remarry."

"I don't think so."

"Why not?" He leaned a little closer. "After all, even though Howard was a bad choice, you still got some good out of the marriage."

She laughed. "You're an optimist, aren't you? I'll bet the glass is always half-full for you."

"I find that life is a lot easier that way."

She laughed, then looked out into the night. "I don't know if I could marry again. In the past few months, I've become a whole different person from what I was. I don't know if I need to be married any longer."

"What do you mean by that?"

"Needing to be married? It was partly a quest for security before. I thought I needed someone to cling to, someone who could support me when I needed it. With the things I've gone through in the past few months, I've found myself becoming so much stronger." She searched for his expression in the shadows. "Maybe I can make it on my own. Maybe I don't need that kind of support anymore."

"Is that all you think marriage is? Support? What about companionship? What about having someone around to listen to your jokes? What about having someone to grow old with, someone to share your memories? What about—" he touched her shoulder with his hand "—having someone to hug in the night?"

For some reason, his words made her shiver. "It's getting a little chilly," she said, not answering his questions. "I think I'm going to go in." She rose and looked down at where he still sat. "Good night, Matt," she said softly.

He didn't look at her. He was staring out into the star-filled night. "Good night," he responded softly.

She stood looking at him for a long moment. She was sure he was thinking about Blair, about how he would never hug her again. Her impulse was to reach for him, to hold him close, to comfort him with her body. But that would be a mistake, wouldn't it? As though she were giving him something just to ease his pain.

She shivered again and went on into the house.

❧

Time was winding down. Claire had a flight out in three days. Howard had already left, suddenly, along with Gregory and the other top administrators. They were on their way to San Francisco to defend their actions of the last nine months. New, local faces were seen in the corporate offices now.

It was probably for the best, Claire was thinking as she took a break from packing and poured herself a tepid cup of coffee. It was early, but she had been working since four in the morning. She hadn't been able to sleep, for something was nagging at her, as though there was something she had forgotten to do, and she couldn't pin it down. So she'd got dressed and begun packing.

She could hear Matt beginning to move around. It was time for him to get into the office. He was working with the transition team and would be staying for another few weeks.

The morning paper, an English language edition, was on the front walk. Yawning, she padded out in slippers to get it and brought it in, spreading it out to read as she had her last cup of coffee. But before she could pick up her cup, she froze. The headline shocked her.

"American Woman Killed by Beirut Gunmen," it screamed.

The minute she saw the headline, she knew. She sat very still for long moments before she could force herself to look at the story below. She knew it was going to be Shareen who had died. And she was right.

Then, suddenly, all she could do was read—every word, every syllable of the story. Her mind kept moaning, "No, no, no," and she searched desperately for some way out, anything that would let her hope this might be a mistake.

Matt came into the room and immediately sensed that something was wrong. "What is it?" he said.

She pushed the paper across the table to him. He scanned the article, then looked up at her. "The woman you've been so friendly with?" he asked.

She nodded. She'd told Matt all about Shareen, and he knew Larry, of course. Larry. Oh, my God, she thought. What about Larry? "I've got to go over and see her husband," she said, her voice curiously stable considering the way she felt. She rose and started for the door. Matt jumped up and came alongside her.

"Do you want me to come with you?"

She looked at him and thought of how much he knew of this sort of pain. He was ready to help—that was clear. But right now, she couldn't accept help, and she knew he would understand that, too.

She shook her head. "I'd better go alone."

She walked quickly down the street and knocked on Larry's door. There was no answer, but she pushed the door open and went in anyway. Kevin was outside, playing on a swing, but she found Larry upstairs, packing a large suitcase. His face was a stone mask. She went to him and put her arms around him. He allowed it, but didn't respond.

"I'm sorry, so sorry," she murmured.

"I am, too." He pulled back. "I'm sorry for the world—no one will get to hear Shareen's laugh again."

"Kevin . . . ?"

"He doesn't know yet. They called me in the middle of the night, but I just can't bring myself to tell him. We only had her for such a short time." He looked as though he were on the verge of breaking down and Claire stepped toward him again. He waved her back, fighting to keep his composure.

"I'm going to Beirut," he said.

She nodded. "But what about Kevin?"

He looked as though he was at the end of his rope. "He'll have to come, too. I . . . we have no family who can take him. I don't have anywhere else to go."

"Let him stay with me."

He blinked at her. "But you're leaving."

"I could stay. I'll take care of him. Don't worry."

He shook his head. "No, Claire, you don't understand. I'm going to Beirut. I'm going to stay there."

She stared at him, not sure she'd heard right. He wanted to go and stay in the country that had just killed his wife?

He nodded slowly, reading her expression. "I know what you're thinking. When I first heard about how she'd been shot in the street, I was full of hate. My first impulse was to go to Lebanon and kill as many people as I could before they gunned me down, too. You know. Rambo in a three-piece suit. Anything to get revenge for what happened to her. But once I calmed down, I realized that was exactly what was wrong with that country in the first place. Relying on the old eye-for-an-eye, tooth-for-a-tooth, just throws you into a spiral of increasing destruction. It's sick. It's got to be changed."

"But, Larry, what can you do to change it?"

"I'm quitting my job with Draxon. It's almost over anyway. And I'm going to donate my legal services to the UN peacekeeping mission in Lebanon. There has to be some way to lessen the tensions, the hatred and the killing. I want to help find that way."

She shook her head. "You're unbelievable," she said, and she wasn't being entirely complimentary. A part of her considered him a saint, but another part thought he was a fool. The conditions in Lebanon had nothing to do with him, not anymore. Why throw himself in the midst of it? But perhaps it was his way of getting over Shareen's death. She hoped it would work.

She looked at Larry and realized there was to be no happy ending here. That was what she'd been waiting for, what she'd gone to Greece for. There had to be a happy ending. Everyone deserved one, didn't they? So where was Shareen's happy ending? Where was Larry's? Kevin's?

Kevin. Oh, Lord, that dear little boy. "You can't take Kevin into that horror of a place."

"I have no choice."

"Yes, you do." She took a deep breath. "Let me take him with me."

He stared. "With you? Back to the States?"

"Why not? I'd love to take him. I've always liked him. I'll be living in my mother's house, just a few doors down from my sister's. He would have lots of other kids to play with. And then when you're ready, settled somewhere, you could come and get him."

"Claire, I can't possibly let you—"

She touched his shoulder. "For Shareen. Please let me do this for her."

In the end, Larry agreed, and when she went back to the house, Kevin came with her. She was keeping him home from school that day. They would be leaving in three days anyway—she'd made a reservation for Kevin.

As she stood in the doorway and watched Kevin play in Katy's room, Matt came up behind her, putting his hands on her shoulders. She turned and, seeing him, burst into tears. He drew her outside of the room and held her close while she cried.

"What am I going to do with this little boy?" she whispered when she could. "How am I going to tell him?"

"You're not." Matt pulled out a handkerchief and dried her eyes, patting carefully, his face intent on his job. "You're going to take him with you to England and home, and when you get to Atlanta, and you're all ensconced in that big old house of your mother's, you're going to hold him close and tell him. His life will be so full of new things, he will be sad, but he won't be overwhelmed."

She looked at him. "That's a good idea. But the only thing is . . . wouldn't that be slighting Shareen's memory?"

"What do you think Shareen would want most, a lot of weeping and wailing, or her son to be happy?"

"Well, of course . . ."

"Of course."

She looked up into his eyes, thankful he was here. "How could this happen?" she asked him, as she had been asking herself for hours. "How? She was so good, so vibrant . . ."

"And she made a major impact on all who knew her, didn't she? A lot of people who live a lot longer do a hell of a lot less than she did."

"You're right."

"Life is for real, Claire. What you do with it is what really counts. We're all playing for keeps."

Playing for keeps. Claire nodded, struck by his wisdom. They were all playing for keeps, and the rules were never certain. It was a tough life. But one worth living.

CHAPTER

"Wow, if it gets any colder, I swear it'll snow." Laura stamped her feet and blew on her hands as she came in the huge front door.

Claire laughed. "You need temperatures a little lower than lukewarm to get snow," she said. "But it's just right for Thanksgiving to have a little nip in the air."

Laura was right, actually. It was cooler in Atlanta than usual for this time of year. But that just made the gathering inside the house seem that much warmer and closer. There was a fire roaring in the big old fireplace, and the aroma of turkey and stuffing filled the air. Children's voices rang through the house, along with the sound of music from the stereo.

"Are they here?" Laura hissed, looking behind Claire searchingly.

"They're here." She helped Laura take off her

coat, then hung it up. "They're out on the porch playing with the model train."

"They" were the two remaining Swedish exchange students. "Our little brother," she said, "must think he's died and gone to heaven."

"He's out there with them?"

Claire laid a hand on her sister's arm and spoke sincerely. "Honey, he's always with them. No matter where they go, or what they do, Gary is right beside them, making sure they are getting along in this big old scary country."

Laura groaned. "Better him than my Jim. Honestly, every time he sees those girls he just about pops his buttons. What was Mom thinking of, letting the prettiest ones stay when the others left?"

"They won't be here forever. Come on into the kitchen. Mom always swears you stir the gravy better than anybody."

They'd only been back for two weeks, but already Claire felt as though she were home, really home, where they belonged. She led Laura into the kitchen and handed her a spoon.

"I've got a surprise for you," Laura announced, beginning to beat the gravy energetically.

Claire threw her a warning glance. "If it's a date with a man, forget it."

"No. Unfortunately, it's just that old gold belt you always liked. I can't wear it anymore and I brought it over for you."

Laura gave the gravy a taste and reached for the salt. "Anyway, from what I hear, you've had enough male companionship lately. You don't really need my help at all."

She turned and looked full at her sister, who was making creamed onions and smiling a secretive smile.

"Well?" she demanded. "Are you ever going to give me the details?"

"Probably not."

Laura shrieked and tossed the spoon into the sink. "That's not fair, and you know it. You've been home for ages now. I've been patient. But enough is enough. I want answers, sister mine. At least a sketchy outline of what went on over there in Greece. And then I hear there was some other man living with you in Saudi Arabia once you got back." She glared at her sister. "Come on. Give."

Claire held back a triumphant smile with difficulty. "There's really not much to tell," she said, gesturing dismissively. "I met Peter Arnold in Saudi Arabia. He invited me to go to Greece, so when I knew my marriage with Howard was really over, I decided to go."

"And then?"

Claire shrugged. "Nothing much. He just . . . taught me how to sail, showed me where he was going to dive for buried treasure, took me to a fabulous party, got me to do some nude sunbathing—"

"Claire!"

Claire smiled at her sister's reaction, then sobered. "He also taught me how to live again, Laura. He made me realize I wasn't dead. He was wonderful."

Laura reached out and took her hand. "Are you going to see him again?"

Claire hesitated. "I doubt it. He's not long-term material, if you know what I mean. But he certainly was wonderful while he lasted."

"I'm glad." She smiled at her sister. "Now go on. What about this man who was living in your house when you got back?"

"Matt Stevens?" Claire's smile was more guarded. "Oh, he was just staying with us because there wasn't any room at the bachelor quarters. He was very nice. Good company. And you know . . ." She shrugged, suddenly reluctant to go on.

"No. I don't know. Otherwise I wouldn't be asking."

Claire laughed. "But that's just it. There's nothing to ask about. He's just a very nice man. But you know him. You must."

Laura's smile was wickedly knowing. "Yes. As a matter of fact, I do."

The arrival of their mother cut off further exploration of that topic. They turned to greet her and Laura gave her a hug.

"How's the gravy coming?" she asked, and Laura went to the sink to retrieve the spoon, letting Claire catch her breath. She smiled, loving her family, glad to be back among them. Her mother had welcomed them all with open arms, including Kevin, and since there were only two Swedish students left, there was plenty of room. And Katy was getting the real Thanksgiving she so desperately wanted.

Kevin was fitting in fine. His story broke the heart of everyone who heard it, and they had all made an effort to be especially kind to him. But he was such a sweet little boy the effort had gone out of it. Now he was one of them.

Claire had done as Matt had suggested and waited until Kevin was in her mother's house and feeling safe and secure before telling him of his own mother's death. It was hard for a boy that age to understand, harder still to know how to deal with the pain. But Kevin was a game little guy, and he seemed to be doing pretty well.

Claire felt responsible for the child's emotional state, his mental framework for the future. She was tempted to pretend Shareen had never existed, so as not to risk bringing up the pain for Kevin. But she knew right away that would be wrong. It had been difficult trying to decide what to do, but finally she'd hit upon a plan. She would bring up Shareen's name at least once a day. That way, he wouldn't be able to blot her out and he would be forced to deal with her death, she hoped, somewhat naturally. When Larry had sent all the legal papers necessary for her guardianship, Claire had asked him to send along any pictures he could spare, any mementoes. She would pull one out every few days, laugh and talk and remember something Shareen had done, or something she had heard about her. Articulating memories of his mother would become such a normal part of Kevin's life Shareen would remain close to him, and not fade away completely.

He and Katy were practically the Bobbsey

Twins nowadays—inseparable. That was good for them both, as Katy was a little shy about changing schools yet again. At her age, friends she'd left for a few months had grown into entirely different people by the time she saw them again. But she would do all right.

Samantha was another story. After barely two months in a British boarding school, she was now sporting an English accent guaranteed to set her apart from the soft Southern drawls all around her. At the moment, it made her seem like a young princess, and the other girls looked at her with a sort of bewildered awe. But that couldn't last; resentment was bound to set in soon. Claire shook her head in dismay. Her contrary child. What was she going to do with her?

But they were all together and cheerful this evening, with Laura's boys and Claire's girls and Kevin and Gary and the exchange students. Her mother loved feeding a crowd, and that was what she was doing.

Suddenly, they needed another plate at the table.

The first Claire knew about it was when her mother called to her from the entryway. "A friend of yours has arrived."

"Matt!" Forgetting everything else, she flew into his arms, laughing. "Oh, it's so good to see you! Come on in. Meet my family."

His eyes were warm as he looked at her. "I missed you," he said simply.

Her laughter faded in her face as she studied

his. "I missed you, too," she replied, almost surprised to realize that was true.

After introductions, Matt sat down and ate heartily. The Swedish students, Kristin and Greta, were quite taken with him, much to Gary's chagrin, and asked all sorts of questions about Saudi Arabia, and then, when they found out he was a geologist, about rocks and mountains and other land-related concerns. Others chimed in and soon everyone was discussing continental drift. Claire laughed. What a topic for Thanksgiving.

Afterward, she and Matt took a walk in the garden, parkas keeping them warm, and talked.

"Have you heard from Howard?" he asked.

Claire looked up, her furry hood framing her face. "The last I heard, he was on his way to Houston to talk to some oil people. I hope he finds something."

"I'm sure he will. Regardless of his missteps in Saudi, he's a good engineer. He'll land on his feet."

"I suppose so." She sighed. "I haven't heard anything from him about the divorce. I'm assuming he would just as soon get rid of us all and not have to think about us again. But you know, if he finds some reason to get angry, he could try to get joint custody of the girls, or something like that."

"How would they feel about that?"

She shot him a worried glance. "You want to know the truth? I think they would hate it. They want to see him sometimes. He's still their father and always will be. But they don't want to live with him any more than I do."

They stopped beside the rose arbor. The roses had all been cut back. Only the thorns remained. The garden looked stark now. But the promise of a bountiful spring was clear in the bulges along the canes.

"And what are you doing with yourself?" he asked.

She smiled. "I'm about to go back to work, thank God. I'm going to be acting curator of the music library at the university. The permanent curator is going on maternity leave. And I only hope, when she gets that baby in her arms, she'll find she can't bear to leave it all day and will give up her job to me for the long haul."

"That sounds perfect for you."

"I think it will be. But what about you?"

"I'm on sabbatical until next fall, so I don't have any classes to teach, but I'll be at the university, too, doing research. And I'm going to write a book."

"A book? Not on the nefarious dealings of a certain oil company in the Middle East, I hope."

"Not a chance." He chuckled. "Although that is a thought. I could throw in some sex and violence and have a bestseller on my hands."

"Please!" Claire dragged the word out exaggeratedly.

"Actually, I'm preparing to publish an analysis of the evolution of electronic music."

"Electronic music." She stared at him in horror. "Why not Satanism? Why not a study of people who torture insects? Why on earth would you want to pick the lowest of the low, the crassest of the crass, the dregs of—"

His eyebrows rose. "Oh-oh, I can see I have an unreconstructed music snob on my hands."

She seemed stunned by the concept. "Is it snobbery to prefer the natural to the artificial? Is it snobbery to prefer faceted diamonds to pieces of gravel?"

"Ah, the blind, narrow-minded prejudices of the traditional music world." His smile was wicked. "You do realize I'm going to be doing a lot of research at the music library, don't you? I'll be asking your help to look up all kinds of things on synthesizers and sound-designing software and digital interfacing. . . ."

"You won't find what you want in a music library," she advised smugly, nose in the air, teasing him like crazy, but only half-joking. "Try the hardware store. They might be able to help you."

He pretended to make a grab for her and she ran, laughing, until he caught her, curling her into his arms and looking down, his eyes smoky with . . . what? She wasn't sure. He's going to kiss me, she thought. Good. It's about time.

But no. He let her go, releasing her almost as though he couldn't wait to get her out of his arms, and they walked along again. She wondered why.

Perhaps it was his wife. But no. Claire wasn't sure how long ago Blair had died, but she was sure it was years. He couldn't still be mourning her, could he?

"I like Katy and Sam," he said, stopping by the

front porch. "They're certainly a couple of beauties. Like their mother."

She smiled. "I kind of like them myself."

He grinned, then his face changed and he frowned. "Samantha is rather aloof, though, isn't she?"

He'd picked up on Claire's major worry right away. "Aloof isn't the word for it. She's in another universe, a universe that doesn't want to recognize ours." It hurt, the distance she felt between herself and her daughter. Joking about it didn't really help.

Matt seemed to sense her pain. "Maybe she's just shy."

"Maybe. But how is one to know when she won't open up in any way, shape or form?" She looked up at him, her eyes full of her unhappiness, and he touched her cheek, then drew his hand away.

"Maybe she just needs an activity to get her going. Is she interested in any sports?"

"She used to be on the swim team when we lived here before, and she loved it. She was quite good, in fact. She made the Junior Olympics in the backstroke. But now she refuses to even go and look at her old team."

He nodded, looking thoughtful. "Have you ever considered synchronized swimming?"

Claire made a face. "You mean those girls who glue their hair down and plaster smiles on their faces and stick their toes out of the water?"

"Yup." He grinned. "My sister coaches a team at the McArthur Center pool. The way Sam moves, with her grace, her poise, her body sense, she'd be a natural."

Claire was intrigued but skeptical. "It sounds great, but I don't know how you could approach her about it. I wouldn't dare bring it up myself. She automatically rules out any of my ideas."

Matt nodded. "That's not unusual for teenagers, if I remember my own teenage years. Let me think it over. I might be able to come up with something."

Laura called from the doorway. "Pumpkin pie is on. Better hurry if you want a piece. The kids have decided they like it this year."

Matt put a hand at the small of her back as they returned to the dining room, and she thought how good it felt. But when she looked at him, there was nothing special in his eyes, and she felt vaguely rebuffed.

Why hadn't he kissed her? And why did she suddenly care so much?

She started working at the library the next Monday. Betty, her middle-aged assistant, helped to show her the ropes and she dug right in, loving the work. She'd been away from music too long. Just handling the aging sheet music, the heavy books on the composers, the drawer after drawer of tapes, gave her chills. When five o'clock rolled around each day, she was surprised and a little disappointed to see that it was already time to go home.

True to his word, Matt came in on her third day. They bantered good-naturedly about his penchant for electronic music, but she helped him find what he needed. As he left, Betty watched him go, then grinned as she turned to Claire.

"He's handsome, isn't he?"

Claire realized she had never really thought about his looks. "Yes. Yes, he is."

Betty put her head to the side and uttered a melodramatic sigh. "It's too bad he never remarried after his wife died. I guess that scandalous affair with that student set him back a bit. I haven't known him to be serious about another woman since."

Claire sat very still in her chair. "Scandalous affair?" she asked carefully. "What scandalous affair was that?"

"Don't you remember?"

"I wasn't here."

"Oh. That's right." Betty's smug smile gave evidence that she'd known that all along, but she welcomed the chance to deliver old gossip. "It happened, oh, quite a few years ago. About a year after his wife died. He started dating a student, very discreetly at first. She was a pretty, popular little thing, homecoming queen and all that. But some fraternity boy, who had a crush on her, got his nose out of joint about it, so he took some of his frat brothers and they caught Matt out behind the stadium and proceeded to try to beat him up—you know, warning him to stay away from the girl. Well, it turned out there weren't enough brothers along. Matt put two of them in the hospital and the third one wore a shiner you could see from here to Thursday. The parents complained, of course, and the board almost fired him. It was touch and go for a while. In the end, Matt kept his job but lost the girl. She quit school and moved to New York, so I heard."

"And that was it?"

"That was it. Kind of sad, don't you think? Every girl on campus thinks so. Any number of them would love to console him. But he keeps his distance these days."

"Well, what do you know," Claire murmured thoughtfully. You learned something new every day.

A few days later, he came in right after they'd opened. She looked up from her ledger and there he was, the morning sunlight streaming in behind him.

"Good morning," she said with a smile. She enjoyed seeing him like this. It reminded her of the breakfasts they had shared in Saudi Arabia.

"Hi." His gaze ran over her conservative green wool suit, the hair in a knot at the back of her head, the glasses on her nose, and he frowned. "Is there some librarians' code or something?" he asked. "Why do you all dress like that?"

This was her best suit. Indignation charged her reply.

"It's a disguise," she returned smartly. "I'm in deep cover here. You see—" she thought fast "—I'm actually an agent for a foreign power that has designs on our electronic-music industry." She gave him a triumphant glare over the glasses. "My real name is Lola, honey, and I really look like this."

It took only seconds to pull the pins out of her hair and shake it into a cloud around her shoulders, to tug off the glasses and put them on the desk, to shimmy out of the jacket of her suit, leaving her in the tight, skimpy little silk blouse and relatively short, snug skirt. She rose and took a provocative pose.

"Is this better for you?" she asked him, chin high, chest thrust out, hand on her hip.

He was laughing, but suddenly she noticed that two students had come in behind him. Their eyes were wide and worried, and they gave the curator's desk a wide berth.

"Oh, Matt, now look what you've made me do," she hissed, shoving the glasses back on her nose. "That was so unprofessional of me! The administration will probably ask me to leave by lunchtime."

"Don't worry, Lola." He tweeked her chin with quick affection. "You can always get a job at the Kitty Kat Klub."

"Strippers R Us?" She couldn't hold back the answering grin as she shrugged back into her jacket. "Will you give me a reference?"

"No problem." He reached out and stopped her hands as they began to gather up her thick hair. "Don't do that," he said softly. "Leave it down. It looks so sexy."

Something warm and exciting shivered through her and she met his gaze with her own. "I . . . I'm not supposed to look sexy. This is a library."

His thumb touched her wrist, stroking across it in a way that tingled. "Just for today," he said, his eyes too deep to read. "I've got work to do in the listening booth. When I look out here, I want to see you like this."

The whole thing was ridiculous, of course. There was no place for "sexy" in the library. And the word had no real business in their relationship, anyway. She and Matt were friends. Where did he get off using this "sexy" stuff on her?

But she didn't tie back her hair. And all morning, while he worked in one of the glass listening booths at the back of the room, she was conscious of his presence, and very careful not to look back and meet his gaze.

Twelve o'clock came and she began to wonder what he was planning to do for lunch. She waited, thinking he might ask her to join him, and then, when he still went on listening to tapes and taking notes, she worked up a little speech of her own to ask him to one of her favorite restaurants. When she had it all prepared, she got up and went back to the listening booth, opened the door and stuck her head in.

"Hi," she said cheerily. "I was just wondering if—"

That was as far as she got. She realized he had a sandwich in his hand and was chewing on a bite at that very moment.

"Oh." The realization fueled her disappointment and caused the snappish tone in her next words. "You're not supposed to eat in here."

He finished chewing and said mildly, "I won't drop crumbs. Honest."

"Well . . . I'm going to lunch."

"Bon appetit."

She'd never noticed before what an annoying man he was. "I'm sure I'll have a wonderful meal," she said, and turned away, letting the door close behind her.

She went to the ice-cream parlor and had a hot fudge sundae, just to make herself feel better. She felt restless and dissatisfied, and she wasn't sure why.

Back at the library, she found it hard to keep her mind on her work. When Matt came out and spoke to her, she was so startled she jumped a foot into the air.

"Sorry," he said. "I just wanted some help finding a reference on Shostakovich. I'm not having any luck."

She steadied herself and looked at the notation he handed her. "Oh, I know where it is. Come on back to the vault. It's an original, and we keep some of the more fragile works back there."

She led him through the stacks and unlocked the door to the vault.

"Shostakovich?" she asked archly. "What do you want with him? He's a *real* composer."

Matt's smile was teasing. "You know how it is. Compare and contrast. I like to cover everything."

She smiled and looked away, and then something drew her gaze back again. There was a new intimacy in the way Matt looked at her. Or was she imagining it?

"It's on the top shelf," she said, looking away again and pulling over the step stool. "I'll get it for you."

She climbed quickly and had the document in her hand, but her attention was still on Matt and this new feeling that seemed to be emerging between them, and she lost her footing.

The sickening sense of space hit her and she cried out, reaching for a handhold and finding nothing but Matt's arms as he caught her and held her and kept her from harm.

She still had the papers in her hand. Looking up into Matt's face, she tried to smile.

"Are you all right?" he asked, but he didn't release her.

"I'm fine," she said in a voice like sandpaper. "I'm . . . just fine."

His arms still held her close. He was looking down at her lips. She could feel his arms tightening, see movement in his eyes.

This time he'll kiss me, she thought, and she waited, breathless.

When his arms loosened, she had that feeling of falling again, only this time she was already standing on the ground and it was only that he was withdrawing his support, taking away his warmth.

"Thanks," he said, taking the papers from her limp hand. "I'll give these back before I leave."

And then he was gone, going back through the stacks and out of her sight. She stood very still, listening to the sound of her own breathing. What was going on here? Was she going nuts? They were just friends, damn it! There was no reason for her to get thrown off the track this way.

Feeling the need to put distance between them, she found a reason to go to the post office. When she got back to the library, he was gone, and she felt as though the sun had gone behind a cloud for keeps.

He came by the house on Friday night, but not to see Claire. It turned out her mother had recruited him to escort Greta and Kristin to an International Center dance.

"Mother," Claire said indignantly when told of the plan, "What are you trying to do? I'm sure the girls would have no trouble finding escorts of their own."

Her mother smiled wisely, like a woman with her cards held close to her vest. "Some of the most unsuitable men chase the poor things all the time. I wanted to make sure they had a nice man with them for a change."

Claire found herself in an unusually grumpy mood when she let Matt in that evening.

"So, you're going out with the Swedish girls." She looked him up and down, and frowned. "Kind of dressed up, aren't you?" She'd never seen him in a dinner jacket before. He looked . . . great.

"I don't want to embarrass Kristen and Greta." He grinned at her, then turned to look at the students, who were making last-minute preparations in front of the hall mirror and hadn't noticed him yet. His eyebrows rose. "Oh, my. Don't they look nice?"

Claire wished she'd thought to remain in her room for the evening. She hadn't realized this was going to be quite so annoying.

"Of course they look nice," she snapped. "They're young. They're blond."

One of them bent over, her low-cut dress revealing an awful lot of breast. "Big, buxom girls," Claire growled, furious with herself for acting so catty, but unable to stop. "Just the way you like them."

He turned to look at her, one eyebrow raised. "Who said I liked big, buxom girls?"

She glared at him. "Don't all men?"

He turned back to examine Greta and Kristen, still chattering away in front of the mirror. His face softened. "Well, you might have a point there. I can't deny I like the look of a nice, round—"

Suddenly he noticed the expression on Claire's face and stopped himself. With one hand, he took her chin and raised her stormy gaze to his.

"But what I really like, lovely lady," he whispered, "is a female form with the elegance of a Japanese brushstroke. As strong and wiry as a length of bamboo. As graceful as an antelope. Know anyone who fits that description?"

The girls saw him and began to giggle and call out to him to join them, and he turned, smiling, leaving Claire standing there, trembling slightly, feeling foolish, but with a warm glow she tried hard to deny.

December came and everything was geared toward celebrating Christmas. At the Duvall house, they got out all the old decorations, and shared the memories tied to each one. If there was sadness in some of their memories, that only served to strengthen them. Claire was glad she was home this year. Home, where she belonged, for the holidays.

Christmas dinner had to be planned; who would be invited, who would sit where. One day Laura stopped by the little office Matt still kept at the university to talk over some plans with him.

"Listen, Matt," she said, flopping down on the only chair not covered with books, "you've got to help me. We've got to find a man for Claire."

Matt's eyes darkened warningly and he didn't smile. "A man for Claire? Why can't she find her own?"

Laura hit the desktop with her hand to emphasize her words as she replied, "Because she just won't. And she needs someone."

He shuffled some papers and put them into a neat stack. "Oh?" he said casually. "What makes you think that?"

"Everyone needs someone. And I want to see her happy."

"I thought she told you in no uncertain terms to stay away from this sort of thing."

Laura's huge eyes were all innocence. "I just want to do this one last thing, and then I'll never bother her again, honest."

That got a grin from him. "I see."

"So you'll help me?"

He shook his head. "Not on your life."

She leaned forward as though she hadn't heard him. "Listen, I know this wonderful professor of ichthyology who's just been divorced. What do you think? Shall I bring him over for Christmas dinner?"

Matt's grin disappeared and his face hardened. "I don't think that would be such a good idea," he said carefully.

Laura batted her eyes in Southern belle bewilderment. "Well, whyever not?"

He leaned toward her, his eyes revealing banked fires within. "Because if you did, I would probably have to punch him out. And that would be so messy for Christmas."

She threw up her hands and laughed with delight. "Why, Matt Stevens, you rough old thing!" She slapped him playfully. "That was just what I was hoping you would say." She got up and started for the door.

"Laura." He came after her and stopped her with a hand on her arm, speaking earnestly. "Please. Stay out of this. Or you're going to ruin things."

She was all innocence again. "Don't you worry about me, Matt. I'll be as quiet as a mouse." She giggled. "You see these lips? They're sealed, honey."

And she was gone in a swirl of skirts. Matt stared after her, shaking his head. Life was a gamble, he thought philosophically.

Claire was glad Matt was around. He was not only
someone she could depend on if ever she needed
him, he was also a lot of fun as a companion. She
found herself thinking about him more and more
often, and watching for him on campus. She knew
where his office was, though she had never visited
it. And she saw him now and then, strolling across
the green, invariably surrounded by a cluster of students.

He dropped by the library every couple of
days, giving her the opportunity to carry on their
running battle between "real" and electronic
music. And he came by the house a few times a
week. But he never asked her out on a date.

That was beginning to irritate her. After all,
what would it cost him to take her to a movie and
dinner? Maybe she should reassure him that she
would pay for her own meal afterward. But some-

how she knew that wasn't going to make any difference. He seemed to like her well enough. But he didn't seem to find the need to see her alone. At night. Under the stars.

The man wasn't shy. And she didn't really think he was still hung up on his wife, not in a way that would preclude another relationship. So what was it? Why hadn't he kissed her? Why hadn't he touched her? Why hadn't he done anything to make them . . . closer?

Well, that was pretty easy to remedy. It was Christmas, wasn't it? With a grim smile, she grabbed a twig of mistletoe and tacked it above the doorway between the hall and the living room.

This is the oldest one in the book, she scolded herself as she worked. But what else could she do without losing all sense of subtlety?

Matt was coming over in a few moments, bringing a wreath he had ordered from a boys' club where they made them up specially. For some crazy reason she found herself flushed with excitement as the time for his arrival drew near. Was she going to get a kiss out of the man tonight?

Greta and Kristen came into the room and her heart sank. If she had to stand back while these two monopolized the mistletoe . . . !

But no, they were giggling and saying good-bye, leaving for a late lecture. She breathed a sigh of relief. And then the doorbell rang, and Matt was there.

"Hi."

"Hello." He held out the wreath. "What do you think?"

"It's beautiful. Leave it here by the door. We can put it up later."

"I could do it now if you get me a hammer and—"

"No, no," she said quickly. "Come on in by the fire. I've made us some hot chocolate."

"Oh. Well, all right." He put down the wreath and followed her down the hall.

"I've been putting up decorations for the last hour," she said, trying to sound light and chatty. "I put the lights in the tree and set out the candles." She paused in the doorway to the living room and looked upward. "And look, I put up some mistletoe."

She was standing right under it and smiling at him. He looked up at it, then down at her and nodded.

"Nice mistletoe," he said.

And that was all. She stared at him, her smile getting strained. He wasn't moving. Oh, Lord! Why wouldn't he kiss her?

"Matt," she said softly, "there's a tradition here you are ignoring."

"Me?"

She nodded. "You. We have the woman. We have the man. We have the mistletoe. There's only one thing wrong with this picture. Why is the man not kissing the woman under the mistletoe?"

He pretended to be shocked, but there was the suggestion of a twinkle in his eye. "What? Is that what you've been hinting around about ever since I walked in the door?"

"Yes!" She grabbed him by the arms, determined, despite the fact her cheeks were hot with embarrassment. "Now come close and do it."

"All right, ma'am," he murmured, his lips only inches from hers. "I'll do it."

She had to admit later, the kiss was worth the wait. Warm and tender, it curled her toes and lasted until she began to think about the fact that, since the Swedish girls had left, there was no one home but the two of them. But just when she thought they had hit a peak from which it would be hard to retreat, he pulled away.

"There's a time limit on mistletoe kisses," he told her. "Come on, let's go have some of that hot chocolate."

She followed him into the living room, sat down on the couch next to him and poured out two cups, still tingling from the kiss. Sitting back, she stared at him, torn between anger and bewilderment.

"Don't you like me?" she challenged at last.

He put down his cup, his blue eyes calm. "Of course I like you."

She took a deep breath and forced herself to go on. "Then why do I have to go to these lengths to get you to kiss me?"

He faced her coolly. "I was waiting for you to be ready."

"Ready?" She shook her head. "What do you mean? Ready for what?"

His eyes were like deep pools, and a look, almost of pain, crossed his handsome features. Reaching out, he laced his fingers through the silky fullness of her hair.

"I don't want to be another Peter in your life, Claire. I don't want to be just a part of your education. If you come to me, you come for good."

His intensity startled her. She hadn't expected that. She was asking for dessert and he was saying she had to eat her dinner first. But what if she wasn't that hungry?

"Can't we just . . . enjoy each other? Have a good time together? Does it have to be so serious?"

He smiled and let her hair flutter through his fingers. "You see," he said softly, his eyes full of regret, "you're not ready yet."

Matt came to Christmas dinner. That made Kristen and Greta happy, but Gary scowled until Matt suggested the two of them take the Swedes out for a drive to show them the holiday lights. Then Gary perked up, but Claire lost her good humor.

Eventually the group returned and everyone gathered around the piano. They sang carols until the little ones fell asleep over their new toys, and the grown-ups were yawning.

Claire walked Matt to the door, and he bent to kiss her softly on the lips, then went off into the night. She closed the door and leaned back against it, closing her eyes.

Her emotions were in a mess where that man was concerned. When he had first told her she wasn't ready, she'd been indignant, refusing to accept that there was something to be ready for. But after a few days' reflection, she knew he was right. There were too many things haunting her—her father's death, her divorce, Shareen's death, and Kevin, Samantha, Peter. She really wasn't ready.

Everyone seemed to have gone to bed. She went into the kitchen and found her mother doing some last-minute washing of dishes. Grabbing a towel, Claire began to dry.

"It was a lovely Christmas, wasn't it?" Her mother sighed. "One of the best we've ever had, I think."

"It was nice. I only wish Dad could have been here to share it with us."

Her mother's hands went still in the dishwater for a moment, then she turned and looked at her daughter. "Claire, I think it's time you faced a few truths. You've been moaning about how much you missed not knowing your father better all those years. I suppose I should have pulled you up short on that subject right from the beginning. But you seemed to enjoy the agony so much, I just let you go on."

Claire stared at her mother. "What on earth are you talking about?"

"The truth is, my dear, your father couldn't deal with you in any way until you were well into adulthood. He didn't like children, Claire. He didn't want children. And he never forgave me for going ahead and having two of them right under his nose."

Claire blinked. "But . . . but if we'd talked, if he had gotten to know us . . ."

"I know a part of you has begun thinking this was all my fault, Claire, but here I go—I'm going to defend myself against a dead man who can't stand up and say his piece. But I can't help that. Your father wanted you out of sight. He wanted to send the two of you off to a boarding school from the time you were born. He lived for his music. Once I had betrayed him by having two girls, he withdrew from me. That was it as far as he was concerned. We lived in the same house, but otherwise our paths hardly crossed."

"But that wasn't the way it was in the last few years."

"You're right. Once we got you two out of the house, he went back to being a normal human being again. Everything was fine. The love we'd felt for each other actually revived. But I don't want you to think that anything could have been different. I'm here to tell you it could not. No matter how lovable you were, little Claire, he wasn't going to love you because you were a child. That was that."

Even though she recognized the truth of her mother's words, Claire rebelled. Wasn't she going to be allowed to keep any of her dreams intact? She left her mother and made her way to her father's den, turning on the light and slipping inside. She touched the worn leather on the chair and looked down at the place under the desk where she had hidden that day so long ago. She felt him there, could almost see his grouchy face.

"So you really didn't like me until about a year ago," she said softly. "You know what? You were wrong to let that happen. Dead wrong. You missed a lot not knowing me or Laura. Mostly your loss. But also ours. You cheated us out of a father. I'm going to hold that against you."

She turned and ran her hand over the spines of books in his bookcase. "I'm not going to do what you did," she went on. "I'm going to stay close to Katy, and work harder at getting to Sam." A sudden smile curled her lips. "Sam takes after you a bit, doesn't she? Stubborn, ornery. But I'll get through to her. I swear I will. I'm not going to let her slip away."

She took a shuddering breath. "I love you, Daddy. I feel cheated, though. You left me too soon, but you also came to me too late. But I love you. I'll always love you."

Tears poured from her eyes and she slumped into the big leather chair and cried until she could cry no more. Don't lose touch—that was the lesson here. Always keep the lines open.

She went back to her mother and they talked long into the night, crying together, laughing together. And she felt renewed. This was what it was all about. Don't lose touch.

She called Howard. He was in Houston and had two job offers he was considering. He was cool but not hostile. He agreed to everything she suggested concerning the custody of the girls. He would see them occasionally but had no interest in having them live with him. Claire breathed a sigh of relief.

"Send me papers," he said. "I'll sign anything."

He was ready to begin a new life without encumbrances.

She wrote to Peter, care of the Hotel Paradissos—just a short note, wishing him well, letting him know where she was. She stopped just short of telling him that she loved him, though she did in her fashion. She would never forget what they had shared. It had changed her life. She chewed on her pen for a long time before she decided how to put it to him. In the end, she wrote, "I'll treasure our time together always," and left it at that.

Matt called. "Would you like to go to a New Year's Eve party?" he asked without preamble.

She never went out on New Year's. Hesitating, she thought of dressing up and going out with him, of staying out all night, of dancing and toasting and laughing. There was something compellingly attractive in all that.

"I'd love to go."

That was all. She didn't see him or hear from him again all week, but early New Year's Eve she spent two hours getting ready. Her dress was slinky, red shot with embroidered gold spears from the fitted waistline. She piled her hair high, a few curling wisps about her face, and put on earrings that dangled almost to her shoulders.

"Wow!" he said when he saw her. "You look terrific."

He seemed oddly uncomfortable, though, and then she noticed that he was wearing gray slacks and a white sweater. No dinner jacket. Not even a tie.

"This is my fault," he said quickly. "I should have told you . . . Listen, never mind. There are a couple of fancy parties we can go to. You need to show this off in the proper setting. The chemistry department members are having a big bash at the Marriott. . . ."

She was still looking him up and down, but she was also shaking her head. "I don't need a fancy party, Matt. I just assumed . . . Tell me what you were planning."

"Well . . ." He hesitated. "You see, my parents always have something at New Year's. It's very casual, just close friends. But we could drop by there later, if you'd rather go to this party at the Marriott."

He wanted to take her home to meet his parents. This man was a master at mixed signals. Did this mean anything? Obviously not. But she didn't care. At least he wasn't ashamed of her. And she wanted to meet his parents.

"Shall I change into jeans?" she asked, only half-joking.

"Are you kidding? You stay exactly the way you are. I want to look at you. You're really something."

He was always wanting to look at her. Why didn't he seem to want to touch?

In the end they skipped the fancy party and drove straight to his parents'. It took almost two hours to get there, a long drive through woods and farmland, where the air smelled clean and fresh and the stars were out in force.

"My father's been the Baptist minister in a small farming community for years," Matt told her as they drove.

"A preacher's son?" She smiled at his profile silhouetted against the traffic from the other side of the road. "Men of the cloth usually produce the wildest children around."

"That's the story," he agreed. "Unfortunately, I was quite a disappointment to everyone on that score. I was just a normal kid. I didn't rob the corner store or wreck my daddy's car or get any girls pregnant or anything interesting."

She laughed. "I bet they still shake their heads to this day over your failure to conform."

"You'd better believe it. Every time I go home I can tell everyone is just waiting to hear if I've been indicted or run off with the chancellor's wife or something juicy."

Claire gasped. "Oh, I get it now. You conned me into dressing up like this so you could take me home and show me off as your new floozy. Right?"

His laugh rang out through the car. "I hadn't thought of it, but what a good idea. Do you mind if I introduce you as Lola?"

The Stevens' home was modest but comfortable and filled with friends and relatives, all of whom wanted to meet Claire. Her head was spinning as she met one after another, dancing with a lot of the men to the music one of the teenagers kept putting on the stereo, chatting with the women. Instead of the usual champagne and wine, the house was filled with the scent of baked goods and homemade apple cider. The children took turns providing entertainment, and just after midnight, Matt's mother took Claire aside to talk to her.

A tall, elegant woman with a warm, lined face, Mrs. Stevens was obviously a force to be reckoned with in the family.

"You know," she began, "you're the first woman Matt has brought home since Blair. Do you know about Blair?"

Claire nodded. "Yes. Matt has told me."

"She was a peach. There was a time when I thought he would never get over losing her. But I see him with you, and I see the old Matt I used to love. He's got that sparkle in his eyes again."

Her words put a glow in Claire's heart. "I'm glad. You know, I . . . I like him very much."

Mrs. Stevens smiled and reached out to give Claire a hug. "Don't hurt my boy, Claire," she whispered in her ear. "He's been hurt enough for one lifetime."

Hurt Matt Stevens? There didn't seem to be much chance of that. He hadn't let her get close enough to do any real damage. And that was just exactly what was so frustrating about the man.

"What was my mother bending your ear about?" Matt asked her as they left the party and went out into the cool night air.

"About Blair." She looked at him quickly to see

if she could catch a hint of tragedy in his eyes, but there was none she could see.

He helped her into the car. "My family loved Blair, and she loved it out here."

"Are you truly over her?" she asked as he got into the driver's seat.

He looked back at her in the dark and said quietly, "I'll never be over Blair. She'll always live in my heart."

Not exactly the answer she'd wanted to hear. But it was the only answer she got. They drove back in silence, until the bright city lights wavered ahead.

"Did you have a good time?" he asked her.

"Yes," she said with feeling. "I had a wonderful time. I like your family. They're . . . real people."

He nodded and she thought she saw a smile on his lips.

It was late when they arrived back in front of her house. "It's late—three o'clock," she said, "but would you like to come in for a nightcap?" she added hopefully.

He shook his head.

Searching his eyes, she asked, "What would you like?"

His grin flashed in the moonlight. "I'll tell you one thing life has taught me, Claire. The longer you wait for something, the more you appreciate it once you get it."

She didn't like that answer much, either, but before she could protest, he was kissing her, his mouth hot and hungry, his arms wrapping around her, holding her tight and hard against him.

"Happy New Year, Claire," he murmured, and the next thing she knew she was standing in her own doorway, watching his taillights disappear around the corner, and wondering why.

21

It was a new year, and for once, it felt new, all sparkly and full of promise. Claire saw Matt almost daily, one way or another. She knew she was becoming addicted to his presence. He was important to her life, vital to her happiness. And to top it off, he was working wonders with Samantha.

Once he'd gotten to know her well enough to gain her confidence, he had talked her into coming with him to help some of his students paint some scenery for a performance. Sam didn't know it was for synchronized swimming until they got to the pool. The team was in the water, practicing, and Matt didn't mention them once, keeping the conversation to the job at hand, painting the scenery.

But Sam's paintbrush moved less and less as she spent more and more time watching the girls work out, and she appeared just as intrigued as he had hoped. When Matt told her the coach was his sister, he could see in her eyes that she would try it. And sure enough, the next day when she drove over with him, she brought her swimsuit.

Claire was pleased about the progress with Samantha, but not about her own progress with Matt. She wanted him to kiss her again, but the mistletoe season was over. She'd begun to think about it all the time. The utter lack of physical intimacy was making her nervous. It was making her tense. What was wrong with a little kissing, anyway? The man had no heart. She wanted him. Badly.

She tried little subterfuges, like being in the right place at the right time, but nothing worked. He acted oblivious. As though they were just friends. And Claire was beginning to hate it.

But what did she want exactly? Had those lazy, crazy days in Greece turned her into a hedonist? Was it sex she longed for?

No. If great sex were all she had on her mind, it would be Peter she lay awake nights thinking about, not Matt.

Lovemaking was definitely involved, though, judging by the way her heart was beginning to pound when she caught sight of Matt in the hallways. She heard his voice behind her in the cafeteria and her hands would begin to shake. She found him talking to a good-looking coed and she would spend the rest of the afternoon in agony. His touch on her shoulder would make her jump, and every time she saw him, she would ache to feel his arms around her.

How could he have kissed her the way he had

on New Year's Eve and then act as though they were mere acquaintances? The more she analyzed it the more she was convinced there had been real passion in that kiss. He wanted her as much as she wanted him. So why was he resisting her?

Finally she couldn't stand it any longer. If he wasn't going to do anything about it, she was going to have to take things into her own hands.

Her decision amazed her. A year before, she could never have thought such a thing. But now, all things were possible. She knew. She'd lived a lot of them.

She picked a Friday evening. Going out against a cold winter wind, she took her car to his apartment, parking in front and sitting in the car for almost half an hour before she got up the nerve to go in.

He answered the door in a black turtleneck sweater and charcoal slacks, looking very handsome and very urbane. Behind him seethed a mass of young faces.

"Oh, hi, Claire," he said cheerfully. "Come on in. We're having a little get-together. These are some of my students from last year. Lately, they've gotten into the habit of dropping by just about every Friday night."

Visiting students had not entered into Claire's plan. "But you're not teaching right now," she complained, letting him draw her into the room.

"Grad students never fade away," he told her with a grin. "They hang on for years and years. And they never forget you. Come on over and meet everybody."

Claire didn't want to meet everybody. She'd spent hours preparing herself for this confrontation, and now her focus was being dissipated by meeting and greeting. All these fresh young faces. She wanted them out of here. But aside from yelling "Fire!" she didn't see how that would be accomplished.

Very well, then. She would have to kidnap Matt.

Excusing herself, she went into his bedroom to use the phone. She made a reservation and gave the person on the other end of the line her credit card number. "Please leave the door unlocked," she said. "I won't need a key. We won't be going in and out."

Returning to the gathering, she called Matt aside. "I need you to come help me with something," she whispered.

He followed her readily enough, looking only slightly surprised when she led him out the door and down the stairs.

"Is there something wrong with your car?" he asked.

She hesitated. "Get in the passenger's seat," she asked without answering his question. She hopped behind the wheel and started the engine.

After they'd gone a few blocks, Matt asked, "What is it? Am I supposed to be listening for something?"

She smiled nervously. "Just a minute." She

pulled the car into the Shady Rest Motel and parked before number thirteen. And then she sat there, frozen, staring straight ahead, not sure she could go through with her plan.

"Claire. What is this? What are we doing here?"

She took a deep, shuddering breath. "I'm trying to seduce you," she said.

"Oh." He waited, but she didn't move. "How are you planning to do that?"

She bit her lip. "I—I'm not sure. The seduction starts when we get into the room, actually. But I can't seem to move." She turned tragic eyes his way. "How do they usually get you into the room?"

His eyes were dark, but she thought she could detect a trace of laughter lurking in them. "I don't know," he said as seriously as he could manage. "I've never actually been seduced this way before."

"Oh." She sighed. "Then I guess I'm just going to have to invite you in."

"That might work."

She turned and smiled tremulously. "Matt Stevens, will you please come into the motel room with me?" Her heart was beating very hard. Surely he heard it. If he told her no, now, if he started yammering about being "ready" . . .

But his face was full of warmth and acceptance. He reached out and cupped the side of her face in his hand. "Claire Duvall, I would love to go into that motel room with you. As long as you promise me one thing."

"What?" she asked warily.

He leaned close and dropped a soft kiss on her lips. "I want a turn." He stroked her cheek. "After you seduce me, I get to seduce you. Agreed?"

She laughed, throwing her arms around his neck. "Oh, yes," she cried. "Yes, yes, yes."

She was nervous when they first went in, but he wasn't. He moved with smooth assurance, as though he had been the one to set this up. When her fingers shook too much for her to deal with her buttons, he took over, murmuring things she loved to hear as he did so. His voice got huskier as they went along, and his movements less controlled as urgency built between them.

The first time was hot and fast and hard, and for Claire it was over too soon, but the next time, he whispered, *"Adagio,"* and they took it slow and easy and she felt a sense of fulfillment that seeped all the way into her soul.

She loved seeing his naked body again. The memory of it had been lurking in the margins of her memory for months, and it looked just as good now as it had that day in the shower. They made love all night and had room service in the morning, and it was so right, so in tune with where she was and who she was, that she never wanted to let him go again.

"Tell me something," she said, lying across him, her cheek to his chest. "How did you know if I was 'ready' this time?"

He chuckled, letting his hand slide down the length of her spine to nestle in the small of her back. "Let's just put it this way, Claire. I was so far beyond 'ready' myself, I was about to self-destruct. Self-control can only take you so far."

She snuggled into his shoulder. "So you do like me," she said happily.

"Like you?" He tilted his head back so he could see into her face. "Claire, don't you get it yet? I love you."

A thrill shot through her, catching at her breath. "But . . . you said the other night that Blair would always be in your heart. . . ."

"And I meant it. But Blair is in my past, Claire." He took her chin in his hand. "You are my future."

She closed her eyes. So this was love. It was almost too wonderful to be true. Had it ever felt this way with Howard? No. Nor with Peter. This was the real thing. And boy, was she ready!

"I knew the minute I saw you walking along the sidewalk that night after the concert that you were for me," Matt went on. "I decided right then and there that I was going to get you. Somehow."

She looked at him, aghast. "I was happily married then."

His mouth twisted in a sarcastic grin. "Right. I could sure tell."

She pretended to punch him in the side. "You're too smart for your own good, Matt Stevens."

"No. Just smart enough. Just exactly smart enough."

They announced their engagement on Valentine's Day. The wedding was planned for June, and in the days and months that followed, Claire knew she was doing the right thing.

Matt was wonderful. He'd helped turn Samantha around. He got along famously with Katy and Kevin. Laura adored him. Jim and Gary both thought he was a great guy. And her mother beamed every time his name was mentioned—which was often.

Claire felt alive as she never had before. She loved her job, and it was beginning to look as though it might be permanent. She loved her children. And she adored the man she was going to marry. Everything was coming up roses. What could possibly go wrong now?

❧

There was nothing prettier than Atlanta in early June. The dogwoods were about done, but every other flower was blooming like crazy, and the scent of spring was strong. The light seemed brighter, more colorful, as though coming through a prism. There was a special freshness in the air that month, and Claire often found herself breathless. She was floating in a heavenly current of happiness. She was going to get married. To the right man.

The house was decorated with flower baskets and violet ribbons, and the yard had been made into the perfect setting, all neatly trimmed and newly planted. Tables and chairs were set up. Food was cooking. There was excitement in the air, with caterers bustling and her mother a nervous wreck.

Claire walked through the preparations and marveled. Now and then she glanced at her father's den and wondered what he would have made of all this. He would have hated having Kevin and Sam and Katy in the house. Would he have approved of Matt more than he approved of Howard?

"Who knows," she said aloud. "It's my life, anyway, not yours, Daddy."

They were having a big wedding. People from all over had been invited—from New York and Alaska and California.

She was delighted when she realized that Princess Nadia would be able to attend. "What a good excuse to come to America!" the princess wrote in her letter of acceptance. "I'll be looking forward to those lessons you promised me."

Even Larry Hunter was coming. He was taking a few weeks to be with his son, visiting Disney World, before he went back to Lebanon. She was going to miss that little boy, even though Kevin would be away only temporarily. He'd become such a part of the family. And every time she looked into his face, he reminded her of Shareen.

"Thank you, Shareen," Claire whispered as she watched him playing with the other children in the front yard, kicking a soccer ball around on the grass. "Thank you for loaning me your wonderful child. And thank you for helping to teach me that life needs to be lived to the full while we have the chance."

Her life was fuller now than it had ever been. She loved Matt with a richness, a completeness, that blotted out what she had ever felt for any other man. She was his. He was hers. She had never been happier.

Time was slipping away and the ceremony was only a little more than an hour from now. Claire went upstairs to her bedroom, her white robe over her silk slip as she surveyed the job the hairdresser had done with her hair. Pretty good, she reckoned. Ringlets piled high and some cascading down, tiny wisps curling around her face. It reminded her a bit of the way she'd worn her hair to the big party in Greece. She sat staring for a moment, remembering.

Her mother knocked on her door. "Claire? You have a visitor."

Who would visit the bride on the morning of her wedding day? Claire frowned. She didn't want her reverie interrupted. "Who is it, Mother?"

"He says his name is Peter, darling. Peter Arnold. Do you know him?"

Claire felt the blood rush from her face. "Oh, my God." What a time for Peter to show up. "Tell him I'll be right down."

Peter. She hadn't heard a thing from him since leaving Greece. And now, here he was, throwing her emotions into a turmoil she didn't need on a day like this. She didn't know what she was feeling. She would be happy to see him, of course—but not now. Not when she was focused on Matt and the life they were setting off on together.

She cinched the belt on her robe more tightly,

took a deep breath, and went down the stairs quickly.

He was standing in the entryway, smiling up at her as she descended.

"Peter!" The moment she saw him, the warmth came flooding back, and she rushed to him, arms wide. "Oh, Peter, how good to see you."

He gave her a bear hug, laughing. "Claire, you beautiful lady. What are you dressing up for?"

She drew back right away and looked at him, ignoring his question. "I can't believe you're here!"

Peter was tanned and strong-looking, as handsome as ever. The devil-may-care light was still in his eyes. All the things that had ever attracted her to him were there, tugging at her again.

And suddenly she noticed something else. Peter was exceptionally well-dressed, his shirt perfect, his slacks tailor-made, his shoes of expensive leather. A large diamond in a thick gold setting sparkled on his hand. Her gaze flew to his eyes, searching for answers.

"How have you been?" she asked tentatively.

"Fine," he replied. "In fact, more than fine." His lopsided grin was broad. "I guess you might say I'm rich these days, Claire. We found the treasure."

He couldn't have said anything that might have surprised her more. "You what?"

"We found the treasure. And we got away with a bunch of it before the authorities caught on."

It was like a fairy tale. She could hardly believe it. "You actually found the treasure from more than two thousand years ago?"

He laughed. "Well, not quite. The one we found had nothing to do with that one. It was only about two hundred years old. But who cares? It was an old galleon, full of old gold coins. We came out okay."

Claire hardly knew what to think. So much for her judgment. "I—I'm so happy for you."

His eyes were bright with excitement. "Remember how I promised to come get you for the celebration when we found it? Well, Claire, here I am." His face was so young, so eager. "You're coming with me. I figure we'll go to Paris first, and then—"

"Peter." She bit her lip.

"What?" He blinked at her, realizing something was wrong.

"Peter, I'm getting married today."

His face fell. "You can't." He frowned. "Who to?"

"You don't know him. Peter—"

His expression was almost comical in its bewilderment. "But that ruins everything. Can't you hold off on this wedding thing? Just come with me for, say a year. You could always get married later if you still want to. I don't want to tie you down with marriage, you know that. It doesn't fit in with my life-style. But I really want you with me, Claire. Just for a while." His grin was as endearing as ever. "I'm not greedy."

Suddenly she was aware that Matt was standing at the back of the room. How much had he heard? Regret surged through her. Not on her wedding day! She wished the earth would open up and swallow her.

She hated to turn her back on Peter, after all he'd done for her, after all they had meant to each other. But she had to.

The members of the small orchestra had arrived and she could hear them beginning to tune up their instruments in the yard. Matt was watching her. Peter was waiting for an answer.

She smiled at him, shaking her head. "Peter, we had such a great time, and you were so good to me. But that was then. And it wasn't real. This is. I was made for this life, not for running off from one place to another. I'm no adventurer."

Reaching up, she kissed him on the cheek. "I love you for asking me," she said with a smile, "and I hate having to turn you down. But that's the way it goes. You off to sail the seas, and me to a house in the suburbs."

Peter took her hand and kissed her fingers, smiling ruefully. "You're missing a really good thing," he reminded her.

She couldn't look into those eyes without smiling. "I know it. Have a wonderful life, Peter."

She turned toward the stairs, then looked back. "I'd love for you to stay for the wedding," she called, then ran up to her room, ignoring Matt completely. What else could she do?

She had a feeling Matt and Peter would talk once she left. She had no idea how that would turn out. And perhaps she would never know. But there was nothing she could do about it now.

Laura had a fit when she heard Matt had seen the bride before the wedding.

"Bad luck!" she screeched as she helped Claire on with her dress.

"No, it's not," Claire replied fiercely. "I'm making my own luck now, Laura. Don't stand in my way."

"Wow." Laura stepped back and looked at her newly determined sister with respect.

Matt was waiting for her as she came down the aisle. His eyes were so full of love she basked in the glow, hardly even hearing the words the minister said. But she answered "I do" at the proper time, and when Matt kissed her, it was like that first real kiss under the mistletoe.

They didn't need a real honeymoon. They felt as though they had been on one for the past six months, during which they had spent almost every moment together. They moved right into their new home, taking Sam and Katy and later Kevin, with them.

"Are you happy?" she whispered that night as she lay in Matt's arms.

"Is this a quiz?"

"Yes. I'm going to ask you every day, and the day you say no, I'm going to—"

He drew her closer. "I'll never say no, Claire. I'm as happy as I've ever been."

Hmmm, she thought. That seemed to leave room for improvement.

"What could make you happier?" she asked, rearing back and studying his face.

He thought for a moment, biting his lip. "Well, we could hire the Swedish girls as housemaids," he suggested. "That might help."

"You!" She poked him and they wrestled gently for a moment, laughing.

"Happiness is no laughing matter," she reminded him once they had settled down again. She looked at him seriously. "I want to know. I want you to tell me if you ever begin to be annoyed by anything I do. I want to keep the lines open. Do you know what I mean? As long as we can always talk to each other, as long as we share our lives, do things together . . ."

"The family that plays together, stays together."

"Exactly."

He rose above her, dropping velvet kisses on her neck. "Do I have some playing in mind for you," he murmured.

She lay back and stretched deliciously, laughing softly. He was so dear to her. "Good," she whispered. "Because I want us to stay together for a long, long time."

He didn't speak again, but his body language made it clear his intentions were just like hers.

She realized she had found the way.

Helen Conrad has written over twenty-five romance novels. She lives in the Los Angeles area with her husband and four sons.

A first novel from the former
Los Angeles bureau chief of
People Magazine

BARBARA WILKINS

ELEMENTS
OF CHANCE

A woman of incredible beauty and talent, Valerie is married to
Victor Penn, one of the richest and most powerful men in the
world. She has everything a woman could want and more …
mansions in London, New York, Paris and Beverly Hills; priceless
antiques; stunning jewels; and a husband shamelessly,
passionately in love with her. But suddenly her destiny shifts
and spins Valerie's privileged world into a web of rivalries,
betrayal and murder. Alone, Valerie searches for the
answers to piercing questions about her past and
the uncertainty of her future.

COMING SOON FROM
HARPER PAPERBACKS